THERESA ON A TIGHTROPE

What was an irrepressible rebel like Theresa doing playing the perfect young lady in the most censorious circles of society? What was she doing playing cards for ruinous stakes against the most skilled sharpers in London? What was she doing as guest of dishonor at one of the notorious weekend gatherings of the Earl of Rusland? And above all, what was she doing daring to fall in love with the daunting Duke of Ashford, famed for being as heartless as he was handsome?

Actually, all things considered, Theresa was doing amazingly well. . . .

Born in Kansas, GAYLE BUCK has resided in Texas for most of her life. Since earning a journalism degree, she has freelanced for regional publications, worked for a radio station and as a secretary, and is now involved in public relations for a major Texas university.

Honor

Besieged

Gayle Buck

A SIGNET BOOK

NEW AMERICAN LIBRARY

A DIVISION OF PENGUIN BOOKS USA INC.

NAL BOOKS ARE AVAILABLE AT QUANTITY DISCOUNTS WHEN USED TO
PROMOTE PRODUCTS OR SERVICES. FOR INFORMATION PLEASE WRITE
TO PREMIUM MARKETING DIVISION, NEW AMERICAN LIBRARY,
1633 BROADWAY, NEW YORK, NEW YORK 10019.

SIGNET TRADEMARK REG. U.S.PAT. OFF. AND FOREIGN COUNTRIES
REGISTERED TRADEMARK—MARCA REGISTRADA
HECHO EN DRESDEN, TN, U.S.A.

SIGNET, SIGNET CLASSIC, MENTOR, ONYX, PLUME, MERIDIAN and NAL
BOOKS are published by New American Library, a division of Penguin Books USA
Inc., 1633 Broadway, New York, New York 10010

First Printing, February, 1990

1 2 3 4 5 6 7 8 9

PRINTED IN THE UNITED STATES OF AMERICA

1

Miss Theresa Thaleman sat in the drawing room, embroidering. The expression on her face was one of utter boredom. Her companion, a worthy lady by the name of Miss Letitia Brown, cast a knowing glance at her charge. She knew that sewing was not one of Miss Thaleman's favorite occupations. As a matter of fact, Theresa cared nothing for any of those accomplishments deemed so necessary to the education of a young lady of breeding. In her seventeenth year, Theresa had quite disappointed her mother by clinging stubbornly to her tomboyish, hoydenish ways. Mrs. Thaleman had quite unreasonably blamed the good-humored squire for Theresa's waywardness.

"As I have perhaps told you before, Miss Brown, there is a want of propriety, I may even say nicety, in the squire that cannot but improperly influence my daughter. Theresa worships her father, as well she should, but he encourages those tendencies of independence that are not becoming in a female. Why, if I had dared to challenge my brothers to footraces or to climb trees in my best frocks, my father would have whipped me within an inch of my life!" said Mrs. Thaleman.

Miss Brown had attempted to give her employer's mind a turn for the better. "Miss Thaleman does dance very prettily," she said quietly.

Mrs. Thaleman's face lighted up. "Theresa does float on a dance floor, does she not? My dear friends do try to disguise their envy when their own flat-footed progeny lumber about like so many graceless hippos, but I am well able to read their feelings, believe me! But I cannot countenance this new dance. The waltz! It is all one hears about. So fast! So

daring! Yes, and so scandalous! I will not have my daughter
clasped to a man's bosom and whirled about with such
abandon!''

Miss Brown, who, as a lover of dance, had often sym-
pathized with Miss Thaleman's frustration at her mother's
old-fashioned notions, made a decided pitch on her charge's
behalf. "Perhaps the waltz is all that you say it is, Mrs.
Thaleman, but I wonder if Miss Thaleman will not become
something of a wallflower when all her young friends have
taken up this latest craze." She left it at that, but was satisfied
by the startled look in Mrs. Thaleman's eyes that she had
pointed out a vastly unpleasant possibility. Mrs. Thaleman
would not desire to see her pretty daughter upstaged by vastly
inferior dancers.

Miss Brown was recalling this conversation, and its
pleasant outcome, as she glanced over at Miss Thaleman.
"Miss Thaleman, I am informed by your mother that she
has reconsidered her objections to the waltz. You are to begin
having lessons next week," she said calmly.

Theresa looked up quickly, amazement in her dark eyes.
Miss Brown smiled at her questioning gaze and nodded.
Theresa threw aside her embroidery hoop and leapt up from
the sofa. "Oh, Miss Brown! It is too, too marvelous! Did
she really? I can scarcely believe it." She grabbed Miss
Brown's hands and pulled that protesting lady from her seat
to dance her about the room. "Dear, dear Miss Brown! I
know it can only be due to you! You are a Trojan!''

Laughing and protesting, Miss Brown was finally let go
by her exuberant charge. Breathless, she sank down once
more in her chair. She tucked back a loosened curl. "You
mustn't use slang, Theresa, dear," she said automatically
and with as little effect as in the past. Theresa continued to
whirl about the room, humming. Miss Brown was startled
to discern a pattern to her charge's steps. "Theresa, where
did you learn to waltz?" she asked slowly.

Theresa stopped and had the grace to look repentant.
"Now, do not scold, dear, dear Miss Brown! I begged and

begged Barbara to show me, which she was very reluctant to do, so you mustn't blame her in the least.''

Miss Brown had no intention of blaming Miss Barbara Trisham, who was Theresa's best friend and confidante. She thought of Miss Trisham as a very good sort of girl and a good influence on Theresa. But Miss Trisham could be, too, somewhat weak of character when it came time to resist some of Theresa's outlandish notions of fun. ''I do not in the least think disparagingly of Miss Trisham. I know very well who is to blame in this,'' she said with a significant glance.

Theresa laughed gaily and with a pert, saucy look curtsied. ''I thank you, ma'am!''

Miss Brown sighed. She had often thought that Miss Thaleman's unspoilt good nature and her outgoing ways were a very dangerous combination. Already there were those who considered Miss Thaleman of a flirting nature, when she was nothing more than an innocent. ''You are incorrigible, Theresa.'' She neatly folded up her completed mending and rose to her feet. ''I am going now to consult with Mrs. Higgins. Pray be so good as to finish that piece I have given you. I should like to show an example of your progress, such as it is, to Mrs. Thaleman this evening. I must earn my keep, you know.'' She spoke the last with a flicker of a smile.

Theresa hugged her companion swiftly. ''You are priceless and you know it, Miss Brown. And so I shall tell Mama if she dares to say otherwise. I shall show her that you have persuaded me to wear a corset. *That* shall win her over!''

''If you must, but I pray not over dinner,'' said Miss Brown dryly. Miss Thaleman laughed at that and promised to finish the hated embroidery. Miss Brown left the drawing room, satisfied that the task would be done. Miss Thaleman was not a shirker of duty once she had given her word.

Theresa picked up the embroidery hoop. Sighing, she resigned herself to an awful morning. She pushed the needle willy-nilly through the linen and stabbed her finger. ''Oh!'' Hastily she dropped the hoop and put the wounded finger in her mouth. Theresa glared at the offending embroidery.

It was simply no use, she thought rebelliously.

The drawing-room door opened. A young man, obviously inclined toward the dandy set, entered. The Honorable George Bennett wore starched shirt points that aspired to hide his high cheekbones. His wasp-waisted coat was padded ridiculously wide through the shoulders. His cravat was intricately tied, but it was his bane that it yet failed to reach the peak of perfection of the Corinthian set.

"George!" Theresa rushed out of her chair, her ill humor forgotten. She flung her arms heedlessly around her cousin's neck.

Her beloved cousin broke her grasp, saying peevishly, "Dash it, Teri! Never grab a fellow that way. Look what you've done to my neckcloth. It isn't nice to muss up a fellow's efforts." He turned to the mirror over the mantel to inspect the damage.

"I am sorry, George. It is only that I have not seen you in months and I have been so bored," said Theresa, her face stricken as she watched him twitch and poke at the cravat.

George's frowning expression dissipated. He was fond of his younger cousin and could not long remain angry with her. "It is not so bad, after all. No need to come the tragic on me, my girl. I know you didn't mean it. What have you been up to this morning? When I arrived last night I was immediately informed by the squire of a new addition to the stables. I quite thought you would have been down inspecting the new mare."

"I have been doing embroidery," said Theresa flatly.

George stared at her with incredulity and revulsion. "No! What the devil do you want to do that for?"

"I don't wish to do it. It is Miss Brown's idea, so that she may show Mama that I am improving," said Theresa, making a face.

"It sounds a waste of time to me," said George frankly. "You've no knack for it, or for anything else, if it comes to that. You'd do much better to throw it over and come out with me to see the mare."

Theresa was sorely tempted, but shook her head. She picked up the embroidery hoop that had fallen to the carpet in her impetuous greeting and sat down on the sofa with it. "I've promised Miss Brown to finish it, George, and so I shall." She gave a huge sigh.

"Why ever did you tell old Brownie that? Mighty cork-brained of you, my girl," said George, turning once more to the mirror to inspect his appearance. He flicked a mote of fluff from his sleeve.

"Mama has agreed to allow me to take lessons in the waltz," said Theresa, industriously plying her needle.

George turned, his brows rising. He whistled in low amazement. "So Brownie came through for you, did she? Now I understand about the embroidery."

"Yes, I felt that I owed Miss Brown at least that much. So you see, George, that I must finish it even if it kills me," said Theresa. She paused to look critically at the stitches she had set. They were not as smooth as Miss Brown's, but she shrugged. Even her mother could not expect perfection from one of her lack of talent.

Looking at his cousin, George was suddenly struck by her appearance. With the embroidery hoop in her hands, her posture appeared perfectly demure. She wore her dark hair in the latest cropped style, and her saffron gown was very prettily finished with lace. The sunlight coming in the window highlighted the fresh lines of her cheek and slender neck. "Do you know, you have changed. It is almost frightening. At this moment you look the very picture of a quiet, well-bred young lady. I am not certain that I like to see my hoyden cousin appearing so grown-up," George said.

"Oh, George! I may look different, but that is mostly Miss Brown's doing. I am still the same inside," said Theresa with a saucy grin.

He laughed and shook his head. "I don't know, Theresa. I suspect that those trappings must rub off on one. You may become a lady despite yourself."

Theresa threw the embroidery hoop at him. He ducked,

but not quickly enough. "There, now! So much for your theory! My aim has not been the least bit affected, George Bennett, and neither has the rest of me," she said, tossing her head.

George rubbed his head where the wooden frame had caught him a smart clip. "Quite," he said ruefully. He bent to pick up the embroidery frame and glanced at the design as he took it over to his cousin. "I do not mean to wound you, Teri, but I cannot quite make out what these are."

"Those are roses," said Theresa with dignity. She took the hoop but set it aside on the sofa. She was tired of embroidering and she promised herself that she would finish it later. "Michael wrote to me and so I know you were to visit at Oxford. Now, tell me how you found the twins. I have not seen them for ages."

"Well, you shall soon enough. They are coming down from Oxford," George said.

Theresa stared at him in dismay. "Oh, no, they have not been given the sack again! Mama will frown ever so hard. What is it for this time?"

"I believe there was a heated dicussion on the merits of permitting donkeys in the classroom," said George. "The twins naturally took the unpopular view that any jackass had a perfect right to enjoy a classical education."

Theresa went into a peal of laughter. "That is just like them! And Father will not be able to say a word about it, for that is just what he is constantly telling the aldermen who begrudge the wages of a tutor for the poorhouse children. But with you to fuss over, even Mama will be less inclined to kick up a dust over Michael and Holland."

"That is one reason for my being here," said George. He laced his fingers about his knee and leaned back on the sofa, wearing a faint grin.

Theresa eyed her cousin. She knew that certain turn of his mouth when he was well-pleased about something. "George, what is it? What have you done? Pray tell me! I am about to go mad, what with lessons and decorum and . . . and . . . oh, everything!"

"I suppose it cannot hurt to let you in on it," George said slowly.

"Pray do not tease me, George!" begged Theresa.

Her cousin was unable to stand against her entreaty. "Oh, if you must know, the twins and I have thought up some very good sport while they are home, but you must promise not to tell a soul about it," George said with a significant glance at the closed door.

"You know that I would not!" Theresa said indignantly.

George leaned toward her and dropped his voice. "You know that there are always grand parties at Rusland Park, and grand visitors too? Well, for a single night Holland and Michael and I are going to masquerade as highwaymen. We shall give some of the guests a scare, I'll warrant!"

Theresa's eyes widened. "Oh, George," she breathed. Her eyes began to shine. "George, might I—"

When he saw the light of excitement in her eyes, George regretted that he had said anything. "No, you may not," he said firmly.

"Why ever not? I can ride and shoot as well as any one of you!" exclaimed Theresa.

"You are a female, dash it! I am sorry, Theresa, but there comes a time when the line has to be drawn. And this is one such time."

There was a mutinous set to Theresa's chin. "I shall do as I please. I will not be set about so by convention and so-called accomplishments! I do not wish to be a lady!"

George took hold of her clenched hands. He said gently, "But you are a lady born, my girl. Nothing can change that."

Her hands trembled in his. Her eyes appealed to him. "But it is not fair, George. You know it isn't. You and the twins have such larks, and I must spend my days at such drudgery. You do not know what it is like with Miss Brown always at my side, unless I can somehow slip away to go riding. I do like Miss Brown, of course! But it is not as though she and I share the same likes and dislikes. Why, I believe she actually cares for that French poetry she rattles off to me."

George laughed and released his cousin's hands. "Perhaps

she does, Theresa. At Brownie's age, reading French poetry must be as much romance as she is ever likely to find.''

"That is unkind, George. Miss Brown is quite nice-looking, even if she is too old to marry," said Theresa. She realized that she had been led off the point. She took a deep breath. "George, I shall be a highwayman. You cannot stop me, you know."

"Oh, yes I can. I shall make a clean breast of the thing to the squire before ever Michael and Holland come home," George said.

Theresa stared at her cousin. "You do not mean it, George." She saw the implacable determination in his eyes. "Really, George, you make it very difficult for me! You *know* that I could not cut up your fun."

"Then you must promise me that you will not try your hand at it, Teri," said George. When she gave a reluctant nod, he smiled and gave her a swift peck on the cheek. "There's a good girl. I am going down to the stables. Are you certain that you do not wish to join me?"

Theresa glanced down at the embroidery hoop. She sighed and shook her head. "I should stay and finish my stitching. Then it will not hang over my head all the day."

George shrugged and rose. "I shall see you next at dinner, I expect. I intend to try out the mare's paces." He left the drawing room, hardly aware of the upsurge of emotions that he had raised in his cousin's breast.

"Damnation!" said Theresa roundly. She was not at all repentant to have used a forbidden word, and she almost wished that her mother had heard her. "How I wish that I had been born a boy!" She picked up the embroidery and stabbed her needle viciously into the linen.

2

The Duke of Ashford sat at his ease in the moving coach. With a weary expression he glanced out the glass window at the passing countryside. It had become a beautiful day. The rain had let up an hour before and the verdant hedges and meadows of the passing estates and farms glistened in the pale sunlight. But the duke had long since forgotten what it meant to enjoy nature for its own sake. He thought only of the fact that the coach would now make better time since the rain had stopped.

"Hugo, do you care for an apple?" The voice was soft and feminine, with an underlying huskiness.

He glanced at his companion and studied her with a sense of detachment. Lady Statten was an astonishingly lovely woman. Her red hair gleamed with fiery highlights and her face had for years turned many heads. As he had good cause to know, her skin was petal-smooth and white and her lush figure was flawless in its beauty. Lady Statten's green eyes met his glance, and there was a decided gleam in their depths. She held out to him a bright red apple. Her tongue touched her lips suggestively.

The duke smiled faintly. He could recall a time when Melanie's slightest glance, the grace of her every movement, had maddened him beyond endurance. He had stopped at nothing to make her his mistress, even to the point of bribing her former lover with one of his best hunters. For a time their relationship had been extremely satisfying, and it had lasted longer than any of his other liaisons. At the zenith of their romance, he had even toyed once or twice with the thought of making Lady Statten his duchess. But inevitably there had come the day when he had begun to detect within

13

himself the familiar weariness. From that point forward it was but a matter of time before he became utterly bored.

This weekend at the Earl of Rusland's country estate was to be his and Lady Statten's last tryst. It would be a good place to end their affair, he thought. The Earl of Rusland offered a brand of hospitality that appealed to those in pursuit of delicate affairs of the heart. Arrangements were such that Lady Statten would have no difficulty in discovering a new lover if she so wished. In the event that she did, there would be a quiet rearrangement of the occupants of adjoining bedroom suites. At Rusland Park discretion and convenience ruled the day.

"One is tempted, of course. But I think not," said the duke.

Lady Statten shrugged. She bit into the apple and matter-of-factly chewed. "As you wish, Hugo. But it is a very fine fruit, firm and juicy," she said. She was no longer playing the femme fatale and she was therefore surprised when the Duke of Ashford laughed. She stared at him in astonishment and then smiled. "Why, thank you, Hugo. I believe you have just paid me a compliment," she said, pleased.

"Not I. You have paid it to yourself," said the duke. "But then, you have never been behind in acknowledging your own beauty."

"No, never. And why should I not acknowledge it?" asked Lady Statten, lifting the tiny mirror that she nearly always carried on her person. She fluffed the artfully placed curls above her eyes.

The duke watched her, his lips lifted in a satirical smile. Lady Statten's large vanity had once been a source of amusement to him. But it had become one of the first of her traits to irritate him. He decided that the moment had come. "My dear Melanie, I have some news that may perhaps distress you to a degree," he said.

Lady Statten glanced at him. What she saw in his cynical eyes made her put away her mirror. "You look quite serious, Hugo. What is it? Have you suffered a reversal in fortunes?

I should like to know at once, for I am counting on a tiara for my birthday.''

The duke shook his head. ''Not quite, my lady. Actually, it is yourself who suffers a financial loss. This weekend at Rusland Park will be our last together.''

Lady Statten's heart beat faster. Her voice sharpened. ''What do you mean, your grace? Speak plain, I pray you.''

The duke sighed and leaned forward to take her hands. Not for the first time, he wondered how a woman so beautiful could have such short, stout fingers. Her hands had always given him an impression of grasping claws. ''I am saying that I no longer wish to continue our affair. We have had a fine run of it, dear Melanie, but it is now to be at an end. Of course, there will be compensation for you. I will not let you go empty-handed, I promise you.''

Lady Statten snatched her hands away. ''How dare you! How dare you simply announce that what is between us is over!'' she exclaimed furiously. Her face and neck began to mottle with ugly reddened splotches. ''And you think to buy me off like some cheap little street whore? No, my fine lord! I think not!'' She began to curse him fluently and quite comprehensively.

The Duke of Ashford sat back, amazed by Lady Statten's transformation. He could not recall ever seeing her in such an enraged state. Certainly she ahd shown him peevishness and irritation, but always there had been that certain air of breeding about her. Now, as he gazed on his former mistress, he felt a growing disgust. Her lovely face was twisted by her fury, and she spat out her insults in a shrill, high voice. Anger stirred in him. Lady Statten was too well-versed in these games to react in such an ill-bred manner. She should have acknowledged the end to their affair with gracious regret and spared them both this embarrassing scene, he thought.

He had not paid attention to her tirade, and when Lady Statten suddenly threw open the carriage window he did not immediately realize her intention. With a twist of her hands, she yanked off the ring that he had given her upon their first assignation and threw it away. The gold circlet caught a flash of sunlight before it disappeared into the road's churned mud. "There, your grace! That is what I think of your flatteries and your promises!" she screamed, her bosom heaving with her panted breath.

The Duke of Ashford sat quite still. The ring had been a special piece that he had commissioned just for her, and it had always seemed to symbolize all that was good in their relationship. When he had presented it to her, he had also come within an ace of asking for her hand. When he spoke, his voice was cold. "I do not believe either of us made any promises, madam."

The utter frigidity of his tone abruptly, effectively dampened Lady Statten's fury. She stared at him, startled, and for the first time in several minutes she read his expression. Her face softened in an instant and she made her voice sound at its most husky. "Oh, Hugo, do not look at me so. Pray try to understand. It is my love for you that has made me behave so wildly." She reached out to caress his sleeve.

He took hold of her wrist and removed her fingers. "I do not believe that we have any more to say to one another, my lady," he said.

Lady Statten felt a renewed spurt of fury, but she swallowed it. She knew herself to be teetering on an abyss. She knew that lofty tone of his grace's. She had heard it used too often on the toadeaters and hangers-on that followed the Duke of Ashford about. It was not the time to try to win him over, she thought, as they were shortly to arrive at Rusland Park. Once she had him in her bed, she was confident that there would be no more talk of severing a relationship that had always proved incredibly advantageous and lucrative to herself.

But the Duke of Ashford had other ideas. The remainder of the drive to Rusland Park was accomplished in silence. Lady Statten felt herself on the verge of screaming with boredom when at last the carriage door was opened and a footman offered her his hand. She stepped down out of the coach and turned to offer a smile of reconcilation to the duke, who followed her. He did not glance in her direction, but at once went up the steps to greet their host. With sparks in her eyes, Lady Statten hurried after his grace.

The Earl of Rusland received the duke warmly. "Ah, Hugo! It is good to see you looking so fit. And here is dear Lady Statten with you, of course." His hard eyes raked her ripe figure with appreciaton. He raised her hand to his lips. "You appear more beautiful than ever, my dear lady."

Lady Statten inclined her head, her feelings somewhat soothed by the earl's leer. "Thank you, dear Charles. It is wonderful to be able to return to Rusland Park. I have always found my visits here most satisfying."

The earl laughed as he led them into the hall. "You will be wanting to freshen up after the journey, of course. I shall have a footman show you up." He started to raise his hand.

The Duke of Ashford forestalled him. "Before you do so, Charles, I should like to arrange a change in my accommodations. Lady Statten understands the necessity," he said quietly. He ignored an indignant gasp from the lady in question.

The earl glanced swiftly from one to the other, and his brows rose. "Of course, Hugo, of course! It shall be just as you wish." He gestured to a footman and gave the man soft instructions. When he was done, he said, "Follow this fellow, Hugo. He will make you comfortable." When the Duke of Ashford had gone on his way, the earl looked down at Lady Statten, who stood pulling her gloves through her hands with jerky movements. "Whatever has happened between you and our Hugo, dear Melanie? He is riding quite high in the treetops this afternoon. Pray do not tell me that you have been cast off!"

She glanced at the earl. "It is no concern of yours, my lord, whatever the case," she said frostily. She turned away to the footman who awaited her at the bottom of the stairs and swiftly left the entrance hall behind.

The Earl of Rusland stared after her stiff back with a thoughtful expression. For years he had admired Lady Statten, but thus far had failed with her. Before the Duke of Ashford had entered upon the scene, he had had hopes of eventually winning her for himself. Now it appeared that the Duke of Ashford and she had suffered a serious rift. "It could prove an interesting weekend," he said aloud. "A very interesting weekend indeed."

Despite the Duke of Ashford's surprising and humiliating insistence on different accommodations, Lady Statten did not abandon hope. There were still two days in an atmosphere of licentiousness and round-the-clock entertainments. As her maid unpacked her belongings and put them away, Lady Statten studied herself in the mirror. She had changed from her traveling dress to a deceptively simple round gown of deep green satin. The décolletage was low, showing to advantage her rounded shoulders and well-endowed bosom, and the skirt was cut in such a way that it clung to her hips when she moved. Lady Statten smoothed the shining fabric, a faint smile on her lips. There were few who could match her in natural beauty. If the Duke of Ashford thought to console himself with another woman this weekend, he would find it difficult not to draw comparisons. "And that is precisely what I wish him to do," she said complacently. The maid glanced at Lady Statten curiously, but she was too well-versed in her place to make the mistake of thinking that her ladyship required comment.

The other guests at Rusland Park were a familiar group, with but a few new faces. It soon became known who was paired with whom and which were free to establish new relationships. Quite a bit of comment was caused by the obvious breach between the Duke of Ashford and Lady Statten. Some believed it only a lovers' quarrel, since the two had been an item for several months and as a consequence had become something of a confirmed couple. But the duke's total disregard for Lady Statten's presence and her less-than-subtle persistence to bring herself to his notice pointed to a permanent break.

It was at dinner on Saturday that the Earl of Rusland leaned over to speak softly in Lady Statten's ear. "My dear Melanie, you make a spectacle of yourself. Surely it must be apparent to you by now that Hugo is made of stone."

Lady Statten shot a glance across the table at the Duke of Ashford. He was addressing the lady beside him with grave courtesy and had not glanced in her own direction for several minutes, though she had done her utmost to appear her most charming. Her fingers tightened about the stem of her wineglass. "I am not rolled up yet, Charles. There is still tonight and one more day," she said determinedly.

The earl shrugged and sat back. He was generally not one to advise his guests of their own follies, and instead derived a great deal of amusement from the maneuverings that went on. But in Lady Statten's case it had become embarrassingly obvious to everyone that she was throwing herself after a lost cause. The earl had wished to save for her a little dignity with his warning, but she refused to take his hint and he could do nothing more. It was only a matter of time before Lady Statten would bring herself to absolute humiliation, he thought regretfully.

Lady Statten's moment of truth came sooner than even the earl had suspected. Early the following morning the Duke of Ashford was discovered to have taken leave of Rusland Park. There was no communication left for Lady Statten, who was, in essence, stranded with no conveyance back to London. It was a blatant message to anyone with the slightest wit that Lady Statten had lost. There was little sympathy for her ladyship within the cynical group. The stakes were high in the games played at Rusland Park, and none of the players could afford compassion.

3

Dinner at the Thalemans' was an informal affair. The squire and Mrs. Thaleman presided at the table with their only daughter and Miss Brown. In many other households, Miss Brown knew that as a paid companion she would have been relegated to a lonely tray in her own rooms. But Squire Thaleman was of a nature unusual among many of his contemporaries and he had insisted from the first that Miss Brown eat at table like any other decent being. "She isn't cranky or ill-bred, is she?" he had demanded impatiently when his wife had objected to his decree.

"Of course not. Miss Brown is of a respectable background. Pray, sir, do you think that I would entrust our daughter's education to someone of mean standards and unpleasant disposition?" Mrs. Thaleman asked indignantly.

"Then Miss Brown will join us in the dining room."

Mrs. Thaleman sighed with frustration. Her husband's blindness to the finer points of polite society was a continual cross to her. She tried once more to bring him to an understanding, at least in this instance. "Squire, as a paid companion Miss Brown does not expect to be treated above her station. I daresay it would embarrass her to be asked to sit at dinner with the family."

The squire had stared at his wife from under frowning brows. "That is the way of it, is it? Poor girl must lead a dog's life. Well, not in my house. I shall explain the matter to her."

And so he had, clumsily and thoroughly, to the quiet amusement of Miss Brown. She had managed to control her smile and thank him with quiet dignity. The squire had emerged from the interview with a heightened respect for

Miss Brown and told his wife that he thought it would not
do any harm for Theresa to have such an example of gentility
set before her, even at meals. At first openly disapproving
of Miss Brown's presence in the dining room, Mrs.
Thaleman had eventually thawed to the extent that she could
think of Miss Brown as a regular guest instead of her
daughter's humble companion. Indeed, before many months
had passed, Mrs. Thaleman began to treat Miss Brown as
more friend and confidante than employee.

The addition of George Bennett to the company that
evening was thought to be a fine treat by all. Even Miss
Brown, who privately considered Mr. Bennett to be a
fashionable fribble, thought that his presence was a welcome
diversion. Mrs. Thaleman in particular held a strong fondness
for her elder sister's only son. He was three years older than
her own sons, but he had always treated Michael and Holland
with friendly forbearance. If he participated in some of their
madder larks, he also managed to bring them off safely from
whatever folly the twins had taken into their heads.

As for Theresa, thought Mrs. Thaleman with a glance at
her spirited daughter, George could not be improved upon
as a cousin. He had always seemed to have a calming effect
on the girl. Not for the first time she toyed with the thought
of promoting a match between the cousins. But she did not
know how the idea would be received by the squire, or for
that matter, by her sister, who she knew, through their
sporadic shared correspondence, had always harbored
inflated social aspirations for her beloved son. With that
thought, Mrs. Thaleman turned to her nephew. "And how
is my dear sister, George? I have not enjoyed one of her
letters in some time."

"Mama is as well as can be expected," George said easily.

The squire and Mrs. Thaleman exchanged a glance. They
were well able to interpret their nephew's gracious reply to
mean that Mrs. Bennett was enjoying her usual indifferent
health. A confirmed hypochondriac, Claudia Bennett had a
taste for wearing ghastly draperies and reclining on a chaise

longue, from which position she ruled her husband and her household with an iron hand. Only her son seemed to have escaped her control. Though Mrs. Bennett was proud of her son's social standing among the dandy set and yearned to see him become a leader of fashion, she was torn by the equal desire to keep him close to her side. Her clinging attitude had only resulted in furthering the distance between herself and her son.

"Keeping your visits far and few between, are you?" asked the squire. "Smart lad. Those die-away airs of your mother's are enough to sap the enjoyment out of any gathering."

"Squire!" Mrs. Thaleman was appalled by her spouse's lack of tact. She was not particularly fond of her sister, having always seen her sister's imagined illnesses as bids for the attention that she should have had as a girl, but she certainly would not say something bound to be be wounding to her nephew.

But George laughed. He enjoyed his uncle's forthrightness. "Quite, sir. As anyone may tell you, I rarely spend much time at m'father's house. And I suspect neither does he these days. I meet him quite often at the clubs. He is forever lecturing me on my attire, you know. I believe that my magnificence shocks his gentler sensibilities."

The squire grunted as he eyed the exaggerated cut of his nephew's coat. He started to open his mouth. Mrs. Thaleman said hastily, "That is just Henry's funning way, I expect. I for one think you look quite splendid."

"Yes, quite top of the trees, George!" said Theresa, who had listened with fascination to the conversation. Whenever George visited, she always learned so much that no one ever told her. Since the squire did not encourage visits by his in-laws, having stated on more than one occasion that Claudia Bennett's dramatics were more then he could stomach, she barely remembered her aunt and uncle from a meeting when she was very small. But she was an intelligent girl and it did not take great insight to realize that Aunt Claudia must be an affliction to her family.

Mrs. Thaleman frowned at her daughter. Miss Brown, easily reading her employer's expression, said gently, "Miss Thaleman, it is perfectly proper to express admiration, but one can moderate one's style of language, don't you think?"

Theresa shot a swift glance at her mother's face. "Oh! I do apologize, George. I should have said, 'How vastly becoming your attire is.' "

George grinned and with exaggerated courtesy lifted her fingers to his lips. "Thank you, Miss Thaleman. I shall cherish your kind opinion," he said in a stiff, formal tone.

The squire snorted laughter. "There, Mrs. Thaleman! As pretty as even you could wish."

Mrs. Thaleman knew that she was being teased, but she could not hold it against her nephew. "You are a wag, George," she said indulgently. "I hope that you mean to make a long stay with us this time. We have been sorely lacking in company these past weeks."

"Of course I shall. I've nothing pressing in London, and it is as good a time as any to discover for myself what all this talk of the Earl of Rusland is about. He is a scandal even in London, you know. I am curious to meet the gentleman."

Theresa waited with indrawn breath, her eyes flying between her parents. The squire was frowning and Mrs. Thaleman's face had gone quite stiff. Theresa had never actually understood the objection that her parents and other older persons in the neighborhood had to the Earl of Rusland. Their vague allusions to impropriety and disgraceful activities sounded to her to be all a hum, and served only to whet her curiosity about the society to be found at Rusland Park.

As did everyone in the neighborhood, the Squire and Mrs. Thaleman regularly received invitations from the Earl of Rusland, but they had never attended even one of his parties. Theresa thought this a rather rude way to treat one's neighbor, but neither parent had ever satisfactorily explained their reasoning to her.

Talk of the Earl of Rusland was usually avoided, but here was George casually announcing that he meant to meet the

earl. Theresa adored her cousin's nerve. She waited to hear
what would transpire next.

It was not the squire or Mrs. Thaleman who spoke up.
"I hope that you will pardon me, Mr. Bennett, but perhaps
it would be appropriate for you to speak later with the squire
regarding the Earl of Rusland," said Miss Brown quietly.
She was aware of the Thalemans' intense dislike of any
mention of Rusland Park within their daughter's hearing. She
did not entirely agree with her employers' policy of sheltering
Theresa so thoroughly from matters of the world by keeping
her in virtual ignorance, but it was not for her to counter
their decision. She could only do her best to prepare Theresa
for her role in life, despite being hedged about by certain
restrictions.

"An excellent suggestion, Miss Brown," said the squire
quickly. George raised his brows in astonishment, but agreed
gracefully to the suggestion.

Theresa's face fell in disappointment. Once again she was
to be treated like a child and relegated outside matters of
interest. However, George was not only her cousin but also
her very good friend. She would wait until he had had a
chance to find out about the Earl of Rusland and then she
would ask him. She was certain that he would tell her. With
that thought, Theresa was able to return her attention with
equanimity to her dinner.

When the ladies rose to exit the dining room and leave
the gentlemen to their wine, Theresa was in a pleasant mood.
Miss Brown was rather surprised. Theresa had never been
backward in voicing her opinion that she was treated more
as a child than an adult. Miss Brown privately held the
opinion that Theresa's frustration was in many instances
justified. But there was little she could do to counter the
situation. When she had guided the conversation away from
the Earl of Rusland, she had known that Theresa would feel
slighted and she had anticipated that her charge would be
seething against her.

Miss Brown had mentally squared her shoulders against

the certain tirade that Theresa would launch the moment the ladies entered the drawing room. But instead, Theresa very prettily offered to play the pianoforte for her mother and Miss Brown. Mrs. Thaleman accepted her daughter's suggestion with every appearance of gratification, and when Theresa had sat down at the pianoforte she said, "Miss Brown, I am overwhelmed. I am certain it is your good influence that has worked this small miracle. I believe this is the first time that Theresa has provided music for us without some form of prodding."

"I doubt that it is due to any influence of mine, ma'am. Theresa is quite capable of forming her own decisions," said Miss Brown. Mrs. Thaleman was vastly pleased by what she took as praise of her daughter, but Miss Brown meant something quite different. She eyed the back of Theresa's head and wondered what that young lady had up her sleeve. But she was not to have her curiosity assuaged.

Miss Brown drew Mrs. Thaleman's attention to the bit of embroidery that Theresa had completed that morning. "I am quite proud of Theresa's latest effort. As you can see, the needlework shows some slight improvement," she said.

Mrs. Thaleman peered doubtfully at the stitching. She could not herself see an improvement, but then, she preferred not to dwell on Theresa's failings as a well-bred young woman. She decided that she must put her faith in Miss Brown's good opinion. "I am vastly pleased, Miss Brown, though I fear that Theresa shall never be able to do her duty toward the church and provide finely worked altarcloths."

Miss Brown smiled as she folded Theresa's embroidery. "It is best not to expect the impossible, certainly," she said.

Theresa listened to her mother's and Miss Brown's conversation with but half an ear. Though she played with skill, the greater part of her concentration was given over to hearing a creak of the door whenever it should open. She was certain that her father and cousin would be coming any minute. But the squire and George lingered long over their wine.

Finally with an incoherent exclamation, Theresa spun about on the bench. "Whatever is keeping Papa and George?" she exclaimed.

"Why so impatient, Miss Thaleman?" asked Miss Brown, raising her delicate brows.

Theresa gave a swift glance at her companion. Her frowning expression smoothed to one of sublime innocence. "Oh, it is just that it has been forever since I have seen George. I am so fond of him, you see."

Mrs. Thaleman smiled with indulgence on her pretty daughter. "And so are we all. George is such a dear boy. I almost think of him as my own son," she said.

Miss Brown, who had guessed Mrs. Thaleman's hope that her daughter and nephew might one day make a match of it, merely shook her head. It was difficult to possess the ability to ascertain the characters of those about her and still maintain her position of neutrality. It certainly would take a more forceful gentleman than Theresa's agreeable cousin to handle her. If only Mrs. Thaleman would resign herself to Theresa's waywardness instead of attempting to mold the girl into a pattern card of submissive respectability. Then a proper suitor for Theresa could be found, one who would accept the girl's free-spirited nature and make her happy.

Miss Brown's troubled thoughts were cut short by the entrance of the squire and George Bennett.

4

Theresa flew up from the pianoforte bench and ran to her cousin. "George! I have been waiting this age to talk to you. Come over to the corner immediately." She tugged at her cousin's arm and, laughing, he followed her obediently to the settee isolated in one corner.

The squire looked after them with a shake of his head. "She has always tagged after poor George like a puppy," he remarked to his wife and Miss Brown as he took a wing chair. Mrs. Thaleman toyed with the notion of feeling out the squire's opinion of George's suitability as a husband for some fortunate young woman, but the moment was lost. The squire picked up his newspaper and at once lost himself in its pages.

Theresa flounced down on the settee and dragged George down beside her. "Now, tell me everything, George. And do not deny that Papa did not fill your ears with ghastly tales of the earl and Rusland Park, for I shall not believe you."

George laughed at her. "You are a clever little monkey. How did you guess?"

"I know Papa very well, and you almost as well. Pray tell me, George! What did Papa say of the earl? He rarely speaks of the gentleman, and when he does, it is with *such* an expression in his eyes! I have been curious for ever so long," Theresa said.

"I don't know that I should say anything if my uncle frowns so strongly on it," said George.

"Pooh! Papa thinks I am a babe. But I am not, you know. I am all of seventeen and quite worldly," Theresa said.

George's upper lip quivered. He cleared his throat. "Of course. How could I have been so blind? Very well, Miss

27

Thaleman. The squire says that the Earl of Rusland is a libertine and he keeps the company of profligates and libertines like himself.''

''Oh!'' Theresa looked at her cousin, wide-eyed. She was not certain what George meant, but she had a hazy vision of wicked amusements. Somehow that did not seem all that bad.

''Do you know what a libertine is, Teri?'' George asked curiously.

She tossed her head. ''Of course I do!'' she said proudly. ''It is a very bad gentleman who entraps young girls into wicked ways. I have learned all about them from Mama's novels.'' Her hand flew to cover her mouth; then she said, ''Oh, Goerge, pray do not tell Mama that I have sneaked her novels. She would scold me so!''

''You are a baggage, cousin. Is Miss Brown aware of this particular predilection?'' George asked sternly.

Theresa gave him a pert smile. ''Miss Brown does not approve of trashy novels. But it is her opinion that one must be well-read to broaden one's knowledge of the world. And in all fairness, she cannot say one word against my romances when she goes into raptures over silly poetry.''

George whistled soundlessly. ''You are a devious one, Teri.''

Theresa took her cousin's observation as a compliment. ''Thank you, George.'' She meditatively smoothed a fold in her muslin skirt. ''I should like to go to just one grand party at Rusland Park, if only out of curiosity. I have never met a libertine before.''

''The squire told me enough of Rusland Park to convince me that his steadfast refusal to associate with the earl is warranted. Believe me, a young lady would not enjoy the sort of entertainments provided at Rusland,'' George said soberly.

''Oh, it is not only Rusland Park, George!'' Theresa heaved a sigh of frustration. ''Whenever the earl is in residence, all of a sudden I am not allowed to accept invitations to any function, except to the stuffiest dinners where nearly everyone is twice my age. I should so like to be out in society like Mary Marling. She tells me of such wonderful parties, where there is dancing, and young gentlemen to pay one compliments. And I can tell her only of the latest novel that I have read on the sly. It is not at all fair,'' Theresa said feelingly.

George was moved by his cousin's unhappy expression. He thought that better than anyone he should understand what it was like to be hedged about by a parent's unpalatable desires and wishes. He put his arm about Theresa's slim shoulders and gave her a brief hug. ''Never mind. I have not met Miss Marling, but I am certain that she cannot compare to you for sweetness of character,'' he said.

''What is the use of that when I am dwindling away into an old maid like poor Miss Brown?'' Theresa asked despairingly.

George glanced over at the lady in question, who was blissfully unaware of the scrutiny. ''How odd that I have not noticed Miss Brown's decrepit years. She appears quite well-preserved for her advanced age,'' said George, tongue-in-cheek.

Theresa gave him a prod with her elbow. ''Oh, George! You know what I mean! Miss Brown is all of nine-and-twenty. Why, she has been on the shelf for ages.'' She, too, glanced at her companion. ''I do think it unfair, for she is truly a dear, and though not a great beauty, she has the most speaking eyes. Do you not think so, George?''

George looked down at his companion, astonished. ''Does she? Cousin, do I suspect correctly that you are making a feeble attempt at matchmaking? For I shall tell you straight to your head that it will not do. I am not at all in the market for a wife.''

Theresa flashed a smile at him. ''I do admit it, George. But if you are firmly set against the notion, I shall not press you. However, if you should have an acquaintance who is gentlemanly and respectable, I would be so grateful if you would bring him to Miss Brown's notice.''

Her thoughts wandered back to Rusland Park. ''George,

do you think that I could accompany you when you call at Rusland Park? I should so like—''

''Most assuredly not! And do not try to wheedle me into it, Teri. The squire and my aunt are quite right not to expose you to that set,'' George said with unusual firmness.

Theresa eyed him speculatively, but she saw that he meant what he had said. ''Oh, very well. I shall not breathe another word about it. But I think it grossly unfair that I am not allowed to do anything of interest. How am I ever to attract an eligible *parti* if I am shut up as though I were in a nunnery?''

Her voice had unconsciously risen as she spoke, so that her parents and Miss Brown were able to hear what she said. When Theresa looked around, it was to meet three pairs of curious, unblinking eyes. She tossed her head defiantly. ''Well, it is true! All I ever do is lessons, lessons, lessons. I am never allowed to go in society or to meet anyone. I am bored to tears, and everyone might as well know it,'' she exclaimed. She jumped up and rushed out of the drawing room.

''George! Whatever has gotten into Theresa?'' Mrs. Thaleman asked, astonished.

George rose and joined his aunt and uncle in front of the grate. He automatically glanced in the mirror above the mantel and twitched a fold of his cravat into place. ''I fear that it is my fault. Theresa asked me about the Earl of Rusland and I told her enough to be certain that she understood it was for her own benefit that she was not allowed to associate with his lordship and his guests. But my cousin has apparently made him out to be some sort of romantic figure.''

''I do not know what is to be done with that foolish girl,'' exclaimed Mrs. Thaleman. She was furious that Theresa had treated her cousin to a fit of distemper. No gentleman liked to see a lady throw a fit, and so she would tell her daughter.

''Theresa is obstinate. If it is as you say, George, I fear what idiotic notion she might next take into her head,'' the squire said with a heavy frown.

"If I may be permitted to make a suggestion?" Miss Brown said quietly. She waited for the squire's nod before she continued. "I believe that Miss Thaleman suffers from the usual girlish fantasies of knights in shining armor and romantic love. Miss Thaleman's forced inactivity merely strengthens her desire for what she thinks is the perfect life. Perhaps a Season in London would redirect her thoughts and give her a more realistic perspective."

"A Season in London? But she is a mere child!" said the squire, astounded.

"That she is not, Squire," said Mrs. Thaleman with unusual asperity. "You are blind to your daughter's budding womanhood, but I am not. I well understand Theresa's feelings. I, too, once yearned for pretty clothes and parties and gentlemen's compliments. I think that Miss Brown has made a very sensible suggestion. Our daughter must be taken to London for the Season." The thought of removing her daughter from the evil influence of Rusland Park and providing her an opportunity to shine in polite society was extremely appealing to Mrs. Thaleman. Theresa had grown to be a pretty young woman ripe for marriage, but she could not be expected to attach an eligible gentleman from a distance, thought Mrs. Thaleman. She would stand a far better chance if she were to mingle in the same circles. Mrs. Thaleman felt a spurt of anticipation as she began to examine ways and means. It was just the sort of problem that she liked.

The squire eyed his wife askance, wondering at her rare tone of forcefulness. "I bow to your superior understanding of a young girl's mind, my dear. However, I must ask how this Season is to be accomplished. We do not run in London circles, you know."

"You may leave that to me, Squire. I shall go up with Theresa, and Miss Brown will accompany us. I expect dear Claudia will be happy to put us up. As for sponsors for our Theresa, I still know a few personages and Claudia will undoubtedly know others," Mrs. Thaleman said, her imagination fired equally by the novelty of a stay in London and by the opportunity of throwing her daughter more in her nephew's company.

The squire snorted. "I wish I might see Claudia exerting herself on anyone's behalf but her own!"

George was enchanted by the thought of his mother's dismay upon learning that Mrs. Thaleman meant to stay with her. His eyes held a distinct look of mischief as he said, "Mama will naturally be delighted to see you again, Aunt. And I am certain that she will exert herself to the utmost in aiding the success of Theresa's first Season."

Mrs. Thaleman smiled at her nephew, gratified by his alliance. "There! You see, Squire? Everything will work itself out to admiration. George thinks Claudia will be delighted."

The squire was still dubious. He thought it highly unlikely that his sister-in-law would feel any such gratifying emotion, but he felt unequal to withstand his wife's importunities and his nephew's firm assurances. Beleaguered, he appealed to Miss Brown. "You are mightily silent, Miss Brown. Have you no opinion to put forward?"

"I stand by my original assessment, sir. Miss Thaleman would undoubtedly benefit by a London Season. It is not for me to say what Mrs. Bennett's feelings may be on the matter," Miss Brown said quietly. George Bennett laughed. The squire grunted, understanding perfectly Miss Brown's reticence, and returned his attention to his wife, who had progressed to the question of monies for a proper wardrobe for their daughter.

Miss Brown felt herself under scrutiny and turned her head to find Mr. Bennett's gaze on her. "Yes, Mr. Bennett?"

George grinned at her. He said quietly, under cover of his aunt's vigorous lobbying of the squire, "You are very quick, Miss Brown. I'll wager that you could give my mother the go-by pretty as you please. Ah, a spark of anger! Do you know, Theresa was quite right. You do have the most speaking eyes."

Miss Brown flushed. She was astonished. She could not

imagine why Mr. Bennett should suddenly choose to flirt with her, but she strongly suspected it must be due to his imbibing too freely of the after-dinner wine. It was certainly not her place, nor her style, to encourage such familiarity from a gentleman, and she rose from her chair, catching Mrs. Thaleman's attention.

"Do you leave us so early, Miss Brown?" asked Mrs. Thaleman.

Miss Brown inclined her head. "If you will excuse me, ma'am, I shall go up now to see to Theresa," she said quietly.

"She will undoubtedly be sulking. You have my permission to reveal to her that we will be going to London, Miss Brown. It will make your life much more pleasant," said Mrs. Thaleman.

Miss Brown went immediately to Theresa's bedroom and knocked at the door. "Theresa, it is Miss Brown. May I come in?"

There was a long moment of silence; then Theresa's voice came from the other side of the door. "If you wish." It was not the most gracious invitation, but Miss Brown decided to accept it without comment. She opened the door and went in, to find her charge reclining across the bed with her feet in the air.

Theresa propped herself up on her elbows and with a defiant air looked at her companion's calm face. "I know that I behaved badly. But I shan't apologize for what I said. *That* was true, every word of it!"

Miss Brown seated herself in a wing-back chair near the bed. "I quite agree," she said.

Theresa sat up. She eyed Miss Brown in astonishment. "You do agree?"

"Oh, quite. You have become far too old to remain in the schoolroom, Theresa." Miss Brown let a flicker of a smile cross her face as she quoted, " 'The heart yearns for what cannot be seen, Aquiver and fragile as a butterfly's wings. Ah, love! Come swiftly.' " She laughed as Theresa made a face. "Yes, it is rather bad poetry. However, it is apropos,

for you are very like that, Theresa. You wish for so much
from life and yet you cannot even define that which . . .
Well, we shan't go into that. I do not mean to lecture tonight.
I came to tell you that the squire and Mrs. Thaleman have
decided you are to have a Season in London.''

The words were scarcely out of her mouth before Theresa
leapt from the bed and ran over to throw tight arms about
her. After emitting a single unladylike squeal, Theresa
exclaimed, ''Thank you so very, very much, Miss Brown!
I know it was your influence that brought it about.'' She
released Miss Brown from her stranglehold and sank down
beside the chair, expressing her heartfelt gratitude by taking
hold of her companion's hand and pressing it to her cheek.

Deeply moved by the rare gesture of affection, Miss Brown
smiled lopsidedly, but she shook her head as she reclaimed
her hand. ''I doubt that my poor powers of persuasion are
as potent as you make out. At all events, I am happy for
you, Theresa.'' The door opened and Theresa's maid
entered. Miss Brown took it as a signal to draw their conversation to a close. With a few other kind words she bid her
charge good night before going to her own room.

Once Miss Brown had left the bedroom, Theresa felt free
to give full rein to her giddy feelings. Her former anger and
frustration were completely forgotten as she whirled around,
narrowly missing collision with the furniture as she passed.
''To London, to London! To London I go!''

The maid watched her antics with a long-suffering
expression. Theresa caught the good woman's expression of
disapproving resignation. She gave a peal of laughter. ''Oh,
Ellie, only think! *London*!''

''Aye, and I'll wager you will set the town on its ear,
miss,'' said the maid with a sour smile.

Theresa turned so that the maid could begin to unfasten
the row of tiny buttons down the back of her gown. She spoke
over her shoulder. ''Oh, I shall, I promise you! Why, what
is the point of having a Season if one does not attend every
amusement one can?'' She gave a small bounce of
anticipation.

"Do stop your wriggling, Miss Theresa," the maid begged, struggling with the last of the buttons.

Obediently Theresa stood still while her day dress and chemise were removed and a fine lawn gown was thrown over her head to fall about her ankles. After her maid had put her to bed and was gone, Theresa scrambled back out of bed to relight the candle. Cupping her hand about its flickering flame to shield it from drafts, she carried the candle to her secretary. By the candle's pale yellow light she unlocked the desk and took out a leather-bound journal. Theresa seated herself and opened the journal to the proper page. She dipped a pen into the inkwell, and as she did each evening before settling herself for sleep, she recorded the day's happenings and her thoughts.

Theresa had been given the journal as a Christmas gift the year before by Miss Brown, who had encouraged her to form the habit of writing as a means of exercise her powers of observation and reflection. Miss Brown had been both gratified and amazed when Theresa had commented that the journal was quite the best gift that she had ever received.

When Theresa was done with the few sentences, she returned the journal to its place and shut the desk securely. She blew out the candle and returned to bed. With a contented sigh she burrowed into the down pillow, and soon she slept.

5

Theresa enjoyed the waltz lessons that she had with Barbara Trisham, but she was always glad when the time came to return home. One could take only so many sighs and heartfelt glances, thought Theresa, not at all sympathetic of her friend's attraction to the dancing master. She rode at a good pace, and since the groom, whom Miss Brown had prevailed upon her to take that particular day, had the good sense to hang back somewhat from his mistress, she was able to forget his presence.

The wood that bordered the squire's estate was ahead, and Theresa slackened the mare's pace so that she could enter the trees without losing her head to an overhanging branch. She was disconcerted when a gentleman rose up beside the bridle path and hailed her. She reined in her horse. "Good day to you, sir. Is there aught wrong?"

As she spoke, she eyed him curiously. The gentleman, who wore dusty riding clothes, was of fair stature and an athletic build. His dark hair served to emphasize his clear gray eyes, which at the moment held a frowning, impatient expression.

"I apologize for waylaying you, ma'am. But as you can see, my horse is lame. He threw a shoe and I have been walking him back to Rusland Park by easy stages," the gentleman said, waving in the direction of a dun gelding grazing nearby. "I wonder, would it be possible for you to send a message to the earl's stables?"

"Of course I shall do so," said Theresa. She was immensely curious about the gentleman, for he was the first person that she had ever met who had actually been to Rusland Park.

Her groom had come up in time to overhear the conversation, and he stared at the gentleman with suspicion. He knew as well as anyone in the neighborhood of the scandalous activities that were said to take place at Rusland Park. This nabob was no doubt one of those rakish sorts, he thought disapprovingly.

"John, pray ride on to Rusland Park and inform them of this gentleman's plight. I am sorry, sir, but I do not know your name," said Theresa, turning an inquiring glance at the gentleman.

He made a brief bow. "I am the Duke of Ashford," he said shortly.

Theresa smiled in the friendly fashion that was habitual to her. "And I am Miss Theresa Thaleman. How pleased I am to make your acquaintance, your grace." She became aware that the groom still sat his horse beside her. She frowned. "John, you may go now."

The groom's face settled into deep lines. He thought he knew where his duty lay. "Miss, the squire would fair have my hide if I was to leave you," he said with a significant glance toward the gentleman he was certain must be a rake.

Theresa flushed, embarrassed by her servant. There was a flash in her brown eyes and she spoke rather sharply. "Then I shall myself ride to Rusland Park for help." She made to turn the mare.

The groom was alarmed. "Nah, nah, miss! I be going." Reluctantly he left her, mumbling to himself and casting back several glances.

The Duke of Ashford had witnessed the exchange with something akin to amusement. "Your man is loyalty itself," he said dryly.

Theresa fingered her reins. She met his gaze. "It is sometimes a nuisance, actually. I much prefer riding alone."

"I sympathize with you. However, being accompanied by one's groom has its advantages. If I had had one with me today, I would not now be afoot," the duke said gravely.

Theresa laughed, her eyes sparkling in appreciation of what she was certain was intended as drollery. "How true! But then I would not have met your grace, which is surely a

pleasant coincidence, for I have never before had occasion
to speak with anyone who is familiar with the Earl of
Rusland. Is his lordship as wicked as they say?''

The duke was startled. He was on the point of delivering
a heavy snub when he realized from the unclouded curiosity
in Miss Thaleman's eyes that she was innocent of any
intended insult. ''The earl is like any other gentleman, though
perhaps he is more used to indulging his whims than are some
others,'' he said cautiously.

''Oh, you are speaking of all the lovely balls. And the
hunts! I have often heard the hounds baying and the call of
the horns on the morning air. I have wished many times that
I was able to participate,'' said Theresa. With a trace of
wistfulness she asked, ''Is it quite, quite wonderful to be a
guest at Rusland Park?''

The duke could not but smile a little at her naiveté. ''At
times it can be very pleasant. However, I find that once the
entertainments have been sampled, it all becomes rather
tedious. One begins to wish for the quiet and privacy of one's
own home and one's own pursuits.''

''Oh.'' Theresa could not imagine anything less likely than
to want to leave round-the-clock gaiety and return to the
drudgery of lessons. Then again, her circumstances were
beginning to change for the better. Only that afternoon she
had completed another lesson in the waltz and Monsieur
Philippe had complimented her on her quick progress.

The sound of hurried hoofbeats caught her attention and
she looked around to see that her groom had returned. It was
obvious from the sweating sides of his mount that he had
ridden it hard, and Theresa felt some annoyance at this
renewed sign of the careful guard that was set over her. Good
heavens, it is not as though I am to be murdered, and by
a duke, no less! in my own father's wood, she thought. She
hoped that the Duke of Ashford would take no notice of the
groom's overweening attention to duty.

''They be bringing a horse from Rusland Park to his lordship, miss,'' said the groom, anxiously eyeing his mistress.

She appeared to have suffered no harm during his absence, and he allowed a sigh to escape him.

"I will bid you good day then, your grace. I am already past due for tea, and my mother shall undoubtedly be wondering at my absence," said Theresa, gathering her reins. She extended her free hand to the duke. "I am most happy to have made your acquaintance, sir. I hope that we shall meet again in the future."

The Duke of Ashford took her gloved hand in the briefest of salutes. "Perhaps we shall, Miss Thaleman. Thank you again for your assistance."

Theresa nodded in farewell and set heel to her mare. She thought over the encounter as she and the groom rode through the trees. It had been most pleasant to converse with such an obviously sophisticated gentleman. She did not often get a chance to put to use her extensive grounding in polite conversation. As she reflected upon that, and the resulting consequences to her small freedoms if the encounter should become known, she drew up a little until the groom came level with her. "John, I think that it would be best if neither of us mentions the Duke of Ashford. I do not think that the squire would be best pleased to learn that someone from Rusland Park strayed onto the estate," she said.

"Aye, miss," agreed the groom. He had no intention of saying a word, for he knew that it would be his head if the squire were ever to learn that the miss had been left alone for several minutes in the company of an unknown gentleman.

Holland and Michael Thaleman arrived home a week later. As Theresa had anticipated, there was an initial explosion from the squire and a severe scolding by her mother. The twins were sufficiently repentant through the uncomfortable interviews to win over their mother, but the squire proved surprisingly recalcitrant. But despite the squire's determination not to allow his sons to get the better of his righteous ire yet again, he was not entirely proof against their penitent apologies.

The worst of the storm clouds eventually blew over and

the brothers quickly regained their usual cheerful spirits, which were not in the least dampened by their cousin George's observation that they could do the devil's own work and still worm their way into the soft places in the squire's and Mrs. Thaleman's hearts.

George recommended that the twins make themselves scarce as much as possible for a few days, since the sight of them was inclined to induce the squire's occasional mutterings. "And in the meantime I shall endeavor to jolly my uncle into a mellower frame of mind," promised George.

"And then we shall see some real sport," Michael said with a mischievous grin. He met his brother's brown eyes and they both laughed.

Seated on the corner of the library table and swinging one booted foot, George allowed a smile to play over his face as he surveyed them. He held a sincere fondness for his cousins, though he was often poles apart from them in tastes. He was the smart London dandy, in the habit of spending hours over his wardrobe, whereas the twins cared little for the correctness of their attire. He was given to attending social gatherings, and the twins preferred the hunt. He was inclined to listen to others' opinions of him, while the twins cared not a fig what anyone might think, Michael even less so than Holland.

Perhaps that was the crux of the twins' fascination for him, thought George. Their lives had been so much more untram-meled than his own. They had the capacity to enjoy life despite the social niceties. George often thought that without their unorthodox example he might easily have fallen into a mundane sort of existence long ago. But it was difficult to remain unaffected by the twins' exuberance and taste for mischief. He knew that his aunt regarded him somewhat in the light of a guardian over the twins, but he felt himself to be more their companion-in-high-jinks. It was true that at times he had attempted to deflate some of their more foolish schemes; but failing that, at least he saw that they came off safely. Thus it was that he fully intended to participate in their latest mad game. He would be a highwayman for a night and he thought that he would probably very much enjoy it to boot.

Theresa was delighted to welcome her brothers home. With the twins in residence, the household's routine could be counted upon to be wonderfully disrupted, not the least of which were her own lessons. The squire took an indulgent view of Theresa's defection from the schoolroom, saying that she would come to little harm in her brothers' company. Mrs. Thaleman was less tolerant. "Pray, sir, do you *wish* your daughter to career over the countryside and become talked up as a hurly-burly female of little distinction?" she demanded.

The squire looked sternly at his wife. "My dear Mrs. Thaleman, I shall certainly know how to answer such errant comments if ever they should arise, which I doubt. My credit is good enough in this county to protect my daughter from such allegations, ma'am! In the meantime, it will not do Theresa a whit of harm to breathe a bit of fresh air. She is looking a trifle peaked, to my mind."

Mrs. Thaleman was silenced, at least within the squire's hearing. But she made known her displeasure to Miss Brown. "For I do not mind telling you, Letitia, that I have grave doubts whether the gossips shall let this wildness of Theresa's go without comment. Why, she is all of seventeen years! It is not as though she were still a girl in pinafore and pigtails and thus could be forgiven a lapse of conduct now and again. No, indeed!"

"Miss Thaleman is known to be high-spirited, ma'am. Her conduct since her brothers' return can hardly be thought unusual," said Miss Brown in soothing accents. Almost as soon as she spoke, she regretted it, for Mrs. Thaleman leapt on her words and placed an entirely different light on her observation.

"That is exactly it, Miss Brown! I could almost wish that my boys had not come down, though I am always happy to see them, of course. But Theresa *will* follow them about like she was always used to!" Mrs. Thaleman lamented. "And what must George think? My nephew is quite the gentleman. He cannot think it other than passing strange that Theresa is allowed to behave in such a hoydenish fashion. I shall be glad to remove to London. At least in town Theresa will see that a lady must behave with circumspection at all times. I do believe that it is the poser. I know that you do your best, Miss Brown, as do I! But we must face it at last. Theresa does not have a respectable female of experience whom she may look up to. Suffice it to say that *we* do not fit the bill!''

Mrs. Thaleman ended on a note of some bitterness, and it took Miss Brown considerable time to soothe her employer's wounded feelings. She emerged from the interview exhausted by her efforts and with a very clear notion of what Mrs. Thaleman desired of her. But between her understanding and the desired results, there proved to be an unbridgeable distance. Miss Brown made a gallant attempt to exercise her considerable authority over Theresa, but her efforts were to little avail against Theresa's desire for her brothers' company.

Theresa felt a pang of guilt for abusing Miss Brown's good nature, but her contrition was not so strong that she would meekly accept internment in the house. She simply avoided Miss Brown as much as physically possible so that that lady could not easily give her a direct command to appear in the schoolroom. It became a game of wits. Miss Brown tried to anticipate her charge's movements so that she could circumvent her escapes, but the contest was from the beginning heavily weighted in Theresa's favor from years of experience in just such circumstances and an intimate knowledge of the house and estate.

Leaving her bed before dawn to sneak away to the stables was only one subterfuge of which Theresa made full use. The loss of a few hours' sleep was a small price to pay when it meant an entire day free to spend with her brothers.

Holland and Michael took it for granted that Theresa would want to tag along with them, as she had always done since she was barely able to walk. Therefore they were never surprised to find their sister waiting patiently for them in the chill morning air at the stables, dressed for riding.

On one such morning, as Holland handsomely acknowledged her presence, he added a caveat to her joining them. ''If we should chance to meet some young ladies, you are to take yourself off, Teri,'' he said firmly, gathering his reins. He harbored particular hopes for just such an occurrence, since he had earlier in the week happened to meet a certain young lady who had mentioned the possibility that she might be out that day.

The trio cantered out of the graveled drive to follow the tree-shaded lane. Theresa tossed her head, setting the feather in her hat waving. "Indeed I shall! I have no desire to watch you mooning over Mary Marling."

Holland reddened. He hoped that he knew better than to give his sister and brother any satisfaction by responding. He leaned from the saddle to open a gate into a field, hoping to deflect attention from his discomfiture. But Michael, who knew him better than anyone, laughed at him as he rode past. "She has you there, twin. And don't attempt to weasel out, because it was plain as a pikestaff last Christmas holiday that Mary had you sitting in her pocket."

"I did not sit in Miss Marling's pocket," Holland said with an assumption of dignity. He followed Theresa into the field and relatched the gate behind them.

"Oh, no. You danced with Miss Marling twice, and thereafter glowered at every other gentleman who came within greeting distance," said Michael, nodding affably.

Holland gave a reluctant grin. It had always been difficult for either twin to hide anything from the other, even if he had really wanted to. But Michael's teasing was not to be tolerated without a fight, and he retaliated with spirit. "Wait until some young lady throws a demure glance your way, Michael, and then we shall see who becomes the mooning calf."

"Not I. I shall hide behind my ecumenical collar when I take Orders," declared Michael. His brother made a rude remark and the twins were well-started on one of their familiar bickerings.

Theresa did not stay to listen, but set heel to her mount. The mare had been jibing restlessly at the bit and answered readily to the command, easing at once into a gallop. Behind her, she heard a shout, but she paid little heed. Her brothers could catch up with her if they wished.

6

Theresa sat the saddle with the ease of long familiarity, slightly bent against the rush of the wind. Riding was exhilarating to her. The swift strength of the horse beneath her, the rapid passing of the ground under the thundering hooves, the air that surged across her face and tugged at her clothing and hat, all combined to give her a sense of unfettered freedom.

Ahead was a stone wall, swiftly looming higher. Theresa sat herself for the jump, her hands and body urging her mount on. The mare rose, hung suspended for an incredible moment of weightlessness, then descended. The mare landed neatly. Theresa gently pulled her into a canter.

It was not long before her brothers joined her and expressed their admiration for her jumping prowess. "You are a true goer, Teri," said Holland with sincerity.

Theresa was warmed by their attention. She had almost forgotten what it was like to be with the twins. She included them both in a happy smile. "I am so glad that you two were rusticated. It has been so deadly dull without your larks and fun. I have had ony Barbara Trisham to talk to, and she is becoming a veritable stick these days. All she talks about are the newest fashion plates and her dancing master, who is rather handsome but not someone at whose glance *I* would swoon away."

Michael laughed, throwing his sister a glance. "Does she actually?"

"What, swoon? Of course not. But she thinks she ought. The man has such beautiful blue eyes, just like a Scottish loch, you know. What rot!" said Theresa disparagingly. She sighed over her friend's inexplicable and boring feeblemindedness. She certainly could not count on Barbara any longer to dispel the tedium of her days. A thought struck her and her eyes brightened. "Michael . . . Holland, *do* say that I may go with you! It would be such good sport to play at highwayman. And I've wanted for ever so long to get a closer peek at the guests who go to Rusland Park. Say that I may go!''

The twins exchanged a swift glance. Their smiles dimmed and their expression had become unusually grave when at last Michael spoke. "George should not have said anything to you.''

"But why ever not? I have always known beforehand of your most funning larks, even when I was too small to be a part of them,'' said Theresa in bewilderment.

Michael kept his gaze fixed on his horse's flicking ears, not wishing to see his sister's hurt expression. "But it is different now, Teri,'' he said.

Theresa looked from one to the other. Michael's face was somber, while Holland wore a deep frown. There was an unfamiliar dread growing slowly within her, which had its origins in her cousin George's refusal a few days earlier to consider her as one of the company. "I don't understand. Why should anything be different? We are still the best of friends and you know what I do not lack courage.''

"We are not questioning your courage, Teri,'' Holland said.

"No, of course not. But you are going to London for the Season,'' said Michael, as though that fact explained everything.

Theresa stared at her brothers. "But so might you, at least until the next term begins. What is there in that?''

Michael gave an explosive sigh. "Teri, you are going up for your first Season. You will be dancing and wearing fine new gowns and setting up flirtations—''

"I am not a flirt!'' Indignation colored Theresa's protest and drove color into her cheeks. The dread she felt was tinged with anger and gave emphasis to her words. Michael looked at her with a troubled expression, for once at a loss for words.

"Of course not," Holland said hurriedly, diving into the breach. "What Michael is trying to say, and badly too, I might add, is that you can no longer be a romp, Teri. You must grow up and act the lady. And perhaps even become affianced to some gentleman."

Theresa pulled up her mare. She stared at her brothers for several seconds. Horrible hurt and anger cascaded through her. Betrayal shadowed her huge soft brown eyes. First George, then Barbara, and now the twins had all changed toward her. But her brothers' defection was by far the most painful. Her familiar world was crashing about her in pieces and she was helpless to stop it. A tight fist seemed clenched about her throat so that she could barely speak. "How dare you," she breathed.

Michael reached out tentatively to touch her velvet sleeve. "Teri—"

She shook off his hand and pulled her horse about. Setting a hard heel to the mare's side, she put it into a swift gallop. Her brothers shouted after her, but Theresa only urged the mare to a faster pace. Within seconds she and the mare had disappeared in the copse of trees at the edge of the tilled fields.

The twins were left with the dreadful feeling that they had bungled things beyond repair. "Now look what you have done with your clumsy words," Michael said disgustedly.

"I! Who was it that said Teri was a flirt?" Holland demanded.

"I said she would set up flirtations. There's nothing in that. Why, only think of Mary Marling. She has dozens of suitors!" said Michael.

"I will thank you to leave Miss Marling out of this," Holland said from between clenched teeth.

"At least I did not say that *Miss Marling* is not a lady, which is what you implied of our own sister," Michael said hastily. His brother retaliated, and the twins plunged into the worst altercation of their lives.

It was several minutes before Theresa at last pulled up the laboring mare. Theresa slid from the saddle, her riding skirt falling down about her boots. She let the reins fall to the ground, and the tired mare dropped its head to begin grazing. Theresa walked a short distance away to lean against a low stone wall. She stared over the countryside and the road weaving into the distance. Tears slipped down her face and she brushed them away with a hasty hand. She could not believe that her brothers could have abandoned her so cruelly. Her mind went back over the years. From her first memories she had toddled after the twins. In the beginning she had been too small to be considered a playmate, but later she had been just as fleet of foot and fearless as they, and she had been accepted. Until the twins had come home this last time from school they had shared every facet of their lives with her.

But now suddenly, simply because she was to have her first Season, they had taken some ridiculous notion into their heads that she was too old to enjoy a lark or two. She was supposed to fill her head with silly thoughts of dances and clothes and the procurement of a husband.

The last horrified Theresa in some vague manner. She had no idea what a husband might require of his wife. She had only her observations of her mother and the other ladies of the neighborhood to judge by, but she suspected that once married, a female was firmly relegated to household duties and babies. There would be no more going out on one's mare whenever one wished, or taking time to walk about the rose garden and breathe in the sweet-scented air. All in all, marriage seemed a thoroughly boring way to finish one's life.

"Not I," said Theresa determinedly. "I shan't marry anyone who will forbid me to go on a lark now and then." Her initial euphoric anticipation of the trip to London had suffered a severe setback with her brothers' view of its consequences. But when she thought of the alternative, which entailed dull months confined to the environs of her father's estate because the Earl of Rusland was entertaining his infamous guests, Theresa could only shudder. She would certainly go to London. And she would enjoy all the dances and fine new clothes. Perhaps she would even flirt with some of the gentlemen, since the twins seemed to think that was what one did to enjoy one's first Season.

But she was decidedly not going to go out of her way to find a husband. She was going to have a wonderful Season, and when it was time to return home, she would simply tell Papa that she was sorry she had not found a proper husband. She expected that he would be disappointed at first, and certainly Mama would scold, but before long everything would be right again and she could go on as she always had. After all, that is the way it happened whenever the twins were rusticated. Theresa reasoned that there should be nothing different in her own case, especially when she knew that her father held a special place in his heart for his only daughter. At least that much had not changed.

"And if I should like the Season, then I shall ask Papa to send me again next year. I suppose one may have as many Seasons as one likes. At least, until one's family realizes that one has dwindled into an old maid," Theresa said with a small laugh. The hard pain in her breast eased a little with her feeble attempt at humor. She contemplated the road a moment. "And if that should become the case, I suppose the female is pensioned off or some such. I wonder if Papa would like to pension me off. I should like that, I think. Then I could go to Rusland Park whenever I wished."

Somewhat cheered by her reflections, Theresa started to turn toward her horse, when her eyes were caught by a bright glint buried in the earth beside the road. Curious, she scrambled over the low stone wall and knelt to brush the gravel and fine dirt away from the spot. A half-circlet of gold was exposed. Digging a little with one finger, Theresa found that she had discovered a fine ring, encrusted with several large stones set into the serpentine pattern of the gold. She held the ring up to the sun. The gems shone even through the coating of dust. "Oh, how pretty! But however did it come to be here?"

She slid the ring onto her slender finger and held up her hand, turning it from side to side so that the stones flashed fire in the sun. Theresa frowned slightly. The ring looked somehow wrong on her hand. She could not think for a moment why, but then realized that the size and diversity of the gems were somewhat gaudy for her taste. "Well, it is certainly nothing that I should like to wear," she said, slipping the ring off. She looked closer at the band, turning it between her fingers, and a delighted smile played over her face. The serpentine pattern was very cleverly done. It was the exact replica of a jolly little snake wending its way through the gem boulders until it swallowed its own tail. "It really is very clever. I wonder whose it is."

After giving the unusual ring a few more moments of contemplation, Theresa dropped it carelessly into her pocket. She went back over the low wall to collect her horse. Theresa used a stone for a mounting block to get back into her side-saddle. She was humming as she turned the mare toward home. The morning had started rather badly, with her falling out with the twins. She still felt hurt and bewildered that becoming a young lady meant that she was to be forced to give up her childhood playmates. But she was beginning to see the outlines of the new role being thrust upon her, and in all fairness, Theresa acknowledged to herself that she was excited by it. There was a certain allure to the talk of entertainments and fancy dress that she had been hearing so much of lately. After all, she had been complaining not a fortnight ago of having nowhere to go to show off her accomplishments.

She would use the London Season and everyone's obvious expectations of it to her own best advantage. When she had tired of it, she would return home. She was confident that the squire would always welcome her back, and though her mother would most likely scold because she had not become engaged, Theresa rather thought that she, too, would be glad to have her daughter return to her.

Holland and Michael would remain her dearest of brothers,

even though they no longer cared to include her in their adventures. Theresa felt a renewed pang of grief at the thought, but she shook her head. It was of no use to repine. Besides, she had thought of a rather brilliant way to get around the promise she had made to George, and take part in the highwayman scheme after all.

On the whole, Theresa thought she was exceedingly fortunate. She had her family and Miss Brown and she was going to London for the Season. She recalled that Barbara Trisham had confessed that she was positively green with envy that it was not she who was about to embark on town life. The memory was a pleasing one, she found. The discovery of the ring but seemed confirmation that the future held only good for her. Her brave reflections helped to soothe Theresa's bruised heart, and if she had but known it, the pain she experienced went far in tearing aside the outworn chrysalis of her childhood.

Holland and Michael were lying in wait for Theresa when she returned to the house. They came out of the billiards room to watch anxiously while she stripped off her riding gloves and dropped them and her crop on the hall table. Theresa said not a word to them upon their appearance, determined that they should feel her full displeasure, but her heart thawed at sight of their mournful expressions. She gave a hand to each and smiled up at them. "I do so love you both," she said.

The twins broke into relieved grins. "We quite thought you would give us up," Holland said. He did the gallant thing and with a flourish kissed his sister's hand.

Michael noted the gesture with approval and quickly followed suit, taking possession of her other hand. "And we would have been justly served, too. We were beasts, Teri," he said with a contrite air.

Theresa giggled at her brothers. They were so utterly transparent, she thought with fondness. She reclaimed possession of her hands and said, "True, and I should disown you. But I have thought better of it, at least for now." She wanted to change the subject, since it impinged too closely on her recent unhappiness. Suddenly recalling her find, she plunged one hand into her pocket to bring out the ring. "Only look at what I have found. It was in the dirt beside the road, as though someone had simply tossed it aside."

Michael took the ring and turned it in the light so that the jewels flashed. "Good God! What a hideous creation. Pray look, Holland. It is fit for the hand of a barbarian queen." He handed it to his brother.

Holland studied the ring in his turn. "Oh, I don't know. The jewels are quite good, and the ring itself is of a distinctive design."

"You will say next that you would not mind that monstrosity at all if it but graced the hand of Mary Marling," Michael said slyly. His twin flushed, opening his lips for a quick retort.

Theresa intervened hastily. "I do not fancy the gemwork myself, but Holland is right about the ring. I do so like that quaint little serpent. But look how he winds about and ends by swallowing his own tail!"

Michael allowed that the gold serpent did have its charm, then asked, "But what will you do with it, Teri? It is not as though you will ever find out to whom it belongs. Why, the ring could have been buried for ages."

"I don't know. I suppose that I shall keep it. But it seems such a waste to have the ring simply tucked away in my jewel box, for I am certain that I shall never wear it," Theresa said. She eyed the gaudy jewels again and made a face. "These gemstones are a bit vulgar, I think. I know Miss Brown would say so, and as for Mama . . . why, she always says that a young girl appears at her best in pearls."

"By Jove! I have a wonderful notion," Holland said, throwing a look at his brother. He took the ring from Theresa again. "What if we were to have it reworked for you, Theresa? These stones here could be removed without destroying the serpent's progress, and it would look much more the thing for a young lady. I'd wager even Mama would approve of it then."

"Yes, and we could have the loose jewels made up into

small earrings. That is, if you should like it," said Michael.

"Oh, I would, above all things! It would be my first grown-up set of jewelry," Theresa said, delighted.

"Consider it done, then. It will be our present to you upon the occasion of your first Season," Holland said with a flash of pomposity.

"Thank you! You are both such dears," Theresa said. "I shall leave the ring with you now. I can scarcely wait to see the set." The hall clock chimed the hour and Theresa jumped, startled. "Oh! I did not realize how late it is. I must change or Mama will scold me for coming to luncheon in all my dirt." She waved happily at her brothers as she ran lightly up the stairs to her bedroom.

The twins watched her until she disappeared. Michael glanced at his brother. "That was well done, Holland. With that small bit of inspiration of yours, we have totally redeemed ourselves with Teri."

Holland grinned. He flipped the ring into the air and caught it again to slip it into his pocket. He slapped his brother on the shoulder. "I say, Michael, let us celebrate by poaching one or two of the squire's partridges."

Michael laughed. "I am with you, twin. We'll persuade Cook to make up our luncheon in a basket, shall we? I should dislike going off when there are meat pies to be had." Holland agreed wholeheartedly, and the brothers, alike in build and carriage but quite different in some respects of character, sauntered off to the gun room.

7

It was pitch dark under the trees on the hillside. But the moon floating overhead, though wreathed in clouds, offered enough illumination to allow Theresa to see the road below perfectly well. The wind brushed the branches overhead, and feeling its questing fingers, Theresa shivered. She knew that she was drawing a fine line with her promise to George, but she consoled herself for the hundredth time that since she was not going to participate, she was not actually breaking her word.

Theresa sat motionless on her horse in the shadows of the wooded knoll. She scanned the scene below once more. From her vantage point she could see the dark forms of her brothers and her cousin as they also sat motionless, a little way back and out of sight of the road. It had been a long wait. The moon had already passed its zenith. Guests traveling to or from Rusland Park were apparently to be scant this evening. Theresa cracked a yawn. She blinked hard, hardly able to keep her eyes open. The thought of her warm soft bed was enticing.

Suddenly the rumble of wheels caught her ears. She straightened abruptly, all drowsiness at an end. Her heart thumping and her nerves drew taut as the approaching coach came into sight. Below her, the men hunched over their mounts in attitudes of anticipation.

When the coach had neared, the trio burst from hiding, their firearms waving in wild display. There was a deliberate shot let off into the air and a puff of smoke bellied toward the moon. ''Stand and deliver!''

Theresa recognized Holland's voice, though it was muffled by design or distance. She leaned over her mount's withers, her fingers tight in the mare's coarse mane. So intent was she on what was happening that, without being consciously aware of it, Theresa nudged her horse forward. The mare began a slow descent toward the drama being played out with such gusto.

The coachman's curses carried plain on the clear night air. He struggled gallantly with the carriage's startled, plunging team. At a colorful and forceful oath from one of the highwaymen, the postilion riding beside the still-cursing coachman threw down his blunderbuss and raised his hands high above his head, bracing himself with his legs against the the bucking of the carriage.

The second highwayman rode around to the front of the equipage. Ramming his pistol in his belt, he reached down to grab the leading rein of the leaders, and at last the beasts began to settle, until they stood shuddering in the traces.

The coachman stared into the horse pistol held by the hooded horseman who had threatened the postilion with such good effect. The coachman was struck by the air of negligence about the highwayman, who sat his mount with consummate ease and an elegant set to his shoulders. "As if it were a blinking tea party," he muttered with disgust.

The remaining highwayman threw a sally to his fellows and reached down to grasp the handle of the coach door. Before he would twist the handle, the carriage window was thrown open. A pistol was thrust out. "Consider yourself warned, fool!"

Even as the suppressed anger in the cold voice punctured the levity of the amateur highwaymen, Theresa desperately spurred her mare to cover the remaining distance to the road. She aimed her mare's shoulder directly into her brother's horse, knocking the animal off balance. Simultaneously there was a deafening explosion.

Theresa's ears rang. A cloud of acrid white smoke burned her nostrils. She saw her brother flinch, and with horrified disbelief she witnessed the rapid bloom of blood on his coat before he slid unconscious from the saddle. "Michael!"

The mare had staggered with the force of the collision, but righted itself within a few steps. Theresa pulled sharply on the reins, dragging her horse around. The unmanned horse shied from the man sprawled on the ground, snorting violently at the scent of warm blood, before it raced away. Theresa threw herself out of the saddle to fall on her knees beside her brother. Holland was already before her, his breath ragged and sobbing as he frantically tore off his twin's mask and lifted his crumpled form in his arms. "Michael, Michael!" he groaned, rocking.

"Put him down, Holland! Let me see," said Theresa. She tried to force Holland's arms open, but to no avail. She looked around wildly. "George!" Immediately her cousin was there, talking urgently but softly to Holland, forcing him away.

Holland stumbled back, his staring eyes riveted on his brother's still form. He raised his hand and glanced at it, puzzled by the sensation of wetness. His face drained white at the dark smear of blood on his palm. His mind was momentarily numbed by a terrible realization. What had begun as a lighthearted lark had ended with tragic consequences.

Theresa found a faint pulse and heaved a sob of relief. But the blood welling through Michael's coat was unbated. She stripped off her neckcloth and folded it against the wound.

"You will need my handkerchief as well." Theresa turned her head, and without a word took the proffered white linen square. Vaguely she wondered at the identity of the calm, oddly familiar voice, but it was not really important. Michael must be gotten home as quickly as possible, but she did not know how it was to be done.

Holland gave a bellow of rage at the sight of the stranger who had shot his brother and then had the audacity to descend from the carriage to speak to his sister. "You! You have killed him, you bastard!"

"Holland!" George Bennett grabbed his cousin, attempting to stop him, but with a stiffened forearm Holland sent him spinning into the road dust. Holland charged, his large hands outstretched to catch his enemy by the throat.

The gentleman stepped back. Coolly he judged the moment, and with perfect timing threw a hard right to his antagonist's chin. Holland met the blow full-on. There was a loud crack. His eyes widened in brief surprise before he crumpled senseless to the ground.

"Oh, damnation!" Theresa said despairingly. She spared a brief unhappy glance for Holland, who lay motionless nearby.

"Quite. It has been a damnable night all round," said the gentleman wearily. He dusted himself off.

Theresa started violently. Her eyes flew to the gentleman's face. She knew now where she had heard his voice. She had spent several minutes in his company while her groom took word of the gentleman's lame horse to Rusland Park. She was appalled by her luck. A well-bred young lady would never be discovered in such a damning situation.

The duke's servants had watched the proceedings with a certain satisfaction, and now the coachman spoke up. "Shall I put the team in motion, your grace?"

The Duke of Ashford contemplated the field of battle. His gaze met that of the young person kneeling beside the wounded man. "Yes, Humphries. We shall wish to convey these two would-be ruffians to their home as soon as possible."

"Your grace!"

The duke ignored the indignant protest of his coachman and addressed the remaining two highwaymen. "If that is agreeable to you?"

The younger of the two shot a swift glance at the other, who had picked himself up, and while dusting himself off, had come forward in time to hear the question. He said firmly, "Indeed, it is most kind of you, sir."

The boy had a well-educated voice, thought Hugo. As he had suspected, the highwaymen were young idiots from the neighborhood, out for a lark. It was a pity that his shot had gone so awry. He had meant only to wing the young fool to teach him a much-deserved lesson. He would have done so but for the interference of the boy. Otherwise the one lad would not now be lying at death's door.

With that grim thought, Hugo set about ordering the ensconcing of the wounded man inside the coach. The youngest lad opted to ride inside the carriage so that he could keep a sharp eye on the still-seeping wound. The ruffian who had been knocked unconscious began to come around once all was settled, and he got groggily onto his horse. The last member of the former band of highwaymen led off the mare belonging to the youngest of the group and that of his groggy companion, who was still too dizzy to direct his own mount.

Once the direction was known and the coach well on its way, the Duke of Ashford slumped in his corner of the coach, occupied by his own thoughts. After he had broken off his liasion with Lady Statten he had deliberately stayed away from Rusland Park for a time to allow the gossip about himself and the lady to die a natural death. He had decided to once again take advantage of the earl's standing invitation and drive down for the weekend's entertainment. But . . . It had been a singularly unnerving evening at Rusland Park, and one that he would not soon repeat. In fact, he thought, it was the last visit he intended to make. The earl's brand of hospitality made it all too easy for Lady Statten to weave her sticky webs, all designed to entrap him again. He wondered how it was that the lady had once appeared so desirable to him.

The carriage with its mounted escort soon reached the manor house. George jumped off his horse and dashed up the front steps to give the bell an urgent pull. He hallooed the house for good measure. A window was thrown open above and the squire sarcastically inquired after his state of inebriation. George stepped back so that he could see the dark outlines of his uncle's bulky form. "Not I, sir! It is Michael. He has been shot and is in a bad way." He heard the squeal of alarm from his aunt and her urgent questionings.

"Shot! Good heavens. I shall be down directly." The squire's head was withdrawn, but before the window could be closed his voice floated down. "My dear lady, calm yourself. It is likely only a scratch. Yes, yes, the doctor—" The sash was firmly shut.

After what seemed an interminable rattling of the lock, the front door was pulled open. The butler blinked with an alarmed air, his white hair disheveled from sleep. He held a lantern high. "Master Bennett! What is it?" Behind him were the household's two footmen. They were half-dressed, their nightshirts tucked any which way into their trousers.

"It is a bad business, Roberts," George said. He brushed by the butler, rapidly explaining the matter and what was required as he stripped off his riding gloves. The footmen rushed outside, one taking the lantern with him. The butler hurried away to the servants' quarters to rouse the household to action.

A heavy tread on the stairs alerted George, and he spun around. His uncle was descending swiftly, heavy brows contracted low over his angered and anxious eyes. He had belted on a voluminous dressing gown of florid character and his sleeping cap still covered his head. Mrs. Thaleman came behind him, wringing her hands. Her voice was raised in unceasing exclamations.

The squire ignored his wife's questions. He looked at George with an unfathomable expression that made his nephew extremely uncomfortable. Then activity at the open doorway claimed his attention. He saw his daughter enter first, attired in breeches and jerkin with her hair coming loose from under a low-crowned hat. She aided Holland, who sported a ripening bruise on his jaw and staggered a little as he came up the steps. Behind them came a stranger attired in evening clothes, who carried a flickering lantern.

When he entered the portal, the Duke of Ashford surveyed the scene with mild curiosity. He recognized the typical furnishings of a moderately well-off country squire and easily surmised the identity of the heavyset gentleman standing in the hall. The squire's stolid worth was evident at a glance, but the sight of the almost hysterical woman who clutched at the squire's arm made his brows rise slightly. At a respectful word behind him he moved aside for the footmen, who carefully carried in their precious burden. Michael's head lolled while the light from the bunch of candles burning in the hall luridly highlighted his bloodied coat.

Throwing up her hands, Mrs. Thaleman shrieked with horror. Her eyes turned up in her head and she proceeded to faint dead away. George leapt forward to catch her. He grunted as he caught his aunt's full weight in his arms.

The squire spared a pitying glance for his overcome spouse. "The silly woman could never stand the sight of blood. 'Tis the damndest thing," he said. He bent over his prostrate son and put his hand in front of Michael's nose to feel for his breath. With a nod of satisfaction, the squire straightened. "Take him up to his room. Ah, Roberts, there you are! I want someone to fetch old Meg, the midwife. She'll do in a pinch . . . She is already here? Good man! I assume that you have given orders that a doctor be sent for, have you not, George?"

"Yes, sir," George said, a slight strain in his well-modulated voice. He heard an exclamation and looked around to discover that the housekeeper and Mrs. Thaleman's maid had arrived, followed immediately by Miss Brown. With relief he gave over his burden to their competent care.

The maid produced a smelling salt and waved it under her mistress's nose with almost immediate effect. Mrs. Thaleman coughed violently and bolted to an upright position. "Michael! Where is he?" she demanded.

Miss Brown spoke in soothing tones. "He has been taken upstairs to his room, Mrs. Thaleman. Pray calm yourself."

Mrs. Thaleman struggled to her feet with her maid's aid. "Calm myself! My son is likely dead and you wish for me to calm myself, Letitia! What kind of unnatural, unfeeling creature do you take me for? I will go to him immediately."

"My dear, might I suggest that you give the men time to

rid Michael of his bloodied clothing and allow old Meg to settle him comfortably?'' suggested the squire. He gazed significantly at his wife, and her face turned a sickly green once more. She wavered on her feet, and had it not been for her maid on one side and Miss Brown on the other, she might have fallen.

''Perhaps a spot of tea is what is needed,'' the housekeeper said.

Miss Brown threw the woman a relieved glance. ''Thank you! Mrs. Thaleman, pray let us go into the drawing room until you are better recovered.''

''Yes, yes. I am feeling quite unwell, now that I think on it,'' said Mrs. Thaleman in a weakened voice. The women, with slowed steps, quit the hall and the housekeeper bustled off, speaking sharply to the chambermaids she caught peeping through the servants'-quarter door.

Meanwhile the squire was casting a cursory glance at Holland's swollen face. ''You've a glass jaw, I see. Whose knuckles did you break, lad?''

Holland pointed a shaking finger at the stranger who stood quite calmly just inside the door. His voice shook with angry accusation. ''That gentleman did it, sir! He shot Michael, too!''

The gentleman stepped forward and swept a bow. ''I am Hugo Ian Ashford, the Duke of Ashford, sir. I fear that I must plead guilty to your son's charges. I meant but to wing the young scoundrel as he sought to force open my carriage. Unfortunately, my aim was thrown off.''

Theresa threw the duke a startled look. She felt a wave of nausea. It was her fault then, that the duke had missed his intended target and Michael had been so badly wounded.

''Highwaymen?'' The squire's voice rumbled ominously. He stared hard at his son and nephew, who shifted uncomfortably under his frosty glare. His glance fell at last on his daughter and he contemplated her thoughtfully. She had said not a word since entering the house, and he saw now that she was rather white of face. ''You may be excused for now, Theresa. But I shall wish to speak with you in the morning.''

"Yes, Papa," Theresa said, her voice unnaturally subdued. She felt eyes upon her and turned her head to meet the duke's startled and rather disapproving gaze as he raked her breeched form. It nettled her that this stranger should show such patent disapprobation, and the spurt of anger served to steady her nerves. With a flash of impudence she bowed as smartly as any young gentleman. "Good evening to you, your grace." She marched away to the stairs with a swaggering gait.

The squire sighed gustily. "I hope that you will excuse my daughter, your grace. She is the very devil to manage at times. Pray come into my study, where we can be private. Holland . . . George, do not go off just yet. I wish you both to join us, if you please. I think it past time that I hear the round tale." He held the study door open for his three companions to enter before him, and then addressed the butler, who hovered nearby. "Roberts, we'll have coffee. And you will let me know when the doctor arrives."

"Very good, sir," the butler said.

Theresa had finished her bath when she heard from her maid that the doctor was examining her brother. Quickly she donned gown and robe and tiptoed into the dressing room adjoining Michael's bedroom so that she could hear the doctor's pronouncement for herself. When she heard that the ball had passed low throgh the shoulder and had not done damage to anything vital, she sagged with relief.

The physician looked across the still white figure in the bed to meet the squire's grim expression. "The lad was fortunate, Squire. Any lower and the ball would have entered his heart."

"Aye, fortunate. But what of the next time?" asked the squire bitterly.

The physician shook his head sympathetically. He was familiar with the Thaleman twins and the consequences of their sense of fun from a long string of such urgent calls, though this night was perhaps the gravest visit he had made in some time. He began to pack his bag. "The loss of blood concerns me, Squire. Michael must have complete rest and quiet if he is to recover quickly."

"He shall have it, I promise you that," the squire said.

Theresa slipped away as quietly and unobtrusively as she had come. Sometime later George found her sitting alone in her sitting room. He stood in the doorway a silent moment, watching her face. Unaware of her cousin's scrutiny, Theresa sat before the fire with her legs curled under her and a shawl hugged about her shoulders. It occurred to George that she appeared unusually small and forlorn.

"Teri, why were you even there?" he asked softly.

Theresa gave a violent start. "Oh! George, you frightened me half to death."

When she said nothing more, but turned around to stare into the flames, George crossed the small room to drop down beside her. "Teri, what was in your head tonight? I had your solemn word that—"

"That I would not play at highwayman. I kept my word, George." Theresa smiled faintly at his exasperated sigh. "I know it's splitting hairs, George. But I saw no harm in it, truly. None of you would ever have known I was there if it had not been for the Duke of Ashford." She paused a moment. Then her voice came very small. "Michael was very fortunate."

George Bennett's shoulders sagged. "Quite fortunate. It is all that I can think about. I should never have agreed to such madness. Michael lies there so pale and still . . ." He ran an agitated hand through his hair, a destructive action so uncharacteristic of him that it spoke volumes.

Theresa put her hand on his arm. "George, do not. If anyone is to blame for Michael's grievous wounding, it is I. It was I who knocked Michael into his lordship's direct line of fire."

George covered her hand with his own and squeezed her

fingers. "Vastly pretty, the pair of us. Shall I scoop up the ashes from the grate or shall you?"

Theresa laughed with a touch of her former spirit. "I wish I could see the dandified Mr. George Bennett wearing sackcloth and ashes!"

"I might as well. I've torn my best coat with this night's work," George said regretfully.

Theresa shook her head at him. "You are such a pattern card, cousin. I thank you, but no ashes, George. Though such a costume might persuade Papa to deal easier with me."

George grimaced. "The squire is in rare form, believe me. I have never seen him so enraged. He gave Holland and me such a trimming that my ears still ring. He threatened to lock us all up as lunatics, and with the Duke of Ashford witness to it all."

"His grace must have been poised to flee," Theresa said with a laugh.

"Not he. The duke attended to the squire with the politest air I have ever had occasion to witness. His grace might have been at the theater, for all the surprise he allowed show. He is an odd one, to be sure. When the squire was done flaying Holland and me, he turned to offer the duke hospitality for the night, whereupon his grace accepted with just the right degree of civility and assured my uncle that it would afford him the greatest pleasure."

"Then I suppose that I shall see his grace at breakfast. With Papa glowering over the table at me, I do not know that I will wish to do the pretty," Theresa said with a sigh.

George rose to his feet. "Oh, I don't think that his grace will be the least bit bothered if you were to neglect him because my uncle chooses to rip up at you over the coffee. I gathered the impression that ice water runs in his grace's veins. Nothing at all moves him to emotion."

After George had wished her good night and left her alone, Theresa went into her bedroom to her secretary and took out her journal. She wrote for several minutes, and when she was done, she reread the lengthy entry. With a sigh, she put away the journal and blew out her candles.

As she settled herself in bed, she reflected that it had been a most educational evening. She did not think that she would again be so eager to jump into the middle of one of her brothers' larks. Indeed, she had learned a valuable lesson and one which Miss Brown would undoubtedly heartily applaud.

The following morning Theresa went out early for a ride. She thought that it would help steady her nerves so that she could meet with her sire in a calm, collected manner. When she returned to the house she went directly to the breakfast room, where she knew that the family would already have assembled for the morning meal. "Good morning, Mama, Papa," she said gaily.

Theresa pretended not to notice when her parents' acknowledgments of her presence were less than enthusiastic. Obviously Mama and Papa were taking a grim view of her involvement in the happenings of last night. Theresa thought it would behoove her to be on her best behavior and try to turn them up sweet before the inevitable lecture she would be treated to after breakfast.

She greeted Holland, her cousin, and Miss Brown before dropping a demure curtsy to the Duke of Ashford. "I had hoped to meet you again in more suitable circumstances, your grace. I am certain you will agree that last night we were all laboring under uncommon tension. For myself, I must apologize for my sad lack of propriety," she said. Theresa took her place at the table, ignoring the quick glances of disbelief among the members of her family.

"I have quite forgotten the incident, Miss Thaleman," said the duke, a faint smile quirking his lips. He studied the daughter of the house with a mild degree of curiosity. It hardly seemed possible that the well-mannered and appropriately dressed young woman seated at the table was the same pert, breeched hoyden of the evening before.

"Could I persuade you to more coffee, your grace?"

Theresa asked. When he assented, she lifted the pot and filled his cup herself. She inquired whether he lived in London, and upon discovering that he did indeed reside in the metropolis, she let drop that shortly she and her mother and companion would be traveling to town for the Season. In a very few minutes the entire company was making civil conversation concerning London and its entertainments.

Mrs. Thaleman leaned over to whisper in Miss Brown's ear, "I have never in my life been more astonished, Miss Brown. Theresa is atually behaving with all the grace of an accomplished hostess! I am quite in charity with her again, believe me."

The Duke of Ashford took his leave of the Thalemans soon after breakfast, saying that he was expected in London. Once the distinguished visitor was seen into his carriage and it started down the graveled drive, the squire turned to eye his daughter. "Aye, you've put on a fine performance, miss. But it did not turn me up sweet, as you no doubt hoped. We shall still have our little talk. Come with me, Teri."

"Yes, Papa," Theresa said meekly.

Mrs. Thaleman hurried to her spouse's side. "Now, Squire, do not be too hard on our dear daughter. As Theresa so winningly told his grace, we were all somewhat at outs, and she did apologize, did she not?"

The squire grunted with sudden amusement. He shot his daughter a swift glance and he was not behind in catching the gleam in her eyes before she could adjust her expression. "So you speak for her, madam?"

Mrs. Thaleman nodded firmly. "Indeed, and I must, Squire. In this instance I believe that Theresa redeemed herself quite well. Though I hope that you will not make a habit of riding about the countryside in your brothers' old breeches, Theresa. It was quite shocking, to say the least, and the Duke of Ashford was amazingly tolerant not to say a word about it. But I took him for a most refined gentleman, not at all like some of those others whom we have observed visiting at Rusland Park."

"No, Mama, I shall not have occasion to wear the breeches again," Theresa said.

"Then we shall not say another word about this most regrettable incident. Shall we, Squire?" said Mrs. Thaleman with a meaningful look.

The squire shrugged, knowing when it was best to give way. It was so rare an occurrence for his wife to champion her daughter that he was reluctant to spoil the unusual harmony.

Mrs. Thaleman smiled and reached out to hug her daughter, startling Theresa to no end, because her mother was rarely demonstrative. "Run along now with Miss Brown, Theresa."

"Yes, Mama," Theresa stammered. She threw a marveling look backward over her shoulder as she left the room.

When Theresa was well on her way, Mrs. Thaleman turned to the squire. "I hope that you may now see the necessity of giving our daughter a Season, dear sir. She cannot go on as she is, wearing breeches and scrambling after her brothers into whatever follies they may concoct. To my mind, it cannot come too early for Theresa to become affianced to some gentleman who will be a steady and guiding influence upon her."

"Perhaps you have a point, Mrs. Thaleman," said the squire in reluctant agreement. But when he recalled years past, it was difficult to accept the thought of his little girl leaving him so soon. The reflection depressed him and, announcing that he had papers to attend to, he went to shut himself up in his study.

8

His grace, reflected the Duke of Ashford's secretary, the Honorable Winfred Herbert Winthrop, was at times a very difficult employer. Winthrop studied the duke's graceful, athletic figure sitting in a pose of ease in the chair, the thin white hands that held the papers, the languid droop of his lids. Only the duke's firm-lipped mouth and the decided cut of his jaw belied his studied attitude of lazy boredom.

The duke was a good five years younger than his own thirty-and-five, but at times it came as a surprise to recall the fact. The Duke of Ashford had already experienced more in some ways than any gentleman of his age should have, Winthrop thought.

Orphaned at an early age, raised by an unloving and careless guardian, the Duke of Ashford had entered his majority and polite society a shy, backward young gentleman. He had been fair game for certain hardened gamesters and rapacious mamas with marriageable daughters.

It was only by the skin of his teeth that the Duke of Ashford had survived his disastrous introduction to gaming. Ever since, he had carefully husbanded his assets until the probability of financial ruin was a thing of the past. He no longer gamed to dissipation as he once had, and now touched the cards only as a social nicety. As for the marriage trap sprung by one ambitious mother, it had only been the young lady's unexpected elopement to Gretna Green with a totally ineligible army officer that had saved his grace from an early and unwelcome marriage.

Winthrop's lips tightened when he thought of the third evil to touch the young duke's life. Though Hugo had grown up lonely and unwanted by his miserly guardian, once he had reached his majority and the extent of his weealth became generally known, there had been a regular parade of distant cousins and the like to descend upon him with claims of undying affection and sad stories of financial difficulties. It had been the disillusioning effects of these people which had laid the final capstone to Hugo's cold cynicism.

An appeal of importunity was still sometimes received, and Winthrop had been given strict instructions on how to deal with the causes presented. In the short three years that the secretary had been with the duke, he had heard such nonsense and outright lies that he had come to understand in a small measure why the duke had become as he was.

The Duke of Ashford had quickly learned to be suspicious and bored by the hangers-on that followed in his wake. He immersed himself in all the entertainments that his position and youth opened to him, but he allowed nothing to disturb his equanimity. His open cynicism was a byword in polite society, and it was said that the Duke of Ashford had forgotten the gift of laughter.

The duke's eyes rose to meet his secretary's gaze, and the illusion of insouciance was completely shattered, for those steel-gray eyes were cold and wintry. "Herbert, do you honestly expect me to lend credence to this claptrap?"

The secretary sighed. His employer's demand was milder than what one might expect, but Winthrop had cherished the hope that for once the duke might be brought to see the importance of the bills being brought before the House of Lords. At heart, Winthrop was a keen student of politics, and it was a constant frustration to him that the Duke of Ashford did not share that interest. "No, your grace. However, I wished you to be aware of the possible consequences if the matter continues to go unaddressed."

The duke put up a hasty hand. "Pray do not enumerate the consequences for me yet again, Herbert!"

"Very well, your grace." There was a hint of reproof in Winthrop's voice, of which he was quite unconscious. He would have been aghast if anyone had accused him of chiding his social betters.

The Duke of Ashford was not insensitive to the nuances of his secretary's voice. When he gave it any thought it all, he recognized that Winthrop's good opinion was important to him. He gave a rare smile. "You are a determined fellow, Herbert. Despite my avowed disinterest, you insist that I be brought to an awareness of my public responsibilities. Very well, dear fellow. I shall lend an ear and perhaps even a word or two in the next session of the House. Will that satisfy you?"

The secretary looked mometarily startled. Recovering, he allowed himself the liberty of a smile. This interview was going unusually well, and he wondered at the duke's sudden tractability. He had not heard any rumors of a new inamorata, and there had been no delicately scented letters written in a new hand for the duke's attention. A frowning expression fleetingly entered his eyes at the thought of those envelopes that *had* come with persistence and regularity. But now was not the moment to bring that correspondence to his employer's attention. "Indeed, your grace. For the moment."

The duke tossed aside the papers. "You will be the death of me, Herbert. The harshest of taskmasters, to be sure! Already I am grown haggard and old from your earnestly voiced appeals."

Winthrop grinned as he neatly gathered up the scattered papers from the desk. "I devoutly hope not, your grace. I should dislike to open the mountains of condolences that your early demise would certainly generate, especially those from prostrated dames whose hopes for their daughters would be quite dashed."

The duke stared at his secretary a moment. Winthrop's brown eyes held a humorous gleam, and not for the first time Hugo appreciated the secretary's sincerity of character. His life was fraught with toadies and climbers of both sexes. He could not think of even one acquaintance that he would unreservedly label a friend. It was ironic that because of his birth it was only with his employee that he could be certain of honest companionship. "I should turn you off without a character, Herbert."

The secretary bowed, not at all concerned. He started to turn away. "Now that you have successfully riveted my undivided attention, Herbert, was there aught else that I should be made aware of?" the duke asked, slumping comfortably into his chair.

The secretary hesitated, a shadow crossing his pleasant features. The Duke of Ashford was quick to catch his indecision. "I suspect that I know the cause of that frown. Have there been further communications from Lady Statten?"

"Yes, your grace. Unfortunately, silence on your part seems not to have dimmed the lady's determination," Winthrop said. He went to his desk and brought a stack of letters out for the duke to view. "I know that my instructions were to consign all billets from Lady Statten to the flames, and so I did until I realized that the sheer volume of the correspondence had to be brought to your grace's attention."

The duke held out his hand peremptorily. The secretary handed him the neatly tied bundle of pale yellow envelopes, from which wafted the unmistakable and familiar scent of lilies. Hugo's mouth tightened. Lady Statten was proving to be more obstinate than expected. It had been more than a month since the unpleasant scene between them. In all that time he had not once willingly communicated with the lady, and yet she still apparently refused to accept that their ways had permanently parted. He weighed the bundle thoughtfully. "I think it time that Lady Statten was given the satisfaction of an answer, Herbert."

The secretary was startled and somewhat dismayed. Surely the duke was not contemplating a reconciliation with one that he had provately characterized from the beginning as a man-eating jade. But when he met the duke's gaze, he was reassured by his employer's unholy smile. "Certainly, your grace. What is it you require?"

The duke tossed him the unopened letters. "Burn them." Then he proceeded to tell his secretary what he wanted done with the ashes.

The package was delivered to Lady Statten's town house by one of the Duke of Ashford's liveried servants. Lady Statten was in her dressing room, and the package was given to her maid, who immediately handed it to her mistress. Her ladyship's fingers curled about the box. "I knew that he could not gainsay me forever," she said in satisfaction. "Inform the man to wait for my reply."

"The man did not stay for a reply, my lady," said the maid.

Lady Statten's plucked brows rose. "No? It is of little consequence. I expect that I shall be seeing the duke quite soon in any event. Here, Louise. Open it and read to me his grace's note." She sat down again at her dressing table to finish applying with a hare's-foot a light dusting of powder to her face. She watched her maid in the mirror, a faint smile caressing her full lips.

"Very well, my lady." The maid carefully undid the string and lifted off the lid of the box. She bit back an exclamation, and a queer look came over her face.

Lady Statten turned sharply away from the mirror. "Give it to me at once!" She snatched the box from her maid's hands, so anxious was she to see inside it. The maid watched her face with an almost fearful fascination.

Lady Statten was seemingly frozen to her seat. She said not a word for several seconds. Her face and neck began to mottle. "The bastard! The rotten, bloody bastard!" Her voice rose on the syllables. With a violence that was frightening in its intensity, she flung the box and its contents against the wall. Gray ash showered the wall and filled the air as an object fell softly to the carpet. Lady Statten paced the room like a tigress, snatching at whatever came to hand and smashing it against the wall or floor. Porcelain jars and bottles splintered. A cloying mixture of perfumes filled the air. Invectives flowed from between Lady Statten's clenched white teeth.

The maid retreated, wide-eyed, coughing on the ash and sickening scents. Lady Statten whirled around to face her.

Her glorious red hair had tumbled down about her face and a streak of dirt marked her cheek. Her green eyes were wild. To the horrified servant, she looked like a madwoman. Her mouth twisted as it worked. "You! Get out this instant!"

"Yes, my lady," gasped the maid. She curtsied hurriedly and fled through the door.

When Lady Statten was alone, she stood with clenched fists, her thoughts murderous. Her slitted eyes fell on the object that had lain on top of the ash in the box. She went over and with her heel she quite deliberately ground the dead lily into the carpet.

Sometime later, Lady Statten left her residence. She had ordered her footman to get a hackney cab for her, and the nondescript vehicle was waiting at the curb. She stepped into the carriage and directed it to a certain address on the fringes of the respectable portion of town. When the carriage came to a stop outside its destination, the lady who descended from it bore little resemblance to the magnificent Lady Statten. This lady was heavily veiled and wore a drab voluminous cloak that disguised her figure. After directing the cabby to wait for her, the lady went up to the door of the small town house and rang the bell. The door was opened by a huge manservant. As the lady swept inside the door, her cloak fluttered open and a brief sight of her fine skirt could have been seen if there had been anyone curious enough to observe it.

Lady Statten did not remove her veil as she was shown into the same parlor where she had been several times before. Lady Statten roamed restlessly around the exotically furnished room, her gloved fingers plucking absently at embroidered draperies or curious figurines that were vaguely Oriental in style. Lady Statten was unconscious that she avoided that corner of the room in which a woven gold-and-red patterned curtain covered a doorway.

The whisper of heavy brocade alerted her, and Lady Statten turned quickly. The mistress of the house had come. The woman allowed the thick curtain to drop behind her and stood motionless for several seconds as she observed her visitor. Her eyes were dark, fathomless, and unnaturally arresting. Lady Statten felt a chill cross her skin under the woman's bright, glittering scrutiny. At last the woman motioned for Lady Statten to be seated.

When they faced one another across the small parquet table, the woman spoke. There was a thread of amusement in her voice. "So, from whom do you hide, Lady Statten?"

"You know very well that I cannot be seen coming here."

"True. But you are here and still you hide," the woman said.

With an abrupt movement Lady Statten pulled aside her veil. She stared at the woman with an unfriendly gaze. The woman smiled slowly and nodded. "Very well. Now we shall begin, my lady." She placed browned hands on the tabletop. Beneath her flattened palm was a deck of oversize cards. She gazed unblinkingly at Lady Statten.

Lady Statten gave a short exclamation. She yanked open her reticule and brought out a small bag tied with a leather cord. The bag clinked dully when she tossed it onto the table. She said angrily, "There you are, you witch, as we agreed. Though I do not know why I should pay you, when—" She broke off, catching her full underlip between her teeth in annoyance.

The dark woman's gaze sharpened momentarily; then her black lashes swept down to her hide her eyes. She picked up the cards. Her hands blurred in brief movement before she began to slowly, one by one, lay out some of the cards. Her expression was impassive as each picture was revealed. Once she frowned and tapped the card that she had laid down, but she said not a word before going on.

Lady Statten's gaze was riveted to the slow play of cards. Her short fingers clenched tighter about the strings of her reticule. An ornate clock ticked loudly in the quiet parlor, and her inner tension became increasingly unbearable with the passing of the long minutes. Just as Lady Statten thought that she must scream, the woman laid down a last card. "Well, madam? What do you see?" demanded Lady Statten.

The woman raised her head to gaze fully into her visitor's face. She watched in satisfaction the expression of near-fear that crossed Lady Statten's beautiful white face. Of all those who had sought her out, this one was least likable, she thought. "It is a strange thing, my lady. You see here"— she lightly touched a card—"this is the man we have spoken of before. But he is not to be taken so easily now."

"What do you mean? I did just as you said! I threw myself after him without regard to pride. Day after day I sent him notes and haunted every event that he could be expected to attend. And yet he still spurned me. He humiliated me!" Lady Statten's voice rose. "You said my pride was the only barrier."

The woman interrupted her with incisive finality. "Something has intruded." Her fingers swept gracefully to another card, and she held it up. Her eyes glittered at Lady Statten. "Perhaps another woman?" She observed that Lady Statten's eyes narrowed to green slits. She laid down the card and her shoulders rolled in a graceful shrug. "Then again, perhaps not. I know only that it is a powerful influence that pulls on this man. It would take much to capture him now." She gave Lady Statten a slow, knowing smile. "Do you still wish for this man, my lady?"

"What must I do? Tell me!" exclaimed Lady Statten hoarsely, staring hotly at the remainder of the cards in the woman's hands. She did not see the expression of contempt that briefly flashed from the woman's eyes. She watched avidly as the woman's fingers gracefully flipped down the remaining cards to the table, and listened to her speak, without once glancing up at her face.

"You must discover the nature of the power that binds the man away from you. Then you must destroy it." A card was suddenly thrust into Lady Statten's face, and she involuntarily jerked back. "Beware, my lady! It is a strong fire that you face. You risk much, perhaps your own destruction."

Lady Statten tore her horrified, fascinated gaze from the card of death. She stared hard at the woman. "But in the end I will have him. Isn't that what the cards say, witch?"

The woman slowly leaned back into her chair. She shook her head. "The cards do not say, my lady. If you choose this path, and survive . . . the cards say only that there may be sanctuary."

Lady Statten stared a moment before she began to laugh. "Sanctuary! Aye, I'll grant you it will be that, madam! A rich, influential sanctuary." Still laughing, she rose from the table and reset her veil. Without a backward glance, she opened the parlor door and swept out.

The woman sat immobile as she listened to the sounds of departure. The front door shut, cutting off the noise of carriages and shouts from the street. She reached out for the small tied bag and weighed it in her palm, smiling faintly to herself. Perhaps Lady Statten would be back, and perhaps not. But if she were to wager on it, she thought that she could count on more of Lady Statten's silver in the future. That kind of woman always sought what could not be had.

9

The gravity of Michael's wound took immediate precedence over the trip to London, and the journey was put off indefinitely. Indeed, Holland announced that he would not be going at all, since his twin would obviously not be able to join him. But Michael was of a strong constitution and he made swift progress. Within a month the physician pronounced himself more than satisfied, saying that rest and quiet were all that were needed by the patient for a complete and speedy recovery.

From the first, Mrs. Thaleman insisted that she could not possibly leave the care of her invalid son in the hands of others. She did not consider the actual cleaning of the wound to be her bailiwick, however, and confined herself to fussing and scolding over her son, so much so that Michael began to endure her innumerable visits with gritted teeth. Holland was aware of his brother's increasing irritability, and he sought out his father to inform him in private that unless something was done, he feared that Michael would go mad.

When gentle hints did not deter Mrs. Thaleman from her perceived duty, the squire was forced to put his foot down. Mrs. Thaleman, you are driving the boy to distraction. Pray leave him be. He will not expire for lack of your cluckings.''

"Squire! What an abominable thing to say. I am positive that I do not *cluck*," said Mrs. Thaleman, hurt in her voice.

The squire recognized that he had deeply wounded her, and he awkwardly patted her shoulder. "Of course you do not, my dear. However, since Michael is no longer in mortal danger, I do think that you neglect your other duties. I have heard nothing further of your plans to give our daughter a proper Season, you know.''

Mrs. Thaleman was immediately flooded with guilt. She could not but agree that her thoughts had been so completely taken up with Michael's plight that she had forgotten her intentions for her daughter. "You are so right, dear sir. I shall immediately set in train preparations for the journey. That is, if you truly think that Michael can do without me?"

The squire assured her with all the diplomacy at his command that Michael, though he would naturally be some-what downcast by his mother's absence, would nevertheless not wish to spoil his sister's chance for a proper come-out that Season. "Besides which, Holland intends to remain here for a while yet, and certainly that must put your mind at ease, Mrs. Thaleman," said the squire. Mrs. Thaleman's expression lightened and she agreed to it almost with relief, for despite her strong sense of duty, she felt herself to be less than competent in the sickroom.

When Michael heard that his mother was once again talking about removing to London for the Season, he rendered heartfelt thanks to his father. "For I don't mind telling you, Papa, that I do not think I could stand much more coddling," he said.

So it was that a couple of days later Mrs. Thaleman made an announcement over luncheon. "Theresa, I have arranged a sitting with the village seamstress for this afternoon. You must be measured for some new gowns and pelisses to be done up before we leave for London. We cannot take a single one of your old gowns, which have become shamefully out-moded."

Theresa flashed a happy smile. "I shall like that, Mama."

The squire cleared his throat. "Dearest wife, did you not tell me that you would be visiting a modiste in London to refurbish Theresa's wardrobe?"

Mrs. Thaleman sent an indulgent glance his way. "My dear sir, we shall still do so. You do wish your daughter to be all the crack, do you not?"

The squire shrugged, confusion on his face. "Of course, of course. But what is the purpose of having gowns done here when—"

"Squire, Theresa cannot travel looking so shabby. And neither, I might add, can I. First impressions are most important," said Mrs. Thaleman, rising from the table.

Holland cracked a laugh, earning for himself a glare from the squire. He had the good sense to swallow whatever it was he meant to say and address himself instead to the remainder of his meal.

"That is undeniably true," said George, a thread of laughter in his voice for the older gentleman's complete bewilderment.

"Thank you, dear George. I believe you must be the only gentleman capable of understanding such nuances. Come, Theresa," said Mrs. Thaleman.

Theresa looked around at Miss Brown, hesitating. She was certain that if she and her mother needed new outfits, then her constant companion must also wish to add to her own wardrobe. "Is not Miss Brown accompanying us to the seamstress, Mama?"

"Miss Brown cannot always be at our beck and call, Theresa. We shall allow her an afternoon's holiday," said Mrs. Thaleman magnanimously. She bestowed a smile on Miss Brown, totally unaware that her gesture was anything but unselfish.

But Miss Brown was too used to being forgotten to make the point that if she was also to go to London she would have at least liked to purchase a few ribbons with which to freshen the look of her bonnets. She sighed inwardly and resigned herself to making a hurried trip to the village just before their departure. She quietly excused herself to the gentlemen and followed the other women out of the room.

The squire had looked after Mrs. Thaleman and Theresa's exit with a lively sense of foreboding. "I only hope that my poor purse is deep enough to stand for the nonsense." When his nephew laughed, he turned a deep frown on him. "It is not at all amusing, George."

"No indeed, sir," said George, quickly sobering his expression. He met Holland's laughing eyes and was forced to cover his own amusement with a cough. He said hastily,

"Holland, you fleeced me finely when last we matched one another at the billiards table. I demand my revenge."

"As you wish, cos. But I promise you that I will not spare you another such drubbing," said Holland, throwing down his napkin and rising from the table.

"Dash it, you make it a point of honor, so you do! Lead on, cousin, for I am right at your heels," George said.

A fortnight later, the squire's antiquated coach pulled up before the walk in front of a respectable London town house. The horseman who accompanied the vehicle swung down to the pavement. The groom, riding on the coachbox with the driver, jumped down to take the gelding's head. The coach window was let down and George addressed the coach's occupants with a smile. "I shall see that we are properly welcomed."

"Thank you, George," said Mrs. Thaleman, nodding. Her nephew bounded up the steps to the front door, which opened at his knock. Mrs. Thaleman rapped on the ceiling of the coach with her walking stick. "John Coachman! We shall descend, if you please." Hearing his mistress, the driver tied the reins and climbed down from his perch to help the ladies out of the equipage.

Theresa hardly noticed the coachman's offered hand, but jumped lightly down to the sidewalk. She glanced at the town house and then gazed with a happy expression at the traffic and pedestrians. "Oh, famous!" she murmured gleefully as she took in two gentlemen sauntering slowly down the opposite side of the street. She felt sure that the gentlemen were what her father would have contemptuously dismissed as macaronis. The gentlemen's exaggerated padded shoulders, wasp waists, and skintight pantaloons all bespoke the extreme of fashion. Their starched shirt points were so tall and their cravats built so high that they were forced to turn their bodies to be able to converse with one another.

"Miss Thaleman, do stop gawking," said Miss Brown quietly as she joined her charge on the sidewalk.

"Do but look, Miss Brown!" begged Theresa. She nodded

in the gentlemen's direction. "Have you ever seen anything like it? And I thought George all the crack!"

Miss Brown blinked at the spectacle, so much startled that she hardly noticed Theresa's lapse into cant. "I think that Mrs. Bennett has better sense than to ape such extravagance," she said involuntarily. Of a sudden realizing how very personal her observation had sounded, she colored. But Theresa only agreed, totally unaware of the inappropriateness of her mentor's statement.

Mrs. Thaleman joined the other two ladies, shaking out her skirts. "Good. The porter is coming down to take in our baggage. Come, Theresa, Miss Brown. We are undoubtedly expected. My sister Claudia must not be kept waiting." She led the way up the steps of the town house, Theresa and Miss Brown bringing up the rear.

The butler came into the hall as George finished giving instructions about the ladies baggage to the footman and porter. "Master George! Why, it has been a long time, sir."

George tossed his hat to the butler and began stripping off his supple leather riding gloves. "Hello, Phelps. My aunt, Mrs. Thaleman, and my cousin, Miss Thaleman, and her companion, Miss Brown, are outside. Pray see that they are comfortably situated, will you?"

"Of course, sir," said the butler, accepting George's gloves with a matter-of-fact air. "Will there be anything else?"

"My father. Is he still at breakfast?" George hardly waited for the butler's confirming nod before he strode off in the direction of the breakfast room.

Mr. Henry Bennett was a gentleman of short stature who had once enjoyed a slim, handsome figure, but who, in middle age, had become rather portly and, like the Prince Regent, had taken to wearing a whaleboned corset. He was savoring his kidney and eggs when his only son walked briskly into the room. He did not often see his son unless it was around the town, and so the visit came as a welcome surprise. "My boy! Glad to see you. Sit down and have some coffee. I know that you breakfast early, but—'' He broke off, watching in open amazement as George filled a plate with a generous portion of eggs, bacon, and biscuits before pouring a cup of coffee.

George caught his father's expression and flashed a grin. "I am devilish hungry this morning. I've just ridden in from the squire's place, playing escort to my aunt and cousin. Theresa will be coming out this Season."

Mr. Bennett was astonished. "Indeed! Why, I recall little Theresa to be a tiny thing with dark ringlets and the most engaging pair of shining eyes. My, my, to think that little Theresa is so grown-up. The years do pass one by. It somehow makes on wish that one had kept in closer touch." He sighed a little in regret.

"You shall have your chance to renew your acquaintance very shortly. My aunt has decided that she and my cousin, along with her companion, Miss Brown, shall be staying with you and my mother for the Season. I assured my aunt that you and Mother would be delighted to put them up," said George coolly.

Mr. Bennett dropped his fork. Alarm registered in his staring eyes. "No, no, dear boy! It is quite impossible. Your mother . . . ! You must tell them it is all a mistake. A hotel would suit better. Yes, that is the ticket. A hotel—"

There was a flurry of voices outside the breakfast room. George smiled and regarded his father with a mixture of impatience and sympathy. "It is too late, Father. I fancy that is my aunt and her party now."

The door to the breakfast room opened and Mrs. Thaleman sailed in with Theresa and Miss Brown in her wake. The gentlemen rose hastily to their feet, Mr. Bennett with the suggestion of a creak. Mrs. Thaleman immediately accosted her brother-in-law. "Dear Henry! No, do not bother to get up on my account. Of course you remember my daughter, Theresa, who is quite the young lady now, as you see. And this is Miss Brown." She reached up to brush a kiss across her stupefied brother-in-law's stout cheek. "How are you, dear brother? Well, I hope. I understand that Claudia is still abed. How very like her. Never mind, I shall go up to visit with her later.''

As she spoke, she seated herself in the chair that Mr. Bennett dumbly offered to her. On the other side of the table George seated both his cousin and Miss Brown before resuming his own seat to await the turn of events. He saw that his father was still speechless, and he stepped smoothly into the breach. ''Would you care for tea, Aunt?'' he asked.

''That will be delightful, George. And perhaps a pastry or two as well. It was such a very long drive, after all,'' said Mrs. Thaleman. George inquired of Theresa and Miss Brown their desires and then signaled a footman to serve the ladies tea and cakes.

Mrs. Thaleman removed her gloves. ''Well, Henry, I know that it comes as a surprise to see us in London. It was a sudden decision, I grant you. Squire wondered where I was to take up residence at this late date, since the Season is already begun. But I told him that my sister will be more than delighted to aid me in seeing that Theresa is properly brought out. Claudia did so enjoy the parties at her own come-out that I am confident she will be thrilled at the prospect.'' She sipped with unconcern at her tea and gave no indication that she heard the groan that emanated from her brother-in-law.

Mr. Bennett gloomily surveyed the remainder of his breakfast. It no longer held any appeal to him, and he pushed the plate away. The morning that had begun so well had sunk to the depths. He dreaded what his wife would have to say to him when she learned of their visitors. The very thought made him swallow nervously.

Theresa had been staring fixedly at her uncle's dejected countenance. She was not a stupid girl, and spoke her mind. ''Mama, I do not think Uncle Henry is pleased that we mean to stay.''

Miss Brown, who had watched the play of emotions over the older man's face, and had been feeling a great deal of pity for him, seized the opportunity that Theresa's words gave her. For once she was grateful for Theresa's abominable frankness. "Indeed, ma'am, until you have spoken to Mrs. Bennett, who I understand is something of an invalid, perhaps it would be best to put up at respectable hotel."

"Crying craven, Miss Brown?" asked a soft voice. Miss Brown ignored Mr. George Bennett, who she was fast concluding was an unfeeling wretch to allow his father to be so bullied.

Mr. Bennett looked up quickly. Hope dawned in his eyes. "A hotel—"

Mrs. Thaleman's soft jaw became amazingly firm. "Nonsense. I am persuaded that Henry will not hear of our taking rooms." She stared at her brother-in-law, who visibly wilted. He sighed and shook his head. She nodded in satisfaction and smiled at him. "Pray do not worry your head over my dear sister, Henry. I have not forgotten what Claudia is like. Even as a girls . . . Well, I am not one to tell tales! I shall explain the matter to her in just such a way that even she will not be able to put fault to anyone. We shall all be very comfortable, I promise you." Mr. Bennett's expression did not lighten, but, if anything, became more lugubrious.

George grinned faintly at his aunt's ruthlessness. He rose from the table. "I apologize for taking leave of you so soon after your arrival, ladies, but I have several engagements to keep. I shall call on you later this afternoon, however."

"Very well, George. You are the dearest boy for putting aside your own plans and waiting a few days so that you could escort us to London." Mrs. Thaleman gave her hand to her nephew and squeezed his fingers in affection.

"I would have it no other way, Aunt," he said. Over his aunt's head his eyes met Miss Brown's dispassionate gaze. He inclined his head slightly before turning toward his cousin. "And you, little baggage, I know that I shall see more of than I wish."

Theresa laughed, not at all affronted by his rude address. "Indeed, George, I am determined that you shall show me the town. And do not think that you shall wriggle out of it, either."

"I know better than to attempt it. I shall take my medicine like a brave soldier and then retire to my bed to recover," George said teasingly. Theresa made a rude face at him, which earned her a look of disapproval from her mother that she chose to ignore. George turned to his father. "I am going up to visit with my mother before I go. Do you wish to accompany me, Father?"

Sunk in gloom for several minutes, Mr. Bennett looked up with a startled air. The thought of confronting his wife so early in the day horrified him. It galvanized him into action and he moved with surprising speed for a gentleman of his girth. "No, no! Much obliged, my boy, but no. I am looked for at the club, I daresay. Ladies, your servant, as always." With that he got to his feet, made his bows, and was out the door.

"Uncle Henry creaks. And he is a bit of a quiz," Theresa observed.

"Miss Thaleman, I must beg you to curb your tongue in public," said Miss Brown with sharp annoyance. Her charge's lack of tact reflected badly on her own ability to instill a sense of what was proper, she felt. Oddly enough, it embarrassed her most to be thought lacking by the dandified Mr. George Bennett, whose polite attentions had gradually become a pleasant diversion to her days.

Theresa's eyes clouded. "I beg your pardon, Miss Brown. I was not aware that my mother and my cousin constituted the public," she said stiffly.

"Pray do not scold my cousin overmuch, Miss Brown. She has a singular knack for cutting through to the bone," George said. Whistling, he followed his father's example in a more leisurely fashon and quitted the breakfast room. Theresa marmaladed a biscuit with a flourish, made triumphant by her cousin's championship. Miss Brown and Mrs. Thaleman exchanged helpless glances.

After the ladies had finished with their tea, Mrs. Thaleman suggested that a rest might be in order for them all after the long drive. Theresa at once objected. "But I could not possibly sleep, Mama. I am far too excited. I wish to go exploring at once.''

Miss Brown smiled at Theresa's enthusiasm. She addressed her employer. ''If you would not frown on it, ma'am, I would be happy to accompany Miss Thaleman on a ride about the city. It would be most enlightening, I am certain.''

Mrs. Thaleman was dubious. ''For myself, I would not wish it. I can hardly keep my head up as it is. But I suppose the younger set does not require as much rest.''

''Oh, pray say that we may! Please, Mama,'' said Theresa.

''Very well, but I will not have you fagging Miss Brown to death. She is very good to give up her own rest to indulge you, Theresa, so see that you mind her well.''

''Of course I shall. I will go up at once to change into my walking dress,'' Theresa said. She flew out of the breakfast room without giving a thought to deportment.

Mrs. Thaleman turned with a sigh to Miss Brown. ''She is such a hoyden. I do not know how we shall endeavor to marry her off, Miss Brown. I know I need not voice my concerns to you, for indeed, better than anyone, you are aware of Theresa's sad lack of polish. I don't mind confiding to you that I have doubts even for a successful Season.''

Miss Brown smiled through slightly gritted teeth. It enraged her that Mrs. Thaleman should sell so short her own daughter's worth. ''You quite put me on my mettle, Mrs. Thaleman. I consider Theresa's behavior a reflection of my training, and therefore I shall strive to impart an even greater awareness of those finer sensibilities to Theresa. Perhaps then your hopes for the Season will come to fruition.''

Mrs. Thaleman was quite incapable of discerning either disapproval or sarcasm in this speech, and she squeezed Miss Brown's hand in gratitude. ''I do thank you for your unswerving devotion, dear, dear Letitia. You are such a comfort to me. Indeed, I do not know how I would go on without you. I am coming to realize that when Theresa is settled I shall wish you to consider staying on as my own companion. It would be such a comfortable arrangement, do you not think?''

Miss Brown felt a wild urge to laugh. She could not imagine anything less palatable than spending the rest of her days at Mrs. Thaleman's beck and call. She cleared her throat and mumbled some meaningless pleasantry before making good her escape. Once outside the breakfast-room door, she paused to lean against it a short moment to collect herself. It would not do to join Theresa when she was still so disconcerted. She had never given much thought to what she would do once Theresa Thaleman had left the schoolroom and embarked on her own life, but now that the moment was nearly upon her, the question demanded attention.

Miss Brown straightened and crossed the hallway to the stairs. She would set aside the poser until she was alone in the privacy of her bedroom, she decided. Until then she intended to enjoy the afternoon without any greater thought than to be certain Miss Thaleman was gotten back to her uncle's residence in time for dinner. But her mind proved persistent and she could not let go of the question of her future.

When Theresa joined Miss Brown for their expedition, she saw at once the tiny frown between her companion's well-marked brows. ''What is wrong, Miss Brown? Have you the headache? Shall we stay in?''

Miss Brown shook her head, giving Theresa a quick smile. ''I am being stupid, Theresa. Only let us embark on our adventure, and I am certain I shall soon be as merry as anyone could wish.'' Theresa was reassured and began immediately talking of the sights she wished to visit.

10

The porter hailed a hackney cab for the ladies. The cabby was deluged with commands from Theresa before Miss Brown could persuade her to enter the vehicle. As soon as they had settled themselves in the cab, it pulled away from the curb into the traffic.

The ladies whiled away the afternoon with a tour of St. George's Cathedral, a visit to the zoo at the Tower of London, and a quick peek at Astley's Circus. After such hard work, partaking of an ice at the famous Gunther's was a necessity.

Finally the ladies agreed to end the day at the lending library. "I shall require a few books of poetry to read in order to steady my nerves during the Season," Miss Brown said.

"And I shall choose a novel or two that Mama may have missed," said Theresa. She pretended not to understand the significance of Miss Brown's raised brows and pointed glance, but she knew that Miss Brown was not fooled into believing that the novels were only for her parent. Theresa's smile was one of complete innocence, though her eyes danced. "Mama does so enjoy romances," she said.

"Indeed? I believe I may name another who enjoys novels just as well," said Miss Brown.

"Pray do not be stuffy, Miss Brown!" Theresa begged. She chose two more volumes to add to her collection of novels.

Miss Brown shook her head. She saw that Theresa's last choices were works by ancient Greek playwrights. Almost she wished that she had never introduced Theresa to Greek tragedy because she felt that the girl's interest in ancient

Greek theater and civilization was not entirely of a scholarly nature. She suspected that Theresa derived a peculiar sense of freedom from being able to study a topic unusual for a female. But at least Theresa was reading something besides those lamentable novels found to be so fascinating by Mrs. Thaleman, she thought. Still, Miss Brown felt somewhat guilt-ridden for allowing her charge to select such books when they stood surrounded by learned treatises and enlightening tomes. "I could wish less frivolous reading material for you, Theresa," she said, glancing around at the filled shelves.

Theresa pointed to the flourishing title of the book of French poetry that Miss Brown had chosen. "Come, Miss Brown! You are entirely capable of rhapsodizing over the most romantic drivel imaginable. Admit that it is so!"

Honesty forced Miss Brown to a reluctant concession of the truth of Theresa's observation. "But my edification is not at issue, Theresa," she said as they went through the library door into the sunlight.

Her attempted lecture fell on deaf ears, for Theresa had glanced down the steps as they left the portals of the lending library and seen a perfectly matched team of grays at the curb. "Oh!" She was enchanted, and without a second thought, she deserted Miss Brown to go to the leaders' heads.

"Theresa!" Miss Brown started to follow with such impetuous haste that she collided with a gentleman. The books flew out of her hands and fell heavily to the pavement. "Oh! I beg pardon. So clumsy of me!" She bent immediately to retrieve the volumes, her color heightened.

"It was my fault, I believe. My apologies, ma'am," said the Duke of Ashford. He helped to pick up the volumes and straightened to hand her the last one, glancing down incuriously at the title as he did so. His brows rose in momentary surprise.

Miss Brown took the book from him, thanking him for his courtesy. They exchanged a few pleasantries as the duke escorted her down the steps and offered to call a hackney cab for her. "I do not see Miss Thaleman with you today. I hope that she is not indisposed," he said politely.

"Miss Thaleman is never ill, your grace," said Miss Brown dryly, and with a nod of her head directed his attention to the carriage at the curb. The duke's expression registered surprise when he saw the slender young girl standing with such unconcern at the head of his team, crooning to them and rubbing their soft noses.

Theresa looked around at their approach. She nodded to the Duke of Ashford in recognition, accepting his unexpected appearance matter-of-factly. She turned an animated gaze on her companion. "Do but look, Miss Brown! What truly magnificent creatures they are! They must be sweet goers."

The duke was astonished that Miss Thaleman handled the high-spirited animals with such complete familiarity. She was holding the leader's bit and scratching his nose. Slender and graceful and without a thought for the state of her walking dress, Theresa presented a striking picture. The duke was particularly struck by the lively expression of pleasure in her eyes. He recovered himself. "I apprehend that you like horses, Miss Thaleman."

Theresa smiled up at him. She gave the horse one last loving pat before she stepped back up on the sidewalk to give her hand to him in proper greeting. "I am quite mad for them, actually. I am used to riding each day, but I suppose that is over until after the Season, when I return home."

"Miss Brown has informed me that your party arrived in town only today. Surely you do not already pine for the country," said the duke with a half-smile. Without his being consciously aware of it, he had relaxed his guard in the face of Miss Thaleman's genuine friendliness.

"Oh, no, it is all vastly exciting. I am certain that the Season will be quite entertaining, especially since it is hoped that I shall contract an eligible *parti*. I shall need to keep my wits about me if I am to escape such a dire fate my first Season out," said Theresa with a confiding laugh.

There was a startled look on the Duke of Ashford's face

that Miss Brown was quick to interpret as one of disgust. She was mortified that her charge had so exposed herself in the eyes of this correct gentleman. The girl had not a shred of discretion, she thought with dismay. "Theresa, we should not keep his grace any longer. I am certain that he must have appointments. And we must return to your uncle's house so that we shall have time to rest before dinner."

Theresa looked at Miss Brown with complete astonishment. "But I never rest before—" Understanding suddenly came to her. She turned to the Duke of Ashford. "Of course. I had not realized. Forgive me for keeping your horses standing about, your grace," she said.

The duke was taken aback by Miss Thaleman's instant solicitude for his team. Unattached ladies usually expressed their concern on his behalf rather than his cattle's. Miss Thaleman was definitely out-of-the-way, he thought. On an odd whim, he said, "Not at all. But since you ladies do not command a carriage, I would count it an honor if you would allow me to drive you home myself. Then, Miss Thaleman, you may judge the team's paces for yourself."

"Thank you! I should like it above all things," said Theresa with alacrity. She noticed her companion's expression of dismay. "Surely there can be no objection, Miss Brown. His grace is known to us, after all. There can be no harm in accepting a seat in the carriage of a gentleman with whom we are friendly."

The Duke of Ashford did not attempt to hide his smile. He looked at Miss Brown. "Come, ma'am. It is an unexceptionable invitation, believe me."

Despite her reservations, Miss Brown allowed herself to be won over. She was tired, and a ride in a well-sprung vehicle was infinitely prefereable to one in a broken-down hackney cab. "If you say so, your grace, then I am persuaded."

"That's the ticket, Miss Brown," said Theresa. She was quite unaware that she had made use of a cant phrase, thus again startling the Duke of Ashford. But his expression as he handed the ladies up into the phaeton registered only pleasantness. He inquired the direction of their destination and then set the phaeton in motion.

"What sweet goers they are!" said Theresa with instant approval.

"I am gratified by your approbation, Miss Thaleman," Hugo said, somewhat amused by her unqualified enthusiasm. He began to point out various personages and sights for his guests. Miss Brown, still torn by doubts on the wisdom of accepting places in the duke's carriage for herself and Theresa, began to enjoy the drive. She had never before been driven in a phaeton. It was nonsensical to waste one's energy on useless anxiety, and besides, it was educational for Theresa to be exposed to the company of such a distinguished gentleman, she assured herself.

The Duke of Ashford addressed her suddenly. "I noticed one of the volumes you hold is a work by Euripides, Miss Brown. I am myself a member of the Dilettante Society, so I assume that we share a common admiration for antiquities," he said.

A curious expression, almost of pride, flashed across Miss Brown's face. "The book you speak of is actually Miss Thaleman's choice, your grace," she said.

The duke was patently disbelieving, but he politely accepted Miss Brown's assertion. He glanced down at the young lady beside him. "I am astonished, Miss Thaleman. I had no notion that a young lady of your years would willingly plow through tomes of Greek tragedy."

"Why is that, your grace?" There was a challenging look in Theresa's eyes. "I really must correct you, sir. As you must be aware, Euripides was the great *comedic* Greek playwright, and something of a scandal. Even to this day he is considered quite shocking."

"I stand corrected, Miss Thaleman." The duke looked to her companion. "Miss Brown, surely you do not endorse such infamous reading for your charge."

"Indeed not, your grace. But Miss Thaleman insists that reading should be a pleasurable experience, not an exercise in piety," said Miss Brown with a half-smile.

Theresa put on a confiding air. "It is quite Miss Brown's fault, your grace. You see, she herself indulges in very bad French poetry."

"Really, Theresa, you are quite adominable," said Miss Brown laughing in protest as a faint flush rose in her face. Theresa sent a sparkling, unrepentant glance her way.

"I apprehend that both you ladies are sunk quite beyond reproach," said Hugo. He recognized the real affection between the two women with something like envy. His circle of acquaintances was wide, but give his deliberate reserve, there were few he chose to call his friends.

"I believe your grace mentioned the Dilettante Society. Pray, what is that?" asked Miss Brown.

"We are a loosely knit group who come together to pursue a mutual appreciation and knowledge of the arts and antiquities. Most of the members, including myself, formed a passion for past civilizations and their treasures during the Grand Tours of Europe we took with our tutors as young boys."

"How I envy you, your grace. I should enjoy being one of such a company. It has been a desire of mine to travel and to see for myself those things that I have but read about," said Theresa.

"I hope that you are able to indulge your wish one day, Miss Thaleman," the duke said.

"Indeed, and so do I," said Theresa. She eyed him. "I suppose that you know quite a bit about Greece, your grace?"

"My travels did not lead me to spend a great deal of time in the Greek islands, though I am naturally as intrigued as yourself by the civilization that flourished there. The architecture alone was magnificent."

"And the pottery and jewelry as well! I have seen only illustrations of such, excepting once when Papa took me with him as a small child to call on an old Cambridge gentleman who had a collection. The old gentleman told me such wonderful stories of his travels in the Mediterranean." Theresa proceeded to share with the duke some of her thoughts on Greek civilization, which prompted him to offer his own opinions.

Miss Brown settled back, her hands resting on the books in her lap. She was pleased that her charge had actually managed to engage the Duke of Ashford in a conversation of worth. She thought that if Theresa did half so well with other gentlemen less reserved than the duke, she would acquit herself quite well during the Season. That would be an astonishment to Mrs. Thaleman and of immense gratification to herself, she thought.

The lively exchange between Theresa and the Duke of Ashford lasted the course of the drive. The duke was once surprised into laughter, and he glanced down at the animated young woman who sat beside him. By the time the Bennett town house came into sight, he decided that he had rarely been more entertained.

As he helped first Miss Thaleman and then Miss Brown down to the pavement, the Duke of Ashford found that he truly regretted to hear their thank-yous and good-byes. He started to take his leave, then turned. "Miss Thaleman, I shall hope to see you again. Perhaps we shall drive together again one day."

"I should like that, your grace," said Theresa. She smiled at him before she entered the house.

When she had gotten upstairs to her bedroom, she was surprised to find that Miss Brown had followed her and firmly closed the door behind them. "Why, whatever is wrong, Miss Brown?" She untied the ribbons of her bonnet.

"Nothing at all, Theresa, except that I think that perhaps you must not refine too much on the Duke of Ashford's flattering attention this afternoon."

"Oh, I do not. I know that gentlemen often forget their best intentions the moment after they have formed them," said Theresa calmly, speaking from a depth of experience with her brothers and cousin. She removed her straw bonnet and tossed it carelessly onto the bed.

Miss Brown sighed. "Theresa, pray attend to me. Mrs.

Thaleman would be quite enraptured to learn that you had apparently attached his grace's notice. To spare you future recriminations when the duke does not come up to inflated expectations, I suggest strongly that you treat our chance meeting this afternoon as inconsequential.''

Theresa regarded her thoughtfully. ''I understand you, of course, Miss Brown. Mama does have a tendency to leap to uncomfortable conclusions. I would never hear the end of it if the Duke of Ashford chooses not to call. She would say that I must have done or said something unladylike that gave him a disgust of me.'' Theresa grimaced even as laughter shone in her eyes. ''Indeed, Mama would have it that I was totally sunk beyond reproach and the only avenue left to me would be to marry my cousin George or some other such idiotic thing.''

Miss Brown gave a start. Her glance was sharp. Surely Theresa was not toying with the notion of building a closer relationship with her own cousin, George Bennett. But Theresa had turned away to remove her gloves, and Miss Brown could not judge her expression. She hesitated, wondering if she should question Theresa about it. But she decided not to interfere. ''Well, that is all that I wished to say, Theresa. I will see you again at dinner.''

Theresa nodded in acknowledgment of Miss Brown's going, and rang the bell for her maid to come and help her out of her walking dress. It was not long before the dinner hour, and Theresa wanted a bath beforehand. While she waited, she thought over the drive home with the Duke of Ashford. A smile curved her mouth. It had been very pleasant in his grace's company. She had sensed that his attention was fixed on their conversation, and it had pleased her that someone should think that she was worth listening to. Besides, he was a handsome gentleman, not nearly so stuffy as she had first thought him, and judging by his team, he was also extremely knowledgeable about horseflesh. Theresa thought she had rarely spent a better twenty minutes.

11

Claudia Bennett did not feel that having guests in the house was sufficient reason to alter her routine, especially when those guests were uninvited. She refused to see her sister that afternoon, sending a message by her maid that she would join the company at the dinner hour. At the appointed time a footman and the maid solicitously supported their mistress to the table. Mr. Bennett rose hastily to offer his wife a chair. Once she had seated herself and arranged her flowing draperies, he took his own seat, somewhat removed from his wife's place.

Theresa had been placed below both her relatives and her mother at the table, and so she had an unobstructed view of them all. She observed that Mr. Bennett at once bent his attention to his plate and spoke little. It did not take much intelligence to see that her uncle disliked his wife, Theresa thought, turning her gaze on her aunt.

Mrs. Bennett was a pale, thin creature with a sharply chiseled face. She had once been much admired for her classical beauty, but now her face appeared to be merely a set of pitched angles. Her eagle glance touched with disfavor on the entrée and she waved it away petulantly. It was the same with each dish that the footman came around to serve. Mrs. Bennett swelled with displeasure. She turned on her husband. "Henry! What has gotten into Cook? I sent down word that I had had a very trying night. She knows that only the blandest of fare will put me right again."

Mr. Bennett appeared harassed. "Why, I do not know, I am sure."

Mrs. Thaleman addressed her sister. "I spoke to your cook this afternoon, Claudia, just to have an idea what to expect,

you know. I am used to providing for the squire, who is a
most exacting gentleman, and it is always my habit to see
that the kitchen prepares those things that he particularly
likes," she said. She raised her fork and calmly took another
bite of an excellent meat pie.

Mrs. Bennett regarded her with incredulity and dislike.
"What has the squire, whom I may remind you is not present,
to do with disrupting my kitchen?"

"Why, everything, dear sister. The squire's culinary tastes
in the beginning were not what one would have hoped, but
with careful cultivation he has become a fair judge of what
makes a good meal. When I visited with Cook, I discovered
that this evening's menu was not what the squire would have
liked. No indeed! So I proffered a few humble suggestions
and it has turned out surprisingly well." Mrs. Thaleman
sighed with satisfaction as she bit into a particularly tender
piece of beef.

Mrs. Bennett's pale cheeks flew stained red flags. "This
is a liberty that I will not tolerate, Charlotte. My constitution
is quite delicate and requires certain dietary considerations
that you, who have always been quite disgustingly hearty,
would have difficulty understanding. I take leave to inform
you that it was only at my dear son's entreaty and for the
sake of our relationship that I have agreed to share my roof
this Season. Of a certainty your visit will constitute the
greatest hardship upon my health, but I hope that I am a
charitable person and I have engaged to do my best.
However, I draw the line at this . . . this *sabotage*, for that
is how I must label it."

Mrs. Thaleman did not appear particularly put out by her
sister's tirade. "Cook told me of your barley water and gruel,
but I could not credit you would prefer such fare when
offered honest meat pie or braised beef. Why, it is no wonder
you are so peaked-looking. You have quite lost your looks
since we last saw one another. But enough said. Here is your
invalid's regimen, dear Claudia," she said, waving in
command to the footman.

Mrs. Bennett sat stiffly, her lips clamped tight, while she

was served. She shot a glance at her husband, who had been listening to the exchange with a increasing sense of dread. "And you, Henry! What have you to say?"

Mr. Bennett jumped. "What? Oh! I agree, naturally." He was rather pleased with himself at so cleverly heading off his wife's displeasure, and he took another mouthful of bread. Really, it was a most excellent dinner. In deference to his guests, and with much foreboding, he had remained at home that evening rather than dining at the club, which was his usual practice whenever his wife was likely to be displeased about something. She invariably demonstrated her displeasure by indulging her taste for invalid's rations and ordering the cook to serve it up to the exclusion of more decent fare. As a consequence, whoever was unlucky enough to be dining with her left the table still hungry.

"Indeed!" Mrs. Bennett's accents were freezing. She stared daggers at her husband, who looked alarmed and confused.

Theresa decided that she could not allow the odious woman to bully her uncle another moment. "Aunt Claudia, how very becoming that shade is to you. Whatever is it called? I do not think that I have ever seen such a purple before."

Claudia Bennett turned, leaving off her prey, and frowned at her niece. "Purple is for the vulgar, girl. I assure you, I do not wear purple."

"Oh. Well, it is a very becoming color, whatever it is," said Theresa, struggling gallantly against her aunt's repressive tone. She tried her most winning smile. "I do hope you may be persuaded to involve yourself in my coming-out, for I am told that you once attended a great many parties, and so you must know just how one must go on."

Claudia Bennett was not proof against flattery. "I admit that I am quite up to the mark." She remembered herself, and the pinched look again descended on her countenance. "But that was before my health—"

"Theresa forgets herself, Claudia. Certainly one should not expect much from you. Why, there is the precariousness of your health to consider," said Mrs. Thaleman. "Pray do

not give another thought to involving yourself in any entertainments on Theresa's behalf. We shall manage splendidly
on our own, I assure you. Henry, do try this dish of Spanish
onions. It is quite the favorite with the squire.''

Mr. Bennett was happy to oblige his sister-in-law and
immediately expressed his enthusiasm. ''Quite, quite
exceptional! I hope that you gave Cook the recipe?''

''Oh, do shut up, Henry! Spanish onions, indeed.
Charlotte, as usual you have leapt to a false conclusion. I
shall be the proper judge of my state of health, thank you.
As for managing on your own, I wish I could see it! You
have not a notion how the thing is to be done. Unfortunately,
I possess too much family feeling to stand by while you make
fools of yourselves and my niece. No, whether you care for
it or not, Charlotte, you are stuck with my assistance,'' said
Mrs. Bennett.

Mrs. Thaleman made a show of reluctant acceptance. ''You
have always wanted your own way, Claudia. However, in this
instance I must confess that I should be more comfortable with
you to support me. But I do not wish to place an unbearble
burden on your constitution, dear sister.''

Mrs. Bennett raised her hand in an imperious gesture.
''Not another word, Charlotte. I insist upon this role. You
may cluck all you wish, but I shall not be swerved from my
duty.''

''Of course not, Claudia. Since you have put it just that
way, I shall not attempt to persuade you otherwise,'' said
Mrs. Thaleman, satisfaction in her voice. She glanced
significantly at her brother-in-law, who sat openmouthed as
he listened to the turn of conversation, and said, ''Now that
that is settled, we may all be comfortable again. Henry, do
help yourself to more of the onions. The squire always says
that they do wonders for his stomach.''

''Heh? Oh, the onions. Yes, I think that I shall. I have
been most enlightened. About onions, that is,'' said Mr.
Bennett. He met his wife's suspicious glance, his expression
as bovine as usual. She turned away from him with a
contemptuous half-shrug of one thin shoulder.

Theresa had said not a word during the fascinating exchange between her mother and her aunt. She had listened wide-eyed to a side of her parent that she had never before witnessed. She wondered that she had not realized previously what a manipulative streak her mother possessed. All in all, it was a remarkable performance that left Theresa most thoughtful.

"Theresa, you have not told me yet of your afternoon in town," said Mrs. Thaleman.

"What? Oh, it was vastly entertaining, Mama. I know that Miss Brown was quite worn out, and even I felt a little wilted. But I revived immediately when the Duke of Ashford was kind enough to drive us home. His grace has such a very fine team."

"Theresa! Why ever did you not tell me that the duke drove you home? But this is wonderful!" exclaimed Mrs. Thaleman. Visions of a coronet danced in her mind's eye. All of a sudden her close-held wish to see her daughter wedded to her nephew seemed a paltry ambition.

Theresa looked up, startled, at her mother's excited expression. She met her aunt's sharp glance of curiosity. She realized with a sinking feeling that through sheer carelessness she had created exactly the complications that Miss Brown had foreseen. She tried to stem her mother's enthusiasm. "I did not think it important, Mama. After all, I am barely acquainted with the duke, and—"

"Important! When a distinguished gentleman extends such a singular honor to a young lady, it is exceptional, let me tell you! Really, Theresa, at times I simply cannot fathom what goes on in that head of yours," Mrs. Thaleman said impatiently.

'I was not aware that you were acquainted with the Duke of Ashford, sister," said Mrs. Bennett, cocking her head.

Mrs. Thaleman waved her hand airily. "We are not altogether *buried* in the country, Claudia. Theresa, I wish you to relate to me every word that was said."

"But, Mama—" began Theresa helplessly.

Miss Brown interposed. "Mrs. Thaleman, it was a most

innocuous meeting outside the lending library. When his grace learned we were about to hail a cab, he very graciously offered us a lift in his phaeton. We spoke only of the sights we had seen this afternoon. Miss Thaleman did not mention the meeting to you before because I advised her that to place too much emphasis on the duke's kindness would be rash. His grace may not again be so inclined.''

"The lending library?'' repeated Mrs. Thaleman, momentarily sidetracked. Her phantasm of the duke's instantly succumbing to her daughter's pretty face suffered a severe attack. The lending library seemed such a common place for a romantic encounter.

"I have heard it said in the clubs that his grace is something of an antiquarian. He was probably after some book or other,'' offered Mr. Bennett.

"Never mind what the duke may have been after,'' Mrs. Thaleman said, beginning to frown with displeasure. "Miss Brown, I rely so heavily on your good sense, but in this instance—''

Mrs. Bennett was swift to side against her sister. "Miss Brown acted exactly right, Charlotte. The Duke of Ashford is certainly not what one might call an eligible *parti*, and to encourage your daughter to set her cap for him would be the height of folly. He is a known libertine, and though I have never heard it said that he dallies with young innocents, it is best to be on guard. Theresa, pray consider yourself well-warned.''

"How can you say so, Claudia? Why, his grace is a well-set, handsome gentleman who presents himself just as he ought. I saw nothing of the libertine in him. I cannot believe the duke to be the bad man that you make him out to be, even though he did shoot my poor Michael. But this is beside the point. I should think the gentleman's income is nothing to be sneezed at,'' Mrs. Thaleman said.

"What was that? Michael shot?'' exclaimed Mr. Bennett, dropping his fork.

Theresa attempted to soothe her uncle's obvious alarm. "The twins were playing at highwaymen, Uncle. They held up the duke's carriage and . . . Well, you may guess the rest. It was a nasty wound, but Michael was recovering nicely when we left home.''

"Highwaymen! I do not know what the squire is about to allow those brothers of yours so much slack. They are a danger to themselves and others and will most likely put your parents in the grave with worry. I am only glad that my son George has never exhibited such a distressing taste for skulduggery,'' Mrs. Bennett said with a sniff.

Theresa stiffened. Without turning she could feel Miss Brown's eyes boring into her head, and she took a deep breath to cool the surge of temper within her, caused by her aunt's disparaging remarks of her brothers. It was not the time to enlighten her odious aunt of the hidden side to her sainted son's character. Besides, it would be a betrayal of her cousin. Theresa thought she could now very well understand why he was so set against his mother. Though George had never discussed the matter with her, Theresa had years before come to realize that he was not fond of his maternal parent.

Mrs. Thaleman was not so forbearing. "Claudia, do not dare malign any member of my family. I shall have you know that—''

"Forty thousand pounds a year,'' Mr. Bennett said. He found himself the object of four pairs of uncomprehending feminine eyes. "The duke's income, that is. One hears things at the club. But I also heard that his grace is a cold one. He'll shy off at the least sign of overture.''

"For once you have spoken sense, Henry. No, Charlotte, the Duke of Ashford is too rarefied a catch for our nets. He is rich, yes, but he is a hardened libertine as well. He merely indulged a whim to offer a ride to Theresa and Miss Brown. Undoubtedly the creature possesses a twisted sense of humor and he hoped to raise just such idiotic notions as you have embraced.'' A superior smile hovered on Mrs. Bennett's lips as she glanced at her sister. "You are still a hen-witted simpleton, Charlotte.''

Mrs. Thaleman flushed. "No matter what your opinion

may be of me, Claudia, I shall continue to harbor suitable ambitions for my beloved daughter. Perhaps the Duke of Ashford is out of our reach, but I shall not whistle away the possibility. Forty thousand pounds and a coronet to boot! No, indeed, Claudia!''

''Mama, pray do not overset yourself. I do like the Duke of Ashford, of course, but I shouldn't wish to marry him,'' Theresa said.

''Not wish to become a duchess? Nonsense! Every woman desires to be a duchess. *I* want to be a duchess!'' Mrs. Thaleman stared at her sister with a challenge in her eyes. ''Claudia, I say that we shall include the Duke of Ashford on the guest list for Theresa's come-out.''

''Of course we shall. His grace is too prominent a figure to slight. However, I warn you in advance that he will not come. He does not attend functions given over to the launching of young women,'' Mrs. Bennett said. ''I shall begin this very night to draw up a list of guests, and among them will be several suitable gentlemen who might be brought up to scratch.''

''And I shall aid you. I do have a few thoughts of my own, Claudia,'' Mrs. Thaleman said.

Miss Brown saw that battle lines had been clearly drawn between the sisters. She had no wish to witness the skirmishing when the ladies retired to the drawing room, and so she set about on her retreat. ''Pardon me, Mrs. Thaleman. If you will be so good as to excuse Theresa and myself, I think it best that we retire early this evening. It has been a very long day and I am certain that you must have plans for Theresa for tomorrow.''

''Of course, Miss Brown. You are right, as usual. I had hoped to do some shopping on the morrow, and I wish you to be well-rested, Theresa.''

''Yes, Mama,'' Theresa said, accepting with alacrity the opportunity to leave the company of her mother and her aunt. She curtsied to Mr. Bennett, who said a fond word to her, and murmured good night to her aunt.

Mrs. Bennett barely acknowledged the courtesy but turned immediately to the attack. ''Shopping, Charlotte! And you never meant to invite me along?'' she asked petulantly.

As Theresa and Miss Brown walked to the door, they heard Mrs. Thaleman's gleeful reply. ''My dear sister, I thought only of your precarious health. You must not overtire yourself, Claudia.''

On that note, Miss Brown closed the door firmly. As she and Theresa climbed the stairs, Theresa said musingly, ''I understand now why Papa did not encourage visits with my aunt and uncle. Mama and Aunt Claudia fight like cats, do they not? I have never seen the like.''

''I believe that in most families there is sibling rivalry of one sort or another,'' said Miss Brown.

''I suppose so. But still, for all their wrangling, the twins at least like one another. I do not think that Mama and Aunt Claudia do.'' Theresa's thoughts turned to her brothers. ''I wonder how Michael is getting along.''

''The squire would never have sent you and Mrs. Thaleman on to London if he was not confident of your brother's recovery,'' Miss Brown assured her.

''That is true. And Holland is with Michael.'' Theresa paused outside her bedroom door. ''It has been a most singular day, hasn't it? I shall have much to put down in my journal tonight.''

''Have you brought your journal with you, then?'' Miss Brown asked, somewhat surprised.

''Of course. I would be quite lost without it. It is queer, really, but the journal has become my closest friend. I may tell it my most intimate thoughts without fearing disapproval,'' Theresa said with a laugh.

''I am pleased that you have continued to keep a journal, Theresa, and particularly now. Believe me, you will find it most comforting when you embark on the Season. London will seem so strange to you at first, I expect. The journal will enable you to better sort out your impressions and experiences,'' Miss Brown laughed a little, realizing how she must sound. ''I am sorry. I never meant to lecture so late in the day. I will say good night before I begin again.''

They parted then, each to seek the quiet of her own bedroom.

12

A few days later, while everyone was still at the breakfast table, the butler entered to announce a visitor. The words were scarce out of his mouth when a youthful gentleman breezed into the room.

"Holland!" Mrs. Thaleman exclaimed, astonished.

"Good morning, Mama." Holland dropped a kiss on Mrs. Thaleman's brow.

Theresa's napkin fluttered to the carpet as she leapt up and ran around the side of the table, her hands outstretched. "Oh, Holland, how good it is to see you."

Holland turned in time to catch Theresa by the hands and hold her away from him so that he could look her up and down. "Teri, you look positively smashing."

"Thank you, Holland!" said Theresa, pleased. There had been a flurry of shopping and visits to an expensive modiste since her arrival in London, so her wardrobe had already taken on a dramatic change in style. She had put on a new morning gown of yellow muslin, trimmed in brown velvet ribbons, and it was pleasant indeed to have one of her brothers voice such approval of her appearance.

Mr. Bennett rose to shake hands with his nephew. "Well, my boy! I have not seen you since you were in short pants. You have grown into a fine young gentleman."

"Thank you, Uncle." Holland turned to his aunt, who was regarding the reunion with an aloof expression. She bestowed her hand on her nephew in a bored manner. Holland easily took her measure. "Aunt Claudia, I am happy to renew my acquaintance at last." He bowed over her fingers, brushing his lips across them as he did so. When he straightened, he was satisfied to see that Mrs. Bennett's face had softened a little.

Mrs. Thaleman had been glancing often at the door, and now she demanded, "Holland, where are the squire and Michael? Are they not with you?"

Holland shook his head. He flashed a mischievous grin about the company. "My twin is still tied to his bed and is a bear for company. I came on alone, leaving poor Michael to the squire's tender mercies."

"Well! However happy I am to see you, Holland, I must express my astonishment. I cannot imagine how you could stand to come away from home when your brother is still in so weakened a state. I would not have thought it of you, Holland, indeed I would not," his mother said.

Holland flushed slightly. "It is not at all what you think, Mama. The squire wanted me gone days past, saying that Michael could not rest easy with me clattering about, but I made one excuse after another, not wishing to leave Michael. But in the end Michael himself positively begged me to go. He said that it fretted him beyond endurance to see me striding about healthy as a horse while he was tied to his bed. He would rather have me in London, where he would not be offended by the sight of my jovial face," he said.

Theresa gurgled on laughter. "That sounds exactly like Michael. He has such a biting tongue when he wishes."

"Exactly so," Holland said, grinning.

"I find nothing amusing in it. It was unkind and ungrateful, too, of Michael to send Holland away in so rude a fashion. But he has never been one for blunt speaking. He is so like the squire in that." Mrs. Thaleman sighed.

"Aye, he has not my gilded tongue," Holland joked. He turned to his sister and his grin widened as he slipped his hand inside his coat pocket. "By the by, Michael asked me to relay his compliments to you when I presented you with this." He drew a jeweler's box out of his pocket.

Theresa took the box, glancing up at her brother's smiling face. "But whatever is it?"

"Perhaps if you open it, niece, all of our curiosities would be satisfied," Mrs. Bennett said acidly.

Theresa did not heed her aunt's tone, having learned that Mrs. Bennett rarely voiced accolades. She opened the box. "Oh! They are beautiful, Holland. Thank you ever so much, both you and Michael." She flung her arm about her brother's neck and kissed his cheek.

Holland laughed, pleased by her gesture. "Put them on, goose."

Theresa put the earrings on and swung her head to feel the small dangling teardrops brush against her skin. There was an elegant gold neck chain with a matching teardrop pendant, and Holland fastened it for her. Last, Theresa slipped on the gold serpentine band with its one remaining stone. She ran to the mirror above the mantel to look at herself. With a light finger she touched one of the earrings. "They came out so very nicely," she said.

"Quite charming," Mr. Bennett said, surveying the reflection of his niece's happy expression with approval. That was what one needed to be exposed to in the morning, he thought. He slid a glance in his wife's direction and sighed.

"I must agree, Theresa. I find the set to be in fine taste. You have my permission to wear it on your coming-out," Mrs. Thaleman said.

"I did not know that you and the squire afforded your daughter such luxuries," Mrs. Bennett said with a sniff.

Holland exchanged a swift look with his mother. Before Mrs. Thaleman could form a proper set-down, Holland stepped into the breach. "The set is a present to Teri from my brother and me, Aunt Claudia," he said easily. He turned to his mother and took her hand. "I must be off now. But I shall return later this evening, if my uncle and aunt will have me to dinner."

"But of course, dear boy. In fact, why do you not postpone your leave-taking and join us for breakfast? I know that the ride to London must have whetted your appetite, and there is plenty yet to be had here," Mr. Bennett said expansively as he gestured at the loaded sideboard.

Holland shook his head. "I am cognizant of your generosity, sir, but the thing of it is, I wish to catch George before he is done with his toilette and leaves his rooms. He'll be able to direct me to the best hotel where I may put myself up."

"You could sit down to a three-course dinner and still have time to catch that puppy in front of his mirror," Mr. Bennett said with a snort.

"Henry, I shall not have you denigrating our son. George is becoming quite a leader of fashion, I shall have you know."

"Just what one wants in the family," Mr. Bennett muttered.

"What was that, Henry?" Mrs. Bennett asked with a sharp glance.

"I was just saying that I might accompany Holland, my dear, at least as far as the club. What say you, boy? Will you allow an old man to bear you company?" Mr. Bennett rose from the table, intent on escaping the threatening storm in his wife's blue eyes.

"With pleasure, sir." Holland took leave of his parent and his sister, giving Theresa a broad wink before he turned to his aunt. He said a pretty phrase or two, and Mrs. Bennett's expression once more seemed to soften slightly. Then he and Mr. Bennett exited the breakfast room together.

"Holland is a most gracious young gentleman," Mrs. Bennett said with grudging approval.

Mrs. Thaleman drew herself up with pride. "Indeed, and Michael is not at all behind him in that. The squire and I have always been at pains to instill the proper manners in our offspring, and I am happy to say that—"

Mrs. Bennett rose sharply. "I have a headache. I knew that I should not have listened to you, Charlotte, and come down so early, against my own established habits. Now I am forced to lie down, when I had wished to go over with Cook what is to be served at Theresa's coming-out. It will simply have to wait, of course. I only hope that I may recover in time to allow the staff proper notice of my intentions."

She motioned to a footman to lend her support, and leaned heavily on his arm as she walked slowly toward the doorway.

Mrs. Thaleman called after her. "Pray do not give it another thought, Claudia. I am certain that Cook and I shall do very well, but if there are any questions that arise that I cannot answer, which I doubt, I shall certainly send in a billet to you to ask your advice. But you may be assured that I shall not countenance an unwarranted disturbance of your rest."

Mrs. Bennett turned about sharply at this speech. It was on the tip of her tongue to let her sister know in no uncertain terms who would do the ordering of the entertainment, but she was in an untenable position. She had already announced that she would be too ill to attend to her duty as hostess, and she could not now turn about her decision without damaging her carefully cultivated persona as an invalid. "I am properly grateful, of course," she said in freezing accents, and continued on her way upstairs. Her maid settled her with soft expressions of concern onto her chaise longue, with a cool towel over her eyes and a vinaigrette close to hand, then quietly left her alone.

Mrs. Bennett usually cherished these times, when she could envision her household suspended without her firm guiding hand, and she always felt much refreshed after an hour or two of solitude. But this time she could not be comfortable. The chaise longue was unaccountably hard, her pillows scratchy on her sensitive skin, and the shawl that covered her legs insisted upon sliding to the floor. And all the while, all she could think about was her sister ordering about her staff—her staff!—to suit her own whims. It was but thirty minutes before Mrs. Bennett threw aside the towel and shawl and vigorously rang the bell on the table beside the chaise.

The maid rushed in with an expression of alarm on her face. "Madam, what is it?"

"Take it away, all of it. I wish to rise," said Mrs. Bennett petulantly. She got up from the chaise and went to her vanity, dropping down on the the silk-covered bench so that she could smooth her hair before the mirror. The maid stared at her mistress's back a long second before she acted, swiftly gathering up the discarded shawl, towel, and vinaigrette.

Within minutes Mrs. Bennett had sailed back downstairs, spurning the arm of her maid or the footman, and reentered the drawing room. "Charlotte, I do not intend to while away the minutes fretting about what you are setiing in train for our ball," she said firmly.

Mrs. Thaleman looked up with a complete lack of surprise. "Pray do join us, Claudia. I was just speaking to Miss Brown about the efficacy of lobster for dinner at Theresa's come-out."

Mrs. Bennett arranged herself in a wing chair. "Pray do not be gauche, Charlotte. Lobster for a come-out, indeed!" And she bent her considerable expertise to showing her backward sister what constituted a proper come-out dinner.

Miss Theresa Thaleman's ball was to be an unqualified success, even by her aunt's estimation. Although a self-proclaimed invalid, Claudia Bennett had an intimate circle of acquaintances whom she received from her chaise longue and from whom she learned the latest *on-dits*. Her visitors could always be assured of hearing some tidbit that had not yet come to their ears, and therefore Mrs. Bennett's sitting room was thought of as something of an information exchange. The arrangement perfectly suited Mrs. Bennett, since she rarely felt inclined to leave her own house to return morning calls.

When Mrs. Bennett announced to her acquaintances that she meant to sponsor her niece's coming-out ball, it created a furor. The news quickly spread beyond Mrs. Bennett's intimates to those who knew of her only by reputation. The very fact that Mrs. Bennett had roused herself to the effort of hosting a ball for her niece had the effect of bringing in many of the curious who would not normally attend a function given by such a minor member of polite society when there were other, more glittering affairs.

Theresa was at her best in the receiving line. She felt not the least bit nervous, contrary to her expectations. She was at last able to practice some of the lessons in etiquette she had been taught. Such as giving her hand to the persons made known to her, and greeting them with an ease of manner that would have done credit to an established hostess.

Mrs. Thaleman was pleased by her daughter's bearing, and even Mrs. Bennett, who had sourly remarked as the first guest arrived that she hoped her niece would not disgrace her by breaking into hysterical giggles, was impressed. Taking advantage of a break in the line, Mrs. Bennett said, "I must commend you, Charlotte. Theresa does very well."

Mrs. Thaleman accepted the compliment graciously. "I am fortunate to have a close relationship with my daughter, so that she is easily guided by example. But I must in turn give some credit to Miss Brown, who is positively marvelous with the girl."

"Quite," said Mrs. Bennett. She had had time in the past weeks to observe her houseguests, and she had long since gathered that it was Miss Brown's influence that motivated Theresa.

Late in the evening, a stir of surprise rippled through the crowd nearest the ballroom door when the Duke of Ashford appeared. He stood for only a moment before Mrs. Bennett became aware of his presence. Her eyes widened in momentary shock before her features settled into smiling confident lines as she went to greet him. "Your grace, this is indeed an honor. I had not honestly expected your presence at my little ball," she said, giving her hand to him.

Hugo bowed briefly over her fingers. "I was on my way to another appointment when I succumbed to the impulse to step in for a few moments and offer my good wishes for a successful Season to Mrs. Thaleman and her charming daughter," he said.

Mrs. Bennett was not unversed in social matters. She knew when she had received a set-down. Swallowing the pique that his words had produced and pinning her smile firmly in place, she took the duke over to her sister and niece. "Charlotte, the Duke of Ashford has come to proffer his respects," she said, and then she left them to it, not wishing to witness the degree of friendliness her sister enjoyed with this most reserved peer of the realm.

Mrs. Thaleman greeted the duke with effusive pleasure. "Your grace, how kind of you, to be sure! I was just mentioning to Theresa my hopes that you would make an appearance tonight, and here you are."

"Quite," Hugo said dryly. He thought he had rarely met anyone who more perfectly suited the description of the ordinary than Mrs. Thaleman. It was a wonder that the daughter was endowed with such captivating character, he thought, turning to Theresa. "Miss Thaleman, I hope that you are enjoying your first ball."

"Indeed I am, your grace. I have met ever so many personages, all of whom have spoken to me with such kindness. I am astonished, for I quite expected that the more exalted would possess a much more defined degree of snobbery." Theresa's eyes were alight with laughter, inviting him to share her fun.

"Theresa, what a thing to say! I am certain that his grace must frown on such frivolity," said Mrs. Thaleman, aghast at her daughter's frank manner. She could not but blame the squire for it, and so she meant to tell him in her next letter.

"On the contrary, I know exactly to what Miss Thaleman refers," Hugo said, appreciative of the gentle irony in her words.

Theresa smiled at him. She was somewhat surprised by her pleasure at seeing the duke again. After all, he had been pivotal in Michael's injury and had also been thoroughly disapproving of her own involvement in the mad highwayman escapade. But she supposed it was because his was a familiar face in a ballroom of strangers. Besides, she liked the way the faintest of smiles made the corner of his mouth quirk. Theresa suspected that behind the duke's grave manner there lurked a gentleman who might appreciate life's oddities as

much as she did. She decided that she would like the chance
to discover if her suspicion was true, especially if it would
bring such warmth to his gaze when his gray eyes rested on
her.

The duke stayed to chat with Theresa and Mrs. Thaleman
a few mintues more before taking his leave. Theresa was
sorry that he left so soon, but she was fully able to set herself
to enjoy the remainder of the evening.

When the last of the guests had taken their leave in the
small hours of the morning and Theresa and Miss Brown
had gone up to bed, Mrs. Thaleman let herself down onto
the sofa and vigorously fanned her warm face. "I declare,
I never thought to see such distinguished attention given to
any daughter of mine," she said with great satisfaction.

"Nor I," said Claudia Bennett from her own seat.

Mrs. Thaleman took umbrage at that. "Really, Claudia!
You speak as though Theresa were a squint-eyed dumpy little
thing. If you had but taken notice, you would have seen that
there were several distinguished gentlemen who were quite
flattering of Theresa. Indeed she was the center of a veritable
company of gentlemen!"

"Indeed. However, the Duke of Ashford was not among
their number," Mrs. Bennett said crushingly.

Mrs. Thaleman had no answer to that, for it was true that
the duke had put in only the briefest of appearances. She
had hoped that he might stay the duration of the ball, if only
to prick Claudia's insufferably superior attitude. She thought
bitterly about gentlemen who so blithely disappointed the
hopes of females. It crossed her mind that Holland had
several times promised to accompany her and Theresa
shopping, but he had always begged off. In fact, she had
seen but little of Holland since he had come to town. His
calls were always brief and he always seemed impatient to
be off to other appointments. Mrs. Thaleman sighed. It was
difficult to watch one's children grow apart from one, but
she supposed that Holland had found any number of amusing
acquaintances whose company was naturally far more

interesting than that of his mother. The thought was a bit depressing to her, and she sighed once again.

Theresa had also noticed her brother's defection, and though she was disappointed not to see as much of him as she would have liked, she hoped that she was magnanimous enough not to fall into childish sulks because her erstwhile playmate was occupied elsewhere. However, the next time her cousin George came to pay one of his frequent visits, Theresa did ask if he had seen anything of Holland.

George shook his head. "Not half as much as I had expected, since it is Holland's first visit to town on his own. I rather thought I would be cast in the role of bear leader, but Holland informed me from the beginning that he wished to wade in without a set of leading strings. You know how Holland is, Teri. He rarely accepts even the most casual of advice."

"Yes, that is what has me in a pucker," Theresa said, her memory vivid of the night her brothers and cousin had played at highwaymen. The very daring of that incident marked the notion as one that had come springing from Holland's fertile mind.

George laughed at her, even as he glanced aside to the mirror to check his cravat. "You look mightily long-faced, cousin, but you know as well as I that Holland can take care of himself, remarkable as that seems at first glance." He adjusted a silken fold and frowned as he measured the effect. He said absently, "If it will ease your mind, I shall step around to Holland's rooms later this week and see what he is up to."

"Thank you, George." Theresa watched her cousin a moment and her thoughts took another turn. "We have seen a great deal of you since we came to London. I am surprised that you do not become bored with our company. Or perhaps it is Miss Brown's company that you find so entertaining."

George swung around. "You are becoming almost catty, dear cousin," he said softly.

Theresa laughed and stepped close so that she could wind

her arm about his waist. "Come, George, I have eyes in my head. But I do wish you would be more circumspect. My aunt is not unintelligent and she already has commented on more than one occasion on the particular attentions you pay to Miss Brown. It is beginning to make dear Miss Brown the smallest bit uncomfortable."

"So my mother disapproves, does she? I find that vastly interesting," George said, his eyes holding an expression of fiendish mischief.

Theresa let go of him and looked up into his face. "George, promise me that you will not do anything that will hurt or embarrass Miss Brown. For I tell you now that I shall not sit idly by if you—"

George put up his hand. "Enough said, Teri. You have my word on it. I know where to draw the line, believe me."

Theresa shook her head, only half-convinced. "George, you really are a cad. What if Miss Brown were to fall in love with you, when all you ever mean to do is to bedevil your mother by paying court to her?"

George lifted her chin and planted a light kiss on her brow. "That would be a settler, wouldn't it? But I suspect that Miss Brown is onto me. She is a surprising woman. Now, I must be off."

Theresa let him go without further demur, and it wasn't until the door closed behind him that she remembered that she had meant to have George give her brother the message that she wished particularly for him to escort her to the theater the following week. It was to be a production of *Hamlet* and she thought that Holland, in particular, would enjoy such sweeping drama. Theresa made up her mind to dash off a note that very instant, and hoped that Holland would reply, even though she knew that he detested to commit to paper even the smallest message.

13

The Bennett household received more than its share of morning callers after Theresa's entrance into society. Mrs. Bennett found to her dismay that she was unable to hold court in her private sitting room, as was her wont, since many of the callers were content merely to visit with Mrs. Thaleman and Theresa in the morning room before going on their way. Perforce, Mrs. Bennett was forced to join the other ladies downstairs if she wanted to hear the latest gossip. This enraged her. She took care to point out her sacrifice at every opportunity, until even Miss Brown dreaded to see her take a breath preparatory to speaking. "It is extremely debilitating to my health, Charlotte. I hope that you and my niece are sufficiently grateful to me," Mrs. Bennett said for the thousandth time, picking at a fold of her flowing skirt.

Theresa and Miss Brown sat in front of the morning-room window so that the sunlight could illuminate their watercoloring. Theresa slanted a glance around her easel to be certain that her aunt and her mother were still situated across the room before she murmured to Miss Brown, "One should not be unkind, but isn't my aunt the most dreadful bore?"

"That is quite enough, Theresa," said Miss Brown, but she could not entirely stifle a laugh.

Theresa smiled affectionately at her. Her mentor was too conscious of what was due her station to openly agree with her opinion of her aunt, but Miss Brown's long-suffering expression told the tale.

Mrs. Thaleman's lips had thinned at her sister's words. "Oh, indeed, Claudia. I am fully cognizant of your selflessness. I would not dream of persuading you to put yourself out another moment," she said in a deceptively mild voice.

"Pray do not feel yourself obligated to stay away from your bed on our account, dear sister. I doubt that there will be more than one or two other callers this morning, and those I shall ask to leave their cards for you." She tossed aside her magazine as she spoke, and went to the door. She opened it and stood waiting, gazing at her sister.

Mrs. Bennett was bereft of speech. After the longest hesitation she rose from the settee and spent an unconscionable time rearranging her skirt as she attempted to think of some way to counter her sister's dismissal. Unable to come up with an excuse to remain, she said finally, "Very well, Charlotte. Perhaps I will join you again later this afternoon."

Mrs. Thaleman ushered Mrs. Bennett out into the hall, adjuring the footman on duty to help his mistress upstairs on the instant. "Rest well, dear Claudia," she called. She closed the door with a snap before she smiled across at Theresa and Miss Brown. "Now we may be comfortable."

"You are the most complete hand, Mama," Theresa said appreciatively.

"Pray do not employ cant phrases, dear. It is very unbecoming," said Mrs. Thaleman, but without her usual heat. She recognized the compliment in her daughter's words and it pleased her. She reseated herself and picked up her magazine once more.

"Yes, Mama," Theresa said, hiding a grin. She did not dare to glance at Miss Brown's face, fearing the lady's expression would overset her. Theresa swept her brush across the canvas with a flourish and regarded the result with surprise. The brushstroke had given dimension to her painting. For once, Theresa actually found a sense of pleasure in the mundane feminine pursuit of watercoloring.

The butler entered to announce another visitor for the ladies. "The Duke of Ashford! My word, what a surprise," exclaimed Mrs. Thaleman, abandoning her magazine.

Hugo strolled into the morning room, greeting Mrs. Thaleman with grave courtesy and bowing briefly over her hand. "I trust that I find you well, ma'am," he said.

"Quite well, for I am never ill. It is otherwise with my sister, Mrs. Bennett. She has just gone upstairs, or otherwise she would be here to receive you as well. How unfortunate that Claudia must miss your visit. But of course you have come to call on my daughter, your grace," Mrs. Thaleman said, gesturing urgently to Theresa to come forward.

Theresa approached the duke with a friendly smile, her hand outheld. "Your grace, I am happy that you have taken time from your schedule to call on us. I have thought often of the treat that Miss Brown and I had in being driven in your phaeton. I believe that you remember my companion, Miss Brown," she said, turning to include the lady in the conversation.

"Of course." The Duke of Ashford bowed to Miss Brown and included her in his glance as he spoke. "It is about driving that I have come, Miss Thaleman. I recalled that I promised to drive you in the park, and this being a good morning for such an outing, I have come to invite whoever should wish it to join me for an hour's drive."

Mrs. Thaleman promptly excused herself, renewed visions in her head of a coronet for her daughter. "For myself, I must beg off. I have a hundred details to take care of today," she said, completely ignoring the presence of the open magazine beside her. "However, I certainly have no objection to your accepting his grace's invitation, Theresa."

"Thank you, Mama." Theresa glanced at the duke. "I will be glad to accompany you, your grace. I miss my mare more than I thought possible, and to be tooled about the park will be a wonderful diversion."

The duke smiled at her before he turned to Miss Brown. "Perhaps you will join us, then, Miss Brown?"

Miss Brown threw a quick glance at Mrs. Thaleman, who frowned heavily at her. It went against the grain to allow a young girl to go out unchaperoned with a gentleman that she was scarcely acquainted with, but Miss Brown felt she had little choice. Reluctantly she declined the duke's invitation. "You are most thoughtful, your grace. But Mrs.

Thaleman undoubtedly requires my services here this morning,'' she said quietly.

"Quite right, Miss Brown. But do not allow our allegiance to duty to spoil your fun, your grace,'' said Mrs. Thaleman. She glanced at her daughter. "Pray do not keep his grace standing about, Theresa. Run up directly for your pelisse, there's a good girl.'' The duke had raised his brows at Mrs. Thaleman's leniency, and now there was a distinctly satirical smile playing about his mouth.

Theresa flushed at her mother's heavy-handedness, but she said only, "Of course, Mama.'' She left the morning room, some of her pleasure in the outing dimmed. In a very few moments she returned wearing a smartly cut pelisse of amber cloth and a chip bonnet. Theresa saw immediately from the Duke of Ashford's frown and the stiff, polite expression on Miss Brown's face that her mother had not done much to retrieve her credit. Theresa was appalled when she realized that her mother was prattling about the ball and the duke's brief appearance at it.

"Such a distinguished company. It is a pity that you did not remain, your grace, for I know that your continued presence would have been the crowning touch for Theresa,'' Mrs. Thaleman said.

Theresa came quickly forward. "I am certain that his grace had a number of other engagements, Mama.'' She turned to the duke. "Shall we go? I am eager to observe what your team may do for a distance.''

It was just the right touch of impersonality needed to lighten the cold boredom in the Duke of Ashford's eyes. His glance warmed slightly as he looked down at Theresa. "I am at your command, Miss Thaleman.'' When he turned to take leave of Mrs. Thaleman, his voice was a shade too polite. "I shall have Miss Thaleman returned to you in an hour, ma'am, so that there will be no cause for anxiety.''

Theresa felt her fingers clench on the strings of her reticule and she saw that Miss Brown was turning away, ostensibly to rearrange the easels. But Mrs. Thaleman was impervious to the slap. "Of course, your grace. You are good to think of my maternal heart. Not that I shall waste a moment worrying over Theresa while she is in your capable hands, for I promise you I shall not," she said, accompanying them to the front door.

Theresa was silent while the duke handed her up into the curricle and climbed in to take his own seat. He flicked his whip at his team, setting the carriage in motion. She stole a glance up at his closed face. Theresa transferred her gaze to her hands, folded in her lap. "I feel that I must apologize for my mother, your grace. I have never before known her to behave in just that fashion."

"Indeed?" Hugo's voice was cold. He was already regretting his lamentable notion to issue this invitation, since it had served to expose him to just the sort of marriage-minded matron that he detested.

It was not an inviting response. Theresa put a tentative hand on his sleeve. "Pray do not be angry, sir. My mother is at times too anxious on my account. I suspect that she hopes much from this Season. I am a sad trial to her, you see. But you have only to disregard it, for I assure you that I do. I have already told you what I expect out of the Season, and if I could count your grace as my friend at the end of it, I shall be well content," she said earnestly.

The duke looked down at her. She met his glance openly but with a hint of anxiety shadowing her brown eyes. He realized of a sudden that she was embarrassed on her mother's account. Hugo allowed the flicker of a smile to cross his face. "You still wish for my friendship, even though I shot your brother?"

Theresa flashed a smile. "Yes. And I am far more at fault for that than you, your grace. I realize that if I had not acted so rashly, Michael would have had but a flesh wound."

The duke sobered and shook his head. "You had no way of knowing what I intended, Miss Thaleman. Your brother Michael—how is he?"

"He was recovering nicely when we left to come up to

London, and Holland has since joined us in town, which he would never have done it Michael were in the least danger. They are twins, you know.''

''I had not noticed. Though your brothers look alike, I trust that they do not share the same hot nature,'' the duke said dryly.

Theresa laughed, knowing that he remembered Holland's abortive attack on him. ''Oh, no, I do not think so. Holland has always been the impulsive one, while Michael is more reflective. Michael intends to take Orders one day,'' she said.

''Good God,'' Hugo said blankly. For once he was completely shed of his polite shield. ''I hope that Michael does not intend to brandish a brace of pistols while in the pulpit.''

''What an infamous thing to say, your grace!'' Theresa said on a delighted laugh. She had not taken the duke as a gentleman given to levity, and it was a pleasure to discover that he had a sense of humor.

''It is, isn't it?'' the duke said, disconcerted. He could not recall ever saying anything half so ludicrous. Casting a glance down at the young lady beside him, he suspected that if he was long in her company he might find himself uttering further inconsistencies. Miss Thaleman appeared to have an odd effect on his usual good sense.

They had entered the park and the carriage began bowling along the green under the tall trees. Theresa looked about with shining eyes. It had not occurred to her that there might be others of like mind who wished to take advantage of the warm sun, but so it was. The park was filled with the equipages of the wealthy, pulled by magnificent teams of horses. The passengers nodded and spoke to acquaintances met by chance or design, so there was much stopping and starting of carriages. A few of the carriage occupants waved in recognition to the Duke of Ashford, but he seemed not to notice and he never slackened the pace of his team. Riders intermingled among the crowded ways, and off on smaller paths the brief flash of muslin skirts and tall beavers through the lacy branches bespoke of pedestrians. Overall the park rendered a charming picture of leisure set against the gleaming greenery.

"It is all so very grand," Theresa said on a sigh. Since coming to London there had been so much that was new that she had felt more content than she had been for some time.

Hugo looked down at her in surprise. He had years before formed the habit of driving in the park, and its sights had long since become commonplace to him. He supposed to someone fresh from the country the activity must seem exciting. "Is it? I suppose to someone like yourself, London is all very fast-paced. One becomes accustomed to it, however," he said.

"You speak as though you are bored, your grace," Theresa said in smiling accusation.

The duke smiled faintly. "If the truth be known, Miss Thaleman, there is little that does not bore me."

Theresa studied his face, suddenly aware that he spoke with the greatest seriousness. She said quietly, "I am sorry for that, your grace. You must miss much that is wonderful to behold." In that moment she caught sight of a pair of riders in full gallop, so she was completely unaware that she had deeply offended her escort. "Oh, do look! It is a race! Stop, your grace!"

Obediently the duke pulled his team to a stop. A sharp retort had been on the edge of his tongue, but when he looked at Miss Thaleman and saw the excitement in her eyes as she watched the impromptu race, he found that he could not utter it. He paid no attention to the approaching racers, but instead watched the enthusiasm in his companion's face. Miss Thaleman's open enjoyment was a revelation to him. The ladies of his acquaintance adhered to a fashionable posture of *ennui*, and if any spoke at all with enthusiasm, it was over a bit of jewelry bestowed upon her by a lover.

The riders were flattened over their mounts, their coats flapping madly in the wind, and snatches of their urgent encouragement to their mounts could be heard. The horses' necks were outstretched to the fullest extent and their thundering hooves flung huge clods of sod into the air. The riders swept past the duke's curricle, and Theresa jumped to her feet, laughing and waving them on. Still laughing, she reseated herself. "That was magnificent!" she exclaimed, glancing at the Duke of Ashford. "Do you not think so, your grace?"

Her eyes sparkled with life and her cheeks had bloomed pink. The duke was utterly arrested by the incredible beauty that obviously eminated from the joy she felt within. "Indeed, Miss Thaleman. I am completely overset," Hugo said slowly.

"Now you are teasing me! Very well, I shall not say another word to persuade you that there is too much of interest to allow oneself to become bored." Theresa folded her hands in her lap, sitting upright and demure on the seat. She spoke with measured primness. "It was quite considerate of your grace to offer to drive me. It is a beautiful day. The weather can be so freakish at this time of year, can it not? But perhaps—"

"Pray do stop going on aobut the weather, Miss Thaleman. I shall expire of boredom before ever we leave the park otherwise," the duke said unthinkingly. Her spurt of laughter brought him to an awareness that he had again spoken his mind without first giving consideration to the polite niceties. "You are an extremely bad influence on me, Miss Thaleman," he accused.

Theresa only laughed again and shook her head. "Not I, sir! It is your own lamentable humor that leads you astray. Actually, I find it most attractive in a gentleman when he is able to let go of his stuffy, formal airs."

"I? Stuffy?" Hugo said, startled.

Theresa was unheeding, her thoughts already leaping on. "Your grace, did you not say before that you were a student of antiquity? I should so like to discover what your thoughts are on Greek tragedy. Do you believe, like some of the writers I have perused, that the Greeks were a discontented, self-destructive lot who were most content when they were dying like flies owing to the gods' displeasure?''

The duke was completely taken aback. He was so startled by her perception of him that he had difficulty rearranging his thoughts to allow for the switch in conversation from the purely personal to such dizzying scholarly heights. "What? The Greeks." He stared at her. "Miss Thaleman, I suspect that you are a bluestocking in disguise."

"Oh, not I. Miss Brown will tell you that I am a most unenthusiastic student." Theresa gave a small laugh and lifted her shoulders in an eloquent shrug. "And my mother is not behind in lamenting that I have no inclination for feminine accomplishment."

The duke did not comment on her statement, but instead chose to voice his opinion on the civilization of ancient Greece. "I hold the Greeks in the highest regard. We must give them just credit for accomplishing so much of genuis. We are the heirs of their successes in philosophy and theater, in architecture and art, as well as in other areas."

"That is just what I think," Theresa said, nodding. She saw that they had left the park and had turned toward her uncle's town house. "Is an hour past already? I would not have thought it. I must tell you that I have truly enjoyed myself, your grace."

Hugo glanced down at her, his expression smiling. "I, too, have thoroughly enjoyed our time together, Miss Thaleman. I hope that you will not think me forward if I suggest another outing in future."

"Not at all, your grace. Though I think it would be best if Miss Brown or my maid accompanied us, do you not agree? I noticed a number of glances given us in the park."

"Acquaintances only, Miss Thaleman," the duke said shortly. He had not been unaware of the interest generated by the sight of himself accompanying an unknown young woman, but to spare Miss Thaleman any embarrassment he had chosen not to acknowledge those who had nodded or waved to him.

Once more he silently cursed Mrs. Thaleman's lack of foresight in exposing her daughter to gossip. If a lady who was accompanied solely by a gentleman was not in some way related to her escort, it was often assumed that she was extremely ill-bred and easily had. However short his acquaintance with Miss Thaleman had been, he did not believe that she was at all experienced. On the contrary, her character was of such an open nature that it brought to the fore chivalric tendencies that he had thought long dead.

He brought the curricle to a stop beside the curb and snubbed the reins before he jumped out to assist Theresa to the pavement. He escorted her up the steps, and when the front door was opened, he bowed over her hand before giving her over to the care of the footman. "Until next time, Miss Thaleman," he said.

"I shall look forward to it, your grace," Theresa said, and went in without a backward glance.

14

Mr. Bennett graciously offered to escort Theresa and Miss Brown to the production of *Hamlet*. As the party was about to leave, he addressed his wife. "Are you absolutely certain that you do not wish to accompany us, my dear?"

"You know very well that I detest Shakespearean tragedy, Henry," Mrs. Bennett said.

Mrs. Thaleman, who was seated nearby with a volume open in her hands, gave an artistic shudder. "And I also. It is beyond my comprehension how anyone could actually *enjoy* the misery endured by the poor characters."

"And yet you are able to positively wallow in the sentimental mush found between those two covers," said Mrs. Bennett, gesturing with disdain at her sister's book.

Mrs. Thaleman was affronted. "I shall have you know, Claudia, that this is a vastly pretty tale and is quite edifying as well." She tightened her lips when she saw her sister's smile of superiority. "I do not know why I even bother to be civil. You have always been a haughty cat."

Mrs. Bennett appeared to swell with indignation. "Well! I know how to reply to that, I hope!"

With his eyes cast in his wife's direction, Mr. Bennett anxiously ushered Theresa and Miss Brown toward the door. "We shall be off, then. Er . . . have a pleasant evening."

"Good-bye, Mama," called Theresa over her shoulder, even as her uncle was closing the door. She thought it doubtful that her mother paid the least heed to her farewell, since Mrs. Bennett was leaned forward in her chair and was speaking with emphatic rancor.

The party emerged from the town house and walked down the steps. They got into the waiting carriage, and as her uncle tapped on the roof for the driver to start the horses, Theresa said, "It is a great pity that Mama and Aunt Claudia do not get on better. Why ever do they quarrel so much, Uncle?"

Mr. Bennett sighed. "I haven't a clue, my dear. They have done so whenever they come together. That is one of the reasons that we did not visit your family more through the years, though George was always the exception. He chooses to do very much as he pleases, of course."

"Mama and Aunt Claudia must positively enjoy their bickering. Otherwise I cannot imagine wasting such energy on it."

Miss Brown laughed a little. "Your insight is quite devastating at times, Theresa."

The drive to the theater was not long, but several times the carriage was forced to a snail's pace due to the traffic. At last the theater was reached and Mr. Bennett handed the ladies out of the carriage to the sidewalk. He offered an arm to each of them and then sauntered into the vestibule with a proud air. "It has been a long time since I was so fortunate as to play escort to a pair of lovely ladies," he said.

Theresa laughed, surprised by his unusually lively countenance and expansive manner. But she thought perhaps it was not to be wondered at after all. It was probably not often that her uncle felt free enough of his wife's suffocating personality to be able to enjoy himself.

"Well met, all!"

Theresa turned quickly and with pleased surprise. "George! I did not know that you were intending to come to tonight's performance."

"It was a last-moment decision, actually. The party I was attending was a frightful bore and I left early. There I was kicking my heels at home when I recalled that you had mentioned the theater for this evening. A quick change of attire, and behold, here I stand," said George, his grin impish. His gaze casually met that of Miss Brown, and then he felt himself seized.

Theresa shook his arm. "Quick change, indeed. Well I know that it takes the better part of an hour for you to do so much as tie your cravat to your satisfaction."

Mr. Bennett snorted laughter. "She has you there, my boy. Such magnificence as that neckcloth deserves a sonnet, no less. But I am always glad to see you, whatever your taste in dress."

"Thank you, sir," George said, amused. He suggested that they find their box, since the performance was soon to begin.

Once they were all seated in the box, it was but a moment or two before the curtain rose from the stage below. Theresa sat on the edge of her chair, excited beyond measure to be attending her first London play. She was instantly entranced and absorbed in the tale of the doomed Prince Hamlet. When the curtain fell for the intermission and the spell was broken, she blinked in momentary confusion. "What a frightfully awful story. One can very nearly see the black tragedy forming about Hamlet's head," she said with every evidence of contentment. "I can scarcely wait to see the end."

"What a bloodthirsty baggage you are, to be sure," George said cheerfully. "After all this high drama, I am for a bit of refreshment. May I bring either of you ladies anything?"

"I should like a lemon ice, please, George," Theresa said.

Miss Brown quietly concurred that she, too, would care for an ice. She pretended not to notice the manner in which George bowed to her, as though she were a grand lady. She had been enjoying the rare evening out and was determined that he would not put her out of countenance. But even as his attentions were bothersome, they were also oddly flattering.

Mr. Bennett heaved himself out of his chair, his corsets creaking. "I shall walk down with you, my boy. I saw an acquaintance of mine in the pit that I should like to speak to for a moment," he said.

When the gentlemen had left the box, Theresa said to her companion, "You should not allow George to tease you so, you know. You have only to tip him a leveler and he will shy off."

Miss Brown felt unaccustomed heat rise in her face. She had thought herself long past the age of the easy blush. That and her discomfiture seemed to unhinge her power of reason. "I hardly know what to say, Theresa."

"If you wish it, I shall hint George away. He is really a dear at heart, and once he understands that you are being made uncomfortable, I am certain that he will behave himself."

Miss Brown pressed a hand to one cheek, appalled by the offer. "No, no, I do not think that will be necessary. I am certain that I am capable of handling the situation," she said unsteadily. She looked at Theresa and wondered when the girl had begun to grow up.

There was a knock on the door. It swung open and the Duke of Ashford stepped inside. "I chanced to see your party from my own box, and I wished to pay my respects. I hope that I am not intruding," he said with a smile.

"Oh, not at all, your grace," Theresa said, her color rising faintly. There was an odd air of shyness in her manner, but the duke did not seem to notice it.

He seated himself in George's vacated chair and nodded pleasantly to Theresa's companion. "Miss Brown, I see that you also are a lover of the theater. I know very well that Miss Thaleman is, for we have debated the merits of Greek tragedy often enough. I have come off several points behind in our discussions, believe me."

Miss Brown laughed, warmed by his courteous attention. "I grant you that Miss Thaleman is perfectly capable of arguing any number of points well, your grace!"

"Really, Miss Brown! You have made me sound the most contrary person alive. And I am really quite easy to get along with, really I am," protested Theresa.

The duke and Miss Brown laughed at her. Theresa had to share in their amusement when she realized that she was arguing. "Very well, I concede the point," she said gaily. "However, I am not the least bit repentant. One must defend one's character from unwarranted slurs, after all."

The duke held up his hand. "Pray give over, Miss Thaleman," he begged. "Miss Brown and I shall both concede that you are not the least argumentative. On the contrary, your universal agreeableness is of the highest order and renowned throughout the kingdom. I shall myself take to task anyone who dares to breathe a word to the contrary.''

Theresa gave a peal of laughter. Her eyes danced with fun when she met his smiling gaze. ''Thank you, your grace.'' She found it difficult to recall a time when the Duke of Ashford had not been her amusing friend. When she was in his company she tended to forget all else but the warmth of his gaze and her pleasure in the teasing manner in which he treated her.

George and Mr. Bennett returned to the box. The duke turned his head, a smile still on his lips. His brows rose at sight of George's face. ''I do believe we have met, have we not?'' he asked.

George flushed, aware of his father's interest and surprise. ''Indeed, your grace. I am Miss Thaleman's cousin, George Bennett. We met one evening when I was visiting with the Thalemans a few months ago.''

The Duke of Ashford nodded. There was the faintest curve to his mobile mouth. ''I recall the circumstances now, yes. It was a very . . . hectic evening.''

George swallowed, but his eyes met the duke's unwaveringly. ''Indeed it was. I do not think the twins and I shall play such a prank again.''

After a swift glance at her uncle's questioning gaze, Theresa interposed. ''Your grace, I do not believe that you have met my uncle, Mr. Henry Bennett. Uncle, this is the Duke of Ashford,'' said Theresa, in full sympathy with her cousin. It was too bad of the duke to tease him so, she thought.

Mr. Bennett shook the duke's hand. ''I recognize your grace from seeing you about the club, of course. What is this about a prank, George?''

The duke smiled. He nodded to George, who had surprised him by that half-admission. The young dandy was made of sterner stuff than he had supposed. ''It was nothing, sir. I see that the curtain is about to rise again, so I shall take my leave. Mr. Bennett, I am happy to have made your acquaintance.'' Mr. Bennett bowed, accompanied by the slightest of creaks. Hugo turned to the ladies. "I hope to see you, Miss Thaleman and Miss Brown, again quite soon. Perhaps we may arrange an outing to the park later in the week. I would be glad of your company as well, George.''

George was startled but gratified. "Certainly, your grace. I shall hold myself ready at your convenience.''

When the duke had left, Mr. Bennett remarked, "I had not expected his grace to be so relaxed in company. He has always given the impression of being a rather standoffish sort of gentleman, even, on occasion, cold and high in the instep.''

"The duke is nothing at all like that, Uncle. His grace has always been kindness itself,'' Theresa said firmly. She turned toward the stage, where the curtain was rising.

Mr. Bennett pursed his mouth in surprise. He turned his gaze toward Miss Brown and his son. "My word,'' he said, and started to make an observation. George shook his head, putting his finger to his lips. Mr. Bennett took the hint. He thought it did not take much intelligence to see that his niece was strongly attracted to the Duke of Ashford. He hoped for her sake that the duke was able to return her interest.

The promised outing took place a few days later. Theresa and Miss Brown rode in a carriage and were accompanied by the duke and George on horseback. It was an agreeable party with good-natured raillery being the order of the day. After an hour or so, Theresa voiced a wish to walk for a time on one of the several paths that meandered through the green park. Miss Brown agreed to accompany her, and the carriage was duly stopped. Theresa was handed out, and with a laugh and a wave of her hand, she slipped alone down a bridle path and was quickly out of sight.

"Theresa!'' Miss Brown was appalled at her charge's lack of manners.

George, who was holding the reins of the duke's mount while he aided the ladies to descend, could not but laugh. "You should know better than anyone how much Teri delights in nature, Miss Brown. She'll be looking about for flowers, I'll be bound, and not a thought of the rest of us.''

The duke helped Miss Brown to the ground and pressed her hand briefly before releasing it. "You need not be so anxious, ma'am, no harm will come to her before we have caught up to her. And if her cousin does not read her a stern lecture for worrying you, then I shall," he said with a half-smile.

Miss Brown returned the duke's smile, but shook her head. "I fear that a lecture only goes in one ear and out the other, your grace. If you will excuse me, I shall go at once to look for Miss Thaleman."

"Of course," Hugo said. He took his reins from George Bennett and quirked a brow at him. "Am I to understand that Miss Thaleman makes a habit of running off?" he asked.

George shrugged and guided his mount in beside the duke's as they began to follow in the direction that Theresa and Miss Brown had already taken. "You must understand, your grace, that Teri was brought up so strictly by my aunt and uncle that she often felt as though she was caged. Actually, I am surprised that she has weathered the Season so well. I rather thought that she would have raised a few brows by now, but I suspect that Theresa is enjoying her social freedom too much to have time to fall into mischief." He realized from the duke's startled expression that he had not done his best by his cousin's character. He said hastily, "There is no harm in her, and never has been. It was always the twins who concocted the mischief, you know."

"Yes, I know," the duke said dryly. His tone caused George to flush as he remembered that better than anyone else outside of the family, the Duke of Ashford had cause to know of what the Thaleman twins were capable.

Theresa found herself alone in the vicinity of some delicate flowering vines. She knelt to sniff appreciatively of the blooms. The woods about her were quiet, so much so that she could hear the hum of insects. She could almost believe herself home in the woods bordering the estate, she thought, marveling.

She did not immediately hear muffled hoofbeats coming up the path behind her. "What have we here? Upon my

word, it is a comely wood sprite! O fair maiden, whither
goest thou? But stay a moment, I beg.'' Theresa had whirled
at the laughing voice and now she stared up at the gentleman
sitting a large bay gelding in the midst of the bridle path.

He laughed softly at her. ''A pretty sight, indeed. No, do
not speak! The spell would be forever broken. Fair maiden,
what have you done to my heart?''

He had dismounted as he spoke, and he took a slow step
toward Theresa. She glanced swiftly about and saw that she
had nowhere to go but further down the path into the trees.
Quite belatedly she realized that she should not have left her
companions behind.

''O fair Persephone, for it must be you, my heart beats
for thee alone,'' said the gentleman in a low, vibrant voice.

Theresa frowned, disliking the comparison. The myth of
the young girl who was kidnapped by the king of the under-
world and ever after condemned to spend a portion of each
year below ground was not one of her favorites. ''You are
speaking nonsense, sir,'' she said.

The gentleman reached out to lightly caress her smooth
cheek. Theresa started, and her eyes widened at his
familiarity. She took an uncertain step backward. The gentleman followed after her, his smile broadening.

''Your delivery is quite good, sir. However, might I
suggest better poetry?'' Miss Brown's voice was astringent
and preceded her into sight.

Theresa heralded her arrival with a certain measure of
relief. ''Miss Brown! How glad I am that you have caught
up with me.'' Instinctively she sought the protection offered
by her companion's presence and flew to her side.

The gentleman cursed under his breath when he took in
Miss Brown's respectable figure. He was not at all surprised
that his delectable quarry greeted the woman familiarly. It
was just his ill luck to be interrupted before he had had a
chance to snatch a kiss. He met the older woman's cool
penetrating gaze and tried a friendly smile. ''A beautiful
day, is it not?''

"Quite." Miss Brown's tone was not encouraging. There was a heavy silence. A slow flush rose in the gentleman's face as it gradually dawned on him that he was not to be vouchsafed the courtesy of conversation. He mumbled a pleasantry, making a bow to the two women, then picked up the reins of his grazing horse. Once mounted, he allowed his gaze to drop once more to the young lady's wide innocent eyes. "Adieu, fair maiden. Perhaps fate will grant us another opportunity to meet," he said softly. He made a deep bow from the saddle before he urged his mount down the path.

"Coxcomb," said Miss Brown roundly. She turned to find Theresa looking after the gentleman with a frowning expression. "Come, Theresa. I think it time that we retrace our steps and join the gentlemen."

Theresa obeyed and was silent a few moments. "Miss Brown, I believe that I owe you an apology. I had no notion that I could be accosted in such a manner. I will do better in future, even after we are returned home," she said quietly.

"Pray do not utter another word, Theresa. You may regret them later," said Miss Brown on a laugh.

Theresa glanced at her, startled, and then she too smiled. "You are too good to me, Miss Brown."

The duke and George were quickly met. The gentlemen dismounted so that they could walk with the ladies. Hugo looked down at Theresa with something akin to a frown. "I hope that you found your excursion enjoyable, Miss Thaleman."

Theresa exchanged a swift look with Miss Brown. She was relieved by her companion's almost imperceptible shake of the head. Miss Brown was not going to reveal her unnerving encounter with the strange gentleman, then. "I am sorry, your grace. It was most thoughtless of me to go off on my own. I hope that you will forgive my bad manners."

Hugo smiled, quite won over by the contrition in her expression. "Quite all right, Miss Thaleman." He made a casual comment on another topic, and the incident was forgotten.

15

Miss Theresa Thaleman had been on the town for more than two months before Lady Statten became aware of her existence. As a rule, Lady Statten paid scant attention to the marrying misses, except to remark what an insipid crop the young ladies were that year. She would never have gone out of her way to actually bring herself to meet any of the backward creatures but for the kind intervention of a catty friend.

Elizabeth Blackhart was a twice-made widow who often frequented the Earl of Rusland's scandalous parties. Her dark, bold beauty was pleasing to the gentlemen and her name had been linked to a succession of peers. She and Lady Statten had long before discovered that when they entered a ballroom together they made perfect foils for one another. That fact and similar tastes in living had formed a loose relationship between the two women that did not include loyalty.

Mrs. Blackhart had patiently waited for Lady Statten's appearance at that evening's soiree so that she could carelessly let drop the information that a Miss Thaleman was sporting a most curious ring. "It is odd how very familiar that ring seemed to me, but I suppose it was the unusual design of the band that arrested my attention. It was a serpentine band, not unlike the one that Ashford presented to you, dear Melanie," said Mrs. Blackhart with a sly smile. "It might not mean a thing. The similarity in the bands, you know. But I suppose you still know better than I what Ashford may be up to." There was a gleam of malice in her pale gray eyes.

After the initial ripple of shock passed over her face, Lady

Statten did not allow her feelings to show. None knew better than she that the circle she moved in was merciless to those discovered to possess vulnerabilities. She showed her even white teeth in a tight smile. "How interesting, to be sure. Have you been to Bath lately, Elizabeth? It has been whispered in my ear that a certain marquess of our acquaintance is taking the waters in the company of his dear wife, who is breeding, if one may believe the prattle. Such a touching tale, do you not think? Of course, if it is true that there is an heir in the offing, his lordship cannot mean to appeal for divorce." She had the satisfaction of seeing her friend pale with rage. Mrs. Blackhart snapped shut her fan and stomped off. Lady Statten watched with scarcely masked spite as Mrs. Blackhart retreated. She stored away the incident in her mind for later airing to their mutual acquaintances.

Though Lady Statten had maintained her composure before Mrs. Blackhart's malicious scrutiny, the news she had been given was disquieting. There had been rumors, of course, that the Duke of Ashford had been seen in the company of an unknown lovely young woman while driving in the park, and that his carriage had been spied several times outside a town house in a respectable district of town. Lady Statten had brushed those aside as idle malice on the part of those who wished her distress. But she realized now that perhaps she had been too complacent, too certain of her own powers. It had never occurred to her that anyone besides herself could possibly engage the Duke of Ashford's interest. If she had considered the possibility, she would have assumed someone of Mrs. Blackhart's ilk would be her most likely rival. The very idea that the duke could be dazzled by a lowly miss was absurd.

Lady Statten's thoughts spun and conjectured. She wished nothing more than privacy to mull over what she had been told, but she could hardly leave the soiree at such an unusually early hour or her defection would be instantly noted and speculated upon. Elizabeth Blackhart would see to that, she thought angrily.

Lady Statten smiled and laughed and endured the dazzling company for what seemed an interminable time. Even the whispered lovemaking of an accomplished rake could not stir more than a passing interest within her. At last she was free to make her exit. After taking leave of her host and hostess, Lady Statten stepped into her waiting carriage. Once safe in the dark vehicle, she allowed her smiling mask to fall away.

The coach bounded over the cobbled street in accompaniment to her leaping thoughts. Surely Elizabeth's insinuation could not be true, she thought. Lady Statten rubbed the naked finger that had once been adorned by the Duke of Ashford's token of affection. The occasion of her regrettable impulse to fling the ring out of the carriage window had since unmercifully plagued her. She had at first slipped other rings on that same finger, but that had only served to point up the absence of the serpentine band with its gaudy stones. The bolder of her acquaintances had more than once openly remarked to her face on the ring's absence. She had laughed off the curious, catty questions until none had bothered push the matter further. Some new scandal had begun to be whispered about and the absence of Lady Statten's well-known ring had been forgotten.

But now, according to dear Elizabeth, who could be counted upon to relate the most acid and factual of gossip, there was another woman who wore the selfsame ring. Lady Statten made an unconscious growling noise deep in her throat. If his grace had indeed commissioned just such another unique band and presented it to a young innocent, it would mean but one thing. Lady Statten's full lips stretched over her teeth in a near-snarl. Hugo never dallied with young ladies; therefore the duke must mean to wed.

"I do not believe it," Lady Statten muttered. But the logic of her conclusion so gnawed at her that she had sunk deep into a black temper by the time the carriage finally stopped. Lady Statten did not acknowledge the driver's proferred hand of assistance, but descended alone to the pavement and swept

up the steps into her town house. The driver looked after
his employer with a shrug of dislike and climbed back up
onto the box to tool the equipage around to the stables.

Lady Statten made it clear by her sharp words and
venomous glances that she wished short shrift from her maid,
who was only too happy to oblige. Alone at last in her sitting
room and attired in a shimmering silk dressing gown that
was belted tightly about her narrow waist, Lady Statten paced
restlessly. The night had grown too long for her. She knew
already what she must do in the next few days. She must
seek out this Miss Thaleman that Elizabeth had so happily
mentioned. She would find out for herself if the Duke of
Ashford's ring adorned the puling girl's finger. And if his
lordship was indeed playing her false, what she would then
do, not even she could guess.

It was at a soiree that Theresa learned why her brother
Holland had been such an infrequent visitor at the town
house. He appeared midway through the evening, his usual
ruddy complexion rather white. When he spied his mother
and sister, he edged his way through the crowd, taking care
to remain out of his mother's sight, while at the same time
attempting to capture Theresa's attention.

At last he was successful, and she went to him, her hands
outheld. "Holland! Where have you been? We have not seen
you for ages. And I so wished you to see *Hamlet* with me,"
she said chidingly.

Holland caught hold of her hands and held her off. "Teri,
I must speak to you in private. Is there someplace we may
go?"

Theresa looked sharply at her brother. There was strain
about his mouth that she had never before seen. "Of course,
Holland. There is a window embrasure over there. But what
is wrong?" A horrifying thought occurred to her and she
tightened her fingers on his as he led her out of the crowd.
"Holland, it is not Michael, is it?"

Holland pulled the heavy drapery closed, isolating them

from the company. "What? No, not Michael. Not anything like that." He rubbed his face and gave a short laugh. "Would that I were back with Michael and all of this was only a nightmare."

Theresa was fully alarmed. She led her brother to the stone bench and urged him to sit. Holland sank down and his head dropped into his hands. "Holland! You must tell me what is wrong. What have you done?" she asked urgently.

Holland raised his head to give a bitter laugh. "How well you know me, Teri. Aye, I have done something foolish. I thought after secretly engaging myself to Mary Marling that I would kick up my heels one last time, to have something to recall once the knot was tied. I have succeeded beyond my wildest dreams! The squire would have my head if he but knew even a fraction of the whole."

Theresa was momentarily stunned by the offhand announcement of her brother's engagement, but though questions crowded her mind, she knew it was not the important issue of the moment. Holland's agony was too plain. "But what is it you have done?" she demanded.

Holland turned his head and stared at his sister. He steeled himself to meet her probable disgust. "I have gambled away my inheritance, Teri. I am floating to perdition on the River Tick."

Theresa gasped, appalled. "My word, Holland! You cannot have gone and put up our home in a card game."

"I was not quite as mad as that, but I may as well have done. I gambled away every pence, Teri, and I could not pay my vowels. A fellow I know gave me the direction of the moneylender in Clarges Street and he advanced me a loan. Then I could not pay that, and so I borrowed from . . . Well, it does not matter from whom I borrowed. The point is that the collectors are hounding me to death. God, I feel all sorts of fool!" Holland pulled at his hair in a tortured gesture. "I should never embroil you in this, but I have nowhere else to turn. Papa—"

"You need say no more, Holland," Theresa said, very well able to understand Holland's inability to apply to their father. After the highwayman incident, the squire had made it clear that his tolerance was at an end. Her mind calculated quickly. "I have some pin money left this month, and I am certain that I can wheedle an advance from Mama. She will assume I have succumbed to some gewgaw or other. Come to the town house around five of the clock. Mama always lies down to rest before dinner. I can give it to you then."

Holland shook his head. "I am a blackguard, Teri. I can hardly stand myself for taking what little you have."

"But you must," said Theresa. She slipped her hand into his and clasped his fingers tightly. "We have always depended upon each other, you and Michael and I."

Holland raised their clasped hands and kissed the back of Theresa's. "You are the best of sisters. Thank you. I shall be around tomorrow just as you say." He stood up, bringing Theresa with him.

As he reached for the curtain, she stopped him. "Holland, will my pin money be enough?"

He smiled crookedly. "It must be, Teri. At least the collectors will be quieted and I can then make some sort of arrangements for the rest. And once I have come clean, I shall be off for home, believe me. I have been given a sharp lesson that I will not soon forget."

Theresa said nothing more, and allowed Holland to leave her. He walked quickly away into the crowd. Theresa turned to locate her mother, and discovered that a lady was watching her. She smiled tentatively, wondering if she had met her before. But surely she would have remembered such a beautiful woman. Theresa thought she had never seen such an incredible shade of red hair.

The lady approached, slowly waving her fan. "Forgive me for staring, Miss Thaleman. I could not but notice that the young gentleman who just left appeared somewhat distressed. A lovers' quarrel, perhaps?"

"My brother," Theresa said automatically, startled to find herself addressed by name by a stranger. "I am sorry, but do I know you, my lady?"

The lady held out her white-gloved hand. "We have not

met before, no. I am Lady Statten. I have taken an interest in your social progress these last weeks since you were pointed out to me as one of our new reigning beauties."

As Theresa shook hands she saw that her first impression had not misled her. Lady Statten was quite the most beautiful woman she had ever seen. "I am hardly that, my lady. Certainly you can lay claim to that title."

"What a kind child you are," Lady Statten said, smiling. She glanced down at Theresa's left hand. "That is an unusual ring band. I do not believe that I have ever seen more than one other of its kind."

Theresa glanced at the serpentine ring and smiled. She had worn it with or without the rest of the set all Season. "I also thought it rather original in design. It has become quite my favorite piece of jewelry," she said.

Lady Statten smiled again. Her green eyes were alight with an emotion that Theresa could not quite fathom. "Indeed. I am happy to have made your acquaintance, Miss Thaleman. We shall see more of each other during the remainder of the Season." She nodded and glided away.

Mrs. Thaleman came up to her daughter. "Who was that lady, Theresa? Why, I have never seen her like, even here in London, where one may expect to find attractive members of both sexes. It is the clothes, of course. One can appear to so much better advantage with the proper outfitting, and naturally one finds the best modistes in the metropolis. I wonder who made that gown for her. Quite shocking, if one overlooks how well it becomes her. For heaven's sake, Theresa, who is she?"

Theresa laughed. "Mama, you have not even drawn breath long enough for me to say! It is a Lady Statten. She was condescending enough to compliment me on my successful Season."

"How vastly kind! Theresa, have you any notion how fortunate you are? Of course not, but let me advise you in this. It is advantageous for one's consequence to be seen in the company of such an obviously exalted personage as this

Lady Statten. Why, anyone with eyes in his head can see that she is a fine lady, though I hope that you will not emulate her style of dress. Quite shocking, that gown, but for all that, very flattering.''

"You need not be anxious, Mama. I fear that I am not quite as well-endowed as Lady Statten, and I should look a perfect freak in such a gown,'' said Theresa.

"And so you should. Not that you will ever have the opportunity to discover it, for the squire would never countenance such a thing. I wonder what that gown cost. It must have come very dear,'' said Mrs. Thaleman. She continued to exclaim over Lady Statten's gown, and then passed on to catalog some of the other ladies' attire. Theresa replied to her mother's queries for agreement with soothing monosyllables, her mind devoted more to her brother's predicament than to the hang of a certain lady's train.

The Duke of Ashford presented himself at that moment and Theresa awarded him a particularly warm smile. "Your grace, how happy I am to see you,'' she said in a relieved voice.

He raised his brows, but most properly first addressed Mrs. Thaleman, inquiring if she was enjoying the soiree. She fanned heself. "Indeed I am, your grace. It has been a very pleasant and rewarding evening. A lady of consequence has been kind enough to take notice of my daughter, and I found it most gratifying,'' she said.

"Certainly a moment of triumph for you, ma'am,'' Hugo said dryly. He was unsurprised when Mrs. Thaleman agreed. Abandoning her, he turned with a smile to Theresa. "And you, Miss Thaleman. Are you also finding it an enjoyable evening?''

"For the most part, your grace,'' said Theresa. She threw her mother a glance as she thought again of Holland's strange appearance. She wondered when it would be best to broach the subject of an advance of her pin money.

The duke misinterpreted her look and immediately set himself to rescue her from Mrs. Thaleman's dull company.

"I believe that you may find my name written on your dance card, Miss Thaleman," he said.

Theresa looked up at him, startled. He had not approached her earlier and so she was certain that he was mistaken. But there was an expression in his gray eyes, so full of uncharacteristic anticipation, that she glanced down at the card. His name was not there, of course, and she felt a sense of disappointment. "But, your grace—" she began, and then met his eyes again. Her own eyes began to dance. "I believe that you reserved this waltz, did you not, your grace?"

The duke bowed in grave acknowlegment and then led her out onto the dance floor while Mrs. Thaleman looked on with complete approval. He put his hand about Theresa's slender waist and his other hand clasped her fingers. "I was almost afraid that you would not be quick enough, Miss Thaleman," he said with a lurking grin.

"I am seized with guilt, sir, and it is quite your fault. What of the poor gentleman whose waltz this actually is?" Theresa asked. She liked the feeling of warmth from his firm hold on her waist. She thought she had never felt happier than at this moment.

"Be damned to him," Hugo said.

"Do you know, I had no notion that your grace could be so quick to set aside convention," Theresa said in a marveling voice.

"Are you disappointed in my character, Miss Thaleman?"

Theresa laughed and shook her head. "No, not in the least. I always enjoy those times that I have been privileged to be in your company, your grace."

"I hope that may influence you to accept my latest invitation, then. There is an exhibition of antiquities from Egypt and from various other points of the Mediterranean at the museum. I wonder if you would care to join me on a tour of the exhibition tomorrow?" Hugo asked.

Theresa accepted the invitation with alacrity. "I would very much like to see the exhibition. Mama is not much for such relics, but I know that Miss Brown will be interested."

The duke frowned. Gone were the days that he had thought

so ill of Mrs. Thaleman for not providing proper chaperonage for her daughter. He had assumed that she would accompany her daughter and that would have suited him perfectly. But Miss Brown was a conscientious chaperone. He could cheerfully consign Miss Brown to the devil, he thought. He wanted to enjoy a lengthy conversation with Miss Thaleman without the constraining influence of Miss Brown's ubiquitous presence. Somehow he must devise a way to distract Miss Brown from exercising her duty in too strenuous a fashion. But he did not voice his disgruntlement. "I shall look forward to your company, Miss Thaleman," he said.

Hugo swept Theresa in dizzying circles about the floor until she was thoroughly disoriented. She began to laugh. "Your grace, pray! You have got my head in such a whirl that I would fall if you were not supporting me," she protested.

He smiled down at her, a certain warmth in his gray eyes. "Indeed, Miss Thaleman? I confess, it is just the object that I strive for where you are concerned."

Theresa's face flamed. Her widened eyes flew to meet his. "You should not say such things, at least to me."

"But I wish to say such things, and especially to you, Miss Thaleman," Hugo said gravely. He saw the uncertainty and confusion in her eyes and he flashed a grin. "You have a most liberating effect on my poor wretched tongue, dear girl. Do you mind it so very much?"

A pleasant haze engulfed Theresa. She did not mind in the least that he chose to address her in such a way. She did not know how it was, but she did like being in the Duke of Ashford's company more than that of any other gentleman. "Not . . . not very much, your grace," she said, a hint of shyness in her voice. Laughter suddenly sprang to her eyes, banishing her uncharacteristic reserve. "Actually, I can hardly protest when it was I who once labeled you a dull gentleman and voiced a wish that it was otherwise."

"I believe the word was 'stuffy,' brat, and let me say that I infinitely prefer to be thought stuffy rather than dull," Hugo said with an exaggerated frown.

Theresa twinkled up at him. "I apologize, your grace. Of

course you cannot be a dull dog at all. You have not the gray head for it as yet.''

"Miss Thaleman, how is it that your unfortunate father has not been driven into the grave long since? Once becoming familiar with you and, however briefly, with your brothers, I am all sympathy for the man,'' the duke said.

"Indeed, your grace, we are a sad trial to Papa and my mother,'' Theresa nodded. Again her brother's strained face came to mind, and a tiny frown puckered her brow.

There was a long moment of silence, during which Hugo realized that his partner's thoughts had taken her far from him. He was surprised by a spark of pique and he determined to bring her out of her reverie. He spoke thoughtfully. "I fear that I must, yes, I really must take umbrage with you, Miss Thaleman.''

"Whatever for, your grace?'' Theresa asked, surprised.

"Just that. I am not 'your grace,' but Hugo.''

Theresa was momentarily bereft of speech. She did not know what she had expected, but it certainly was not this. She had been taught that it was not done to address a gentleman with such familiarity. She could not think of a graceful way to turn aside the Duke of Ashford's request, and so she was blunt. "I cannot. Surely you can understand that, your grace.''

"On the contrary, I acknowledge no such understanding. My friends all refer to me as Hugo,'' said the duke firmly.

"Oh.'' Theresa thought it over for a moment. She was inordinately pleased that he should consider her on such an intimate footing. Surely even Miss Brown would not object to making use of the gentlemen's Christian name under the circumstance of proferred friendship. Theresa found the decision easy when it ran parallel to her own inclinations. She smiled at the Duke of Ashford. "I am honored to be considered one of your intimates, your gr . . . Hugo.''

Hugo was satisfied with the headway he had made, and thereafter made light conversation until the waltz was done and he returned her to Mrs. Thaleman's chaperonage. Mrs.

Thaleman waited until the duke had walked away and then turned to her daughter. "I am not yet in my dotage, whatever the duke may think. I know very well that his grace never signed your dance card, so he must have had a particular reason for wishing to stand up with you. Tell me at once, did the duke say anything of moment?" she asked in an expectant tone.

Mindful that her mother was wont to jump to uncomfortable conclusions, Theresa decided instantly not to disclose that she had been requested to make use of his grace's Christian name. "Why, no, Mama. Should he have?" she asked casually.

Mrs. Thaleman's face registered disappointment. Her hopes of a title for her daughter were dashed. She had thought that surely if the Duke of Ashford meant to come up to the mark, he would have done so this very night. "I suppose not. It is just that his grace has been so attentive these past weeks that I hoped . . . Well, never mind. I shall have nothing extraordinary to write to the squire after all."

Theresa was on the point of pursuing her mother's curious statement when another gentleman came up to claim the next dance on her card. In the ensuing activity she completely forgot what she meant to ask.

16

The following afternoon Theresa waited impatiently in the drawing room for the Duke of Ashford's promised arrival. For the third time in as many minutes she went to the window and parted the lace curtains to look down hopefully at the street below.

Miss Brown sat on the settee, whiling away the time with her embroidery. "A lady is careful not to be discovered staring out the window like one of the vulgar," she said quietly.

Theresa paid no heed to her companion's gentle observation. Her vigil had just been rewarded. A carriage, its doors emblazoned with a ducal crest, pulled over to the curb before the town house steps. "The duke is here at last!" she exclaimed in delight. "But who is that gentleman with him?"

The top-hatted gentlemen disappeared from view as they went up the steps of the town house. Theresa dropped the curtain and moved swiftly to settle herself in a prim pose on the settee beside Miss Brown. She picked up the embroidery yarns and began sorting the colors. When she felt Miss Brown's glance of amusement, Theresa looked over at her with a bland expression of innocence. "Am I not the very picture of gentility, Miss Brown?" she asked provocatively.

Miss Brown's eyes lit with the light of battle, but she had no chance to retort before the drawing-room door was opened and the gentlemen were ushered in. Miss Brown turned her head, a smile on her lips, prepared to greet the Duke of Ashford and to make his companion welcome. Her eyes traveled beyond the duke and she met the unknown gentleman's glance. There was a look of honesty, of immediate warmth, in the gentleman's eyes that she instinctively recognized. Her face whitened, even as a shiver of acknowledgment coursed through her. Miss Brown's white-faced shock was mirrored in the gentleman's own countenance. She and the gentleman stared at one another, unmoving.

Unaware of her companion's sudden stillness, Theresa greeted the Duke of Ashford warmly. "Good afternoon, your grace. I had almost despaired of you, you know."

The duke laughed. He derived enjoyment from Miss Thaleman's open manner toward him. "I am not so shabby as to cry off, Miss Thaleman. And may I remind you that it is Hugo? I wish you to meet my secretary, the Honorable Herbert Winthrop. He will be accompanying us this afternoon."

"I am delighted to make your acquaintance, Mr. Winthrop," said Theresa, holding out her hand in a friendly way. "I assume that you also share an interest in artifacts."

"Mr. Winthrop dragged his gaze from Miss Brown's face and took Theresa's hand. With an effort he managed a reply. "Quite, though I prefer more modern periods. I am likewise happy to meet you, Miss Thaleman. His grace has mentioned your name on more than one occasion." His employer shot him a glance of startled amazement, for he had just committed the first indiscretion of his career. Oblivious of the duke's reaction, Winthrop let go Theresa's hand and his eyes turned once again in Miss Brown's direction.

Theresa followed Mr. Winthrop's gaze, and she was amazed to see that her unflappable companion was blushing. Theresa realized that Miss Brown was taking notice of Mr. Winthrop to the exclusion of all else. It was almost as though the two had no need of words, exchanging volumes with their eyes alone, thought Theresa. "Mr. Winthrop, I should like you to meet my companion, Miss Letitia Brown," she said. She curiously waited to see what would happen.

Mr. Winthrop stepped forward quickly to take Miss

Brown's hand and carry her fingers to his lips. "Miss Brown," he said quietly.

"Mr. Winthrop," said Miss Brown. She said nothing more, and neither did he, both seemingly content to simply gaze at one another.

After a moment the duke cleared his throat. "Let us depart, then. It will take more time than we have allowed this afternoon to see all that the museum has to offer." As he escorted Theresa toward the door, Hugo said in a low voice, "I was under the impression that Miss Brown and Mr. Winthrop were to be our chaperones, but I strongly suspect that the roles have been reversed."

Theresa glanced over her shoulder. The couple in question was following her and the duke out to the carriage, still silent and self-absorbed. "Indeed! I have never known Miss Brown to act so queerly upon meeting anyone, no matter how exalted. She is the most collected creature alive, but your Mr. Winthrop seems to have completely bowled her out."

"I must say the same for Winthrop. He is usually the most reliable fellow one could wish, but I wouldn't trust him at my back in a row just now." He glanced down at the young lady on his arm and a faint smile curled his mouth. "I hope you do not dislike it, Miss Thaleman, but it appears that we shall be thrown entirely on our own."

"Oh, I shan't mind it *excessively*," Theresa said.

"Brat," Hugo murmured appreciatively. He handed her up into the carriage and stood aside while his secretary performed the same service for Miss Brown. The gentlemen stepped up into the carriage and the duke signaled the driver.

The outing took longer than anticipated but Theresa did not realize it until the party had returned to the town house. The butler handed her a paper screw, saying, "Master Thaleman came to call, miss. He left this note for you."

"Holland! I completely forgot him," exclaimed Theresa. She had that morning gotten her pin money from her mother and had been carrying it in her reticule since. She hoped that Holland meant to return later that evening. Theresa swiftly untwisted the paper and gave the note a hasty glance. In Holland's distinctive, hasty scratching, the note read, "You were my last hope, Teri. I must run for it now. H." Theresa's face whitened. She stood, her mind working furiously, having completely forgotten where she was.

The Duke of Ashford had observed the gamut of expressions cross Theresa's face. Mindful of their companions, who were calmly conversing nearby, he stepped close and said quietly, "Is there aught wrong, Miss Thaleman?"

Theresa crushed the note quickly between her fingers. She turned a bright smile on him. "Nothing at all, your grace."

Hugo raised his brows at her sudden formality. She had become comfortable that afternoon with addressing him by his Christian name. He thought it a measure of her obvious distress that she retreated so thoroughly to their former footing. He took possession of one of her hands and held it gently between his own. "Miss Thaleman, pray call on me for anything you may require. I hold myself ready at your service."

"Yes, yes. I do thank you, your grace," Theresa said hastily. Realizing how she must sound, she made an effort to pull her thoughts together. She must appear as usual, she thought. Bestowing a hurried smile on him, she said, "Thank you for a lovely time, Hugo. I enjoyed myself prodigiously. I shall look forward to our next meeting, I assure you."

It was a dismassal. The duke accepted that she was not going to confide in him. He kept his bows brief and left with Winthrop in tow. Theresa was not inclined for conversation, so perhaps it was fortunate that Miss Brown rather vaguely announced that she was going up to her room. Theresa waited in the hall long enough to be certain that her companion was ascending the stairs before she turned and went into her uncle's private library. She knew that there were stationery and pens always kept ready at his desk.

Theresa dashed off a note to her cousin, urgently requesting that he wait on her that very evening. She gave the note to

the footman with instructions that it be delivered to Mr.
Bennett's rooms and that the manservant was to wait for an
answer. Then she settled herself as best she might in the
drawing room to await George's arrival. Surely between the
pair of them they must be able to think of where Holland
could have bolted to and be able to help him, she thought.

However, the footman returned with the unwelcome news
that Mr. George Bennett was away from his lodgings and
it was not known when he would return. "But what of my
note?" Theresa asked sharply. The footman assured her that
he had impressed upon Mr. Bennett's valet that her note was
to be given without delay to Mr. Bennett whenever he did
return. With that Theresa was forced to be satisfied.

Hugo regarded his lovely visitor over the edge of his book.
His expression was weary. With exaggerated courtesy he
said, "Good evening, Lady Statten. I trust you have been
well."

Lady Statten stripped off her gloves and stood yanking
them between her fingers. Even at this sign that she meant
to make a long visit, the duke did not offer her a chair. Her
mouth tightened. So be it, she thought. "I think we know
one another well enough to dispense with the empty
pleasantries, your grace!"

The duke sighed and lowered his book to his knee. "As
you say, Melanie. Since you have quite literally browbeaten
my poor servant into allowing you into my private library,
I suppose that I must hear you out."

Lady Statten had moved to the mantel and now she swept
around to confront him, her expression watchful. "I have
come with but one object, and that is to learn what you know
of a young lady by the name of Miss Theresa Thaleman."

Hugo had been musing minutes before on the pleasurable
two hours he had spent that very afternoon in accompanying Miss Thaleman about the museum, as well as idly
wondering about the contents of the note that had distressed
her. He was therefore startled beyond measure to hear the

young lady's name, especially from this particular woman's lips. "Miss Thaleman? I am acquainted with her, of course. What of her?"

Lady Statten, who had been watching his face closely, saw his startlement before he was able to smooth his expression. She gave a cry of mingled rage and triumph as she leapt to her own conclusion. "So it is true! You mean to wed the chit. You have given that bit of fluff my serpentine ring. You need not deny it, Hugo, for I have seen it for myself. My ring! How are you insult me in such a blatant fashion. I—to be replaced by a green girl! You think to make me a laughing-stock, and that is one thing that I shall not tolerate. I warn you, Hugo! I shall not stand for it!" Lady Statten turned on her heel and swept out of the room, slamming the door behind her.

The Duke of Ashford did not stir in his chair. He stared at the still-vibrating door, his expression one of sheer amazement. After several long moments he spoke his thoughts aloud. "Extraordinary. I really must see this ring that I am supposed to have bestowed upon Miss Thaleman. I had no notion that the young lady was such an intimate of mine." As he reviewed the abrupt scene again, a slow smile began to play about his mouth. "I do believe that for once Lady Statten has proferred a worthwhile notion."

17

During her usual afternoon rest, Mrs. Bennett chanced to glance out her sitting-room window and saw that a carriage was sitting at the curb. She did not recognize whose it might be, and when no one was ushered into her presence, she was miffed that the visitor had chosen to call on her relations rather than herself. When several moments later a lady, accompanied by Theresa, got into the carriage and it drove away, Mrs. Bennett simply could not contain her curiosity. She went down to the drawing room with the express purpose of learning who it was that had come to visit.

Mrs. Thaleman was very willing to impart the information that a lady of consequence had been so kind as to extend an impromptu invitation to Theresa to accompany her to a card party and dinner. "She was so taken with Theresa when they met at the soiree two days ago that she wished to further her acquaintance. What do you say to that, Claudia? It would appear that my daughter is steadily ascending the social ladder, and nothing but good can come from that. Why, I would not be a bit surprised if Theresa was to receive several unexceptionable offers before the Season is out," Mrs. Thaleman said triumphantly.

"How fortunate for Theresa if it should so happen," said Mrs. Bennett. "But you still have not told me the lady's name. You have talked all around the question, as usual, and not imparted anything of particular importance."

Mrs. Thaleman decided to let her sister's ill humor pass without challenge. She was feeling more than magnanimous at the moment. "It is a Lady Statten. I thought her manner of dress quite shocking when I first laid eyes on her, but for all that, one could not but notice how well she carried herself.

At a glance, I knew that she was a personage of consequence, and that she would harbor such kindly feelings toward Theresa is quite a feather in my cap. Claudia, my dear! Are you quite all right?''

Her alarm was well-warranted, for Mrs. Bennett had abruptly collapsed onto the settee, and her face had turned chalk white. Mrs. Thaleman rushed to her side. She lifted her sister's limp hand and began to slap it in an agitated manner. ''Claudia, pray . . . Whatever has overset you so? Shall I call for a physician?''

Mrs. Bennett shook her head quickly and managed to gasp for a glass of wine. Mrs. Thaleman turned to the decanter table and poured her a generous portion of the first wine that came to hand. She held the glass to her sister's trembling lips so that Mrs. Bennett could swallow it down. Of a sudden Mrs. Bennett started up, her face purpled and her breath wheezing. She spluttered indignantly, ''Port! For heaven's sake, Charlotte, have you *no* common sense?''

Mrs. Thaleman smiled at her. ''Oh, I *am* relieved. For a moment I believed that you meant to expire in my arms.''

Mrs. Bennett looked at her balefully. ''Really, Charlotte. I would never do anything half so vulgar. I shall die in my bed like a true gentlewoman.''

''Of course, dear Claudia. But it gave me a frightful start when you fell over in such a way! My heart practically *leapt* into my throat, I promise you,'' said Mrs. Thaleman.

''What rot! You have read too many of those trashy novels, Charlotte. But never mind that. Have you gone quite mad? Whatever were you thinking of, to allow Theresa to go off with Lady Statten? She should not even be seen in that woman's vicinity, let alone be in her company!''

''What are you talking about, Claudia? Her ladyship is kindness itself, as I told you. I cannot see that associating with someone of consequence can be in the least harmful to Theresa,'' Mrs. Thaleman said, surprised.

''Can you not? Then let me tell you that your ignorance may ruin my niece. In one stroke you may have wrecked

all her chances, and especially any hope that the Duke of
Ashford may be brought up to scratch,'' Mrs. Bennett said
grimly. ''Dear God, Charlotte, have you not listened to any
of the gossip? Lady Statten was the Duke of Ashford's
mistress! And she still may be, for all I know.''

It was Mrs. Thaleman's turn to pale. She stared in dismay
at her sister, for once quite defenseless against Mrs. Bennett's
harsh manner of speech. ''Oh, dear! I had no notion. But
what are we to do, Claudia?''

''We can do nothing, except hope that no one of
importance sees Theresa with her, though I doubt that we
shall be so fortunate,'' snapped Mrs. Bennett.

Lady Statten introduced Theresa around to those in the card
room. They were all strangers to Theresa, though she thought
she had seen one or two of their faces at other functions.
Lady Statten urged Theresa to take a chair at the table. ''For
I shall not have you merely an observer, my dear. I mean
to teach you to play deep,'' she said with a tinkling laugh.

Theresa flashed a smile in appreciation of her ladyship's
teasing manner. ''Very well, my lady, but I warn you that
I know next to nothing about the pasteboards.''

A gentleman leaned over her shoulder. ''Never fear, Miss
Thaleman. I shall appoint myself your mentor and guide your
faltering first steps.''

''Beware, Miss Thaleman! Wilson has not a feather to fly
with and it was a lamentable lack of skill which brought him
to that sad state,'' said another gentleman. There was a round
of good natured laughter, with Theresa's mentor making an
ironic bow to his decrier.

The raillery soon gave way to business, and the card room
gradually quieted so that every flip of the cards and chink
of coin could be heard. Theresa found that she had to
concentrate firmly on the play to keep a grasp on what was
happening. She was thankful more than once for the soft
advice of the gentleman behind her whenever she hesitated.
So involved was she in the game that she did not notice when

Lady Statten folded her hand and quietly withdrew from the game.

It was only when the stakes were raised, and then raised again, that Theresa began to wonder at the wisdom of allowing herself to be cajoled into playing. She was an inept player and was barely holding her own. No one else seemed to be made uneasy by the raising of the stakes. On the contrary, there were even complaints by one or two of the players that the game was still too tame to suit them. Theresa looked around to tell Lady Statten that perhaps she should withdraw from the game, and it was only then that she became aware that she was alone at the table among strangers.

Theresa glanced swiftly about the card room, hoping to see Lady Statten's face among the bystanders. Surely her ladyship had not abandoned her. Theresa did not know what she should do to withdraw gracefully from the game, which was becoming distinctly uncomfortable for her. When she did not see Lady Statten, she began to feel a flutter of panic.

Her searching eyes met a familiar gaze. Immediately a wave of relief washed over her. Theresa's smile radiated gladness as the Duke of Ashford made his way around the table toward her. "Your grace! How happy I am to see you," she said, holding out her hand.

Hugo took her slender fingers in his clasp. He noted that the desperate strain that he had seen but a moment before in her face had all but disappeared. Obviously Miss Thaleman had not been enjoying her time at cards. His lips tightened momentarily and his gaze swept those at the card table. He recognized most of the players. These were all hardened gamesters. He had no idea which of those seated round the green baize had persuaded Miss Thaleman into such an unpalatable situation, but he had every intention of extricating her from it.

"Miss Thaleman, do you play?" inquired one lady, raising a coy brow in the duke's direction.

Theresa looked about her swiftly. She flushed when she saw that the game waited on her. "Oh!"

The Duke of Ashford interposed before she could make a movement. "I believe that Miss Thaleman is promised to me for the next quadrille." He held out his hand to Theresa and automatically she placed hers in his. His hand closed about her fingers with a reassuring pressure. Theresa abandoned her cards and rose from the table.

"In that case, take her away then, Ashford. We have an empty place. Wilson, do you care to take a hand?" said a gentleman.

"Aye, and I call for a raise in the stakes. A shilling more a point, my friends," Wilson said, sliding into Theresa's vacated place. The duke and Theresa were forgotten before ever they left the card room as the players returned their attention to the game.

Theresa looked up at the Duke of Ashford. "I must thank you, sir. I had begun to realize that I was in too-deep waters, but I had no notion of how to extricate myself. If you had not come into the card room, I do not know what I would have done. Your appearance saved me from making a complete cake of myself. I am only embarrassed that you found me in such straits."

"We have all made the same mistake, Miss Thaleman, and often it was because at the time we were more guileless than our companions," said the duke. He guided her toward the refreshment table. "I assume that you came under the aegis of someone worldlier than yourself. May I inquire who?"

"It was Lady Statten who invited me to join her this evening. But I do not see her about," said Theresa. She accepted the lemon ice that he offered to her, and so did not witness the startlement that entered his eyes.

Hugo swiftly regained his equilibrium. But he was disturbed that it had been that particular lady who had misled Miss Thaleman into such fast company. Surely she would not actually make good on her dramatic promise regarding Miss Thaleman, he thought. Aloud he said, "I am well-acquainted with Lady Statten. Perhaps I might offer an

unasked-for word of advice, Miss Thaleman. Lady Statten
is associated with a faster circle than one such as yourself—
or, for that matter, any other young lady or gentleman—
should be exposed to. I hope that you are not offended when
I suggest that your association with her ladyship is perhaps
unwise.''

Theresa was very aware of the warmth of his hand on her
elbow. She wondered at the racing pace of her heart. ''Oh,
no, I am not in the least offended, your grace,'' she said,
meeting his gaze. The duke smiled at her, and she had the
oddest feeling of breathlessness.

''If you are finished with your ice, perhaps I could be
permitted to escort you come, Miss Thaleman,'' Hugo
said.

''I am quite finished, your grace.'' Theresa did not know
if Lady Statten would miss her when it came time for the
lady to call for her own carriage, and at this point Theresa
did not much care. Nevertheless she requested the porter of
the establishment to let Lady Statten know that she had been
escorted home by an acquaintance. Then with a light heart
she allowed the duke to hand her up into an equipage standing
at the curb.

The duke had come in his own elegant carriage and Theresa
was certain that she had never seen anything to compare with
its rich comfort. She settled back on the velvet seat as the
duke swung in to sit beside her. The carriage rocked as it
started away from the curb, then settled quickly into smooth
well-sprung motion. Theresa found that she had not much
to say. The dark inside the carriage was relieved by
intermittent flashes from the streetlamps and bestowed
mystery to the duke's shadowed figure. She felt that he had
become somehow an enigma, at once compelling and incredibly dangerous. She did not know why she should couple
him with danger, but it could only have something to do with
the swift hammering of her heart. How perfectly idiotic,
when he has been all that is kind, she thought in a futile
attempt to persuade herself.

"Miss Thaleman." Theresa started violently, and gasped when she felt him take hold of her fingers.

"I am sorry that I startled you," said the duke from the shadows. His voice was shaded with strong amusement.

"Not at all, your grace. I am a creature of strong nerves." Theresa had meant to sound firm, and she was dismayed by the slightest of tremors in her voice.

"I am glad of it, for I do not carry a smelling salt." The laughter in his voice was unmistakable. Theresa was disconcerted to feel his breath warm on her face, and then she forgot everything as her lips were found by his. The kiss was warm and leisurely. His arms drew her close and one hand slipped up into her hair. Time melted away.

When at last Theresa felt her mouth freed, she came back to awareness of time and place with a jarring thump. She discovered that she was half-reclining in an extremely compromising position. Her head rested against his shoulder and her fingers clung to his lapel. Her face flamed. She sat up abruptly, and her forehead cracked against the duke's chin. He bit off a sharp exclamation. "I . . . I am sorry, your grace. I had not meant to hurt you," Theresa stammered. She should slap his face or . . . or scream out in protest, she thought confusedly, not apologize to him.

"I undoubtedly deserved that," Hugo said, gingerly fingering his chin. There was a painful throb, and he hastily dropped his hand. He sighed, wondering what madness had come over him. He had been thinking idly of Miss Thaleman's expressive eyes, and then she had made that ridiculous statement about her nerves, which had very nearly caused him to laugh. He wished now that he had done so, rather than have happen what had just transpired. "Miss Thaleman, I deeply apologize. I have completely overstepped the bounds of propriety. I shall understand if you decide that you do not wish to continue our acquaintance."

Theresa did not know what to say. On the one hand, she knew that she should be outraged, but certainly she was not that. Nor was she particularly frightened by what had occurred. She felt herself blush hotly and she was glad for the shadows in the carriage. Indeed, if the truth be known, she had rather liked being kissed by the duke. She certainly did not wish to bid him farewell, and she wondered if she was not in the slightest bit rakish. With her thoughts tumbling, she said slowly, "I suppose that is the reason one is always supposed to be accompanied by a chaperone."

Hugo was taken aback. Of all things that she could have said, he had never expected her to voice such a matter-of-fact observation. "Miss Thaleman, do you quite understand what I have said to you?" he asked.

"Of course, your grace. However, I think that I may weather the experience quite nicely, thank you. I have not been given a disgust of you, if that is what you fear," Theresa said calmly.

She heard him let out his breath on a soft sigh. "My dear Miss Thaleman, you amaze me," he said, and she was not certain whether he complimented her or not.

The carriage slowed and stopped. The duke opened the door and jumped out, turning at once to offer his hand to her. Theresa accepted his aid and descended out of the carriage to the walkway. She looked up at him as he escorted her up the steps to the town house door, but she could read nothing in his polite expression.

The porter opened the door in answer to the pulling of the bell, and his swift glance was all that expressed his surprise at seeing Theresa in the company of the Duke of Ashford. The door to the drawing room opened and Mrs. Thaleman rushed into the hall. She stopped abruptly at the sight of the duke. She had the most lowering feeling. "Your grace!"

Hugo made a brief bow in her direction. Then he raised Theresa's hand to his lips. "I shall call on you later in the week, if I may," he said quietly.

It was more question that statement, Theresa knew. She smiled up at him. "Of course, your grace. I shall look forward to it."

The duke nodded to a stupefied Mrs. Thaleman. "I bid

you a fair evening, Mrs. Thaleman,'' he said, and then he was gone.

Mrs. Thaleman found her voice. ''Theresa, come this instant into the drawing room.''

''Yes, Mama.'' Theresa preceded her mother, who closed the door firmly behind them. Theresa began to draw off her white gloves, pausing to smother a pretended yawn. ''I am quite exhausted by this evening. I had no notion Lady Statten meant to tarry so long, or I would not have accepted the duke's offer to drive me home.''

''Pray, did his grace know whom you were with at the card party?'' Mrs. Thaleman asked anxiously.

''I told him that I was with Lady Statten, of course.'' Theresa felt only the mildest curiosity at why her mother should ask such an odd question. She was much more concerned with her memory of those oddly exhilarating moments with the Duke of Ashford.

Mrs. Thaleman sat down abruptly on the settee. ''Then we are undone, indeed,'' she said. She saw that her daughter was looking at her with a surprised expression. ''Theresa, I have learned that Lady Statten is not a particularly good companion for one to cultivate. I am afraid that your association with her ladyship can only be frowned upon by a personage such as the duke. I think it best that you do not spend much time with her ladyship.'' She saw that her daughter was about to speak and, fearing an argument, she hurried on. ''I do not like to curb your natural friendliness, my dear, but I fear that in this case I must insist. If he but knew of this, the squire would positively insist upon my warning you away from Lady Statten. You see, her ladyship is . . . Drat it, I am of no use at this! Theresa, one may say that Lady Statten is one who is undoubtedly of the same ilk as those who are invited to Rusland Park. And you are aware of how the squire feels on that score!''

Theresa took in her mother's stricture with a thoughtful expression in her eyes. For the moment she was diverted from her former preoccupation as she wondered if Lady

Statten was indeed an occasional guest at Rusland Park. She knew that the Duke of Ashford was friendly with the earl and he had claimed acquaintanceship with her ladyship there. Theresa could not but wonder whether Lady Statten was the sort of woman that the Duke of Ashford would find entertaining. She decided that she would make a point of observing Lady Statten. Perhaps she could learn something from her ladyship, though certainly she would not again place herself alone with her. Theresa had no desire to earn for herself a reputation for keeping fast company, not when the Duke of Ashford was so set against it. Theresa realized that her mother was watching her with an anxious air and she smiled reassuringly. "I do understand, Mama. Now, if you will excuse me, I think that I shall retire for the evening. I found card playing to be extremely fatiguing."

Mrs. Thaleman was relieved that the interview had gone so well. "Of course, Theresa. Good night, my dear."

18

When Theresa heard that her cousin had called, she hurried at once to the drawing room. She opened the door and rushed in. "George—" She stopped abruptly.

Her cousin and Miss Brown stood before the occasional table. Roses and carnations were strewn over the tabletop, while a few stems had been placed into a large bowl. Miss Brown held a long-stemmed red rose in one hand. Her other hand was in George Bennett's firm clasp. There was an odd expression on her face. At Theresa's entrance, Miss Brown snatched back her hand, her color heightening. When she spoke, her voice was a trifle unsteady. "Theresa, here is Mr. Bennett come to visit. I shall leave you alone so that you may be comfortable with your cousin. Do not mind the flowers. I shall finish arranging them in the bowl later." She hurried past the younger woman and exited the drawing room.

Theresa looked after her in surprise. Then she looked thoughtfully at her cousin. "George, have you been teasing Miss Brown?"

He curled his fingers over his palm so that he could study the polished nails. "I have, rather. Actually, I believe that I come here as much to call on her as I do you, Teri."

"Well, I wish you would not. My aunt dislikes it and she makes positively catty remarks whenever you have seen Miss Brown." Theresa was annoyed when her cousin laughed. "George! It is not like you to be so unfeeling."

"Believe me, I am far from unfeeling." His voice had been contemplative, but then he seemed to shake free of his reflections. "But it is not about myself and Miss Brown that

I wish to talk to you.'' George crossed to the still-half-open door and shut it firmly. "Wouldn't do to let the servants get wind of this. Your mother shouldn't hear of it just yet. If ever.''

"Whatever are you talking about, George?'' Theresa demanded with a sinking feeling.

He took her hands. "Theresa, it is Holland. I went to see him just as you asked me to, but he wasn't at his lodgings. I went back several times, but to no avail. Finally I asked Holland's landlord of his whereabouts and the man said that Holland had been taken off.'' George paid no heed to Theresa's swift intake of breath as he recalled the less-than-pleasant interview. His voice became affronted. "Would you believe it? The rascal refused to tell me any more until I had paid the rent Holland owed him. The heartless skinflint! But I've got Holland's direction now. The only thing is, I can't get in to see him.''

Theresa's mouth was dry. She cleared her throat. "Where is he?''

"I thought it would be Newgate after what you imparted to me, but he is held in a private gaol. It seems Holland was indiscriminate in choosing his lady friends. He borrowed a huge sum from an actress. The woman signed a complaint against him for nonpayment in the district where her uncle is the justice. Awful cheek, that, considering what sort of woman she is. In any event, even though this woman is an actress and as vulgar as you may imagine, she still has family connections that stand to serve her well in this instance.'' George drew his breath and tightened his hold on Theresa's trembling fingers. "Teri, the family means to see their precious black sheep firmly wed, thus throwing a much-needed cloak of respectability over her. And she is quite willing that it should happen.''

Theresa was white-faced. "Surely she does not really wish it. If someone were to talk with her, George . . . Perhaps if I were to see her, to plead with her—''

George shook his head. "I have already seen the lady, and I use that term loosely in this connection, believe me. It was of no use. Holland has finally run his neck into a tightened noose. The woman stands firm. It is to be wedding papers in exchange for Holland's freedom.''

''But what of Papa? And Mama and Michael? And Mary Marling! Holland blurted out to me that he has become secretly engaged to her.'' Theresa's mind reeled with the implications. She stared at her cousin. ''What shall we do, George?''

''I am off immediately to consult with an acquaintance of mine who is knowledgeable on points of law. Perhaps he may think of something. If that fails . . .'' George shook his head despondently. ''I think that you may gain a different sort of sister-in-law than you ever expected.''

Theresa made George go over his story again and again, asking questions and proffering suggestions that her cousin gently dismissed as unworkable. Theresa eventually could not think of another thing, and after a few more minutes George decided to take leave of her, recommending that she tell no one of the disaster.

''What sort of ninny do you think me?'' she asked on a spurt of anger. ''I can hardly reveal such a story to Mama! And whom else in London can I confide in but you?''

George was properly chastened. He kissed her cheek. ''I am frightfully sorry, Teri. This thing has me on edge. I shall be in touch as soon as I am able.'' He gave a wave and then he was gone.

Theresa sat down in a wing chair and contemplated the fire in the grate. She could not let go of Holland's dilemma. As her mind fretted this way and that for a solution, it slowly dawned on her that there *was* one person that she might confide in who could conceivably be of help to her brother.

During their long talk, George had unintentionally let drop more information than he intended. Theresa had soon remembered enough to put together the district where Holland was being held and the name of the actress. As soon as she was certain that she had recalled as much as she could, Theresa pulled on the bell and stood waiting impatiently.

When a footman entered to inquire as to her needs, she requested a hackney cab to be hailed for her.

Without bothering to explain her reasons to the astonished footman, she hurried out of the drawing room and up the stairs to her bedroom. She had learned enough during her first Season to know that she could not do openly what she intended. She would need a cloak and bonnet to disguise her identify if she were to visit a gentleman's abode in broad daylight.

The porter at the Duke of Ashford's residence was too well-versed with such demands to express hesitation whether the veiled young woman should be allowed in to see his master. Without a word, the manservant showed the visitor into a deserted drawing room and closed the door. Then he went in search of Mr. Winthrop.

While she waited for the duke's appearance, Theresa moved about restlessly. She had thrown back her veil immediately, since it proved to be hot underneath its concealing folds. When the drawing-room door opened, she turned swiftly, hope in her brown eyes. Upon seeing Winthrop, her expression fell. She glanced beyond his shoulder. "Mr. Winthrop, is the duke not at home, then? I had hoped particularly to speak with him."

Winthrop, who had expected to find himself in the company of another of the duke's inopportune relatives, was utterly flabbergasted. He snapped shut the door so that the servants in the hall could not overhear. "Miss Thaleman! Whatever are you about? You should not be here!" he exclaimed.

"I know that I am risking scandal and social ruin and all the rest. But it is of the utmost importance that I speak to his grace." Theresa saw the hesitation and half-formed denial in his eyes. She clasped her hands together in an unconscious pleading gesture. "Pray do believe me, Mr. Winthrop. I would not have come if it was not of the direst importance."

Winthrop could not withstand the plea in her eyes. "Very

well, Miss Thaleman. I shall tell the duke of your presence. But I beg of you, do not allow any of the servants to glimpse your face. Even a loyal household will gossip.''

"Thank you, Mr. Winthrop!'' Theresa said gratefully. She had to let down her veil again before he would leave her.

It was not many moments before the door opened again, this time to reveal the Duke of Ashford's graceful figure. He regarded her with raised brows. "My dear girl, this is a bit dramatic, is it not?'' he asked, nodding at the black veil.

"Oh, Mr. Winthrop made me promise to keep it down in the unlikely event that I might be recognized. He is concerned for my reputation,'' Theresa said with a laugh.

The duke closed the door. "As he should be. Miss Thaleman, I must take leave to scold you. I have on several occasions received female visitors, and some have even been veiled. Believe me, your credit does not lend itself to this sort of thing,'' Hugo said, advancing toward her. He gestured to a chair, inviting her to be seated.

"I cannot sit, Hugo. I am sorry, but it is just such a muddle and I hoped that you might help me, you see. And I simply cannot be still,'' Theresa said, throwing back the weighty veil that she was fast coming to despise.

Hugo was startled by the look of strain in her expression. He took her hands and felt them tremble in his clasp. "Miss Thaleman, pray tell me what the matter is and I shall certainly do all in my power to help you.''

"It is about my brother Holland, your grace. He is in the greatest straits imaginable, and I could not think of anywhere else to turn. Geroge is doing all that he can, of course, but I fear very much that it is all up for Holland.'' Despair washed over Theresa of a sudden and tears welled in her eyes. She freed her hands and fumbled in her reticule. "I do apologize, your grace. I detest watering pots and here I am . . .'' She found the small linen square at last. "Damnation, it is so small!''

The duke choked back a laugh. He handed his own hand-kerchief to her, thinking that he had never seen a more adorable look of frustration. "Come, Miss Thaleman. I insist that we make ourselves comfortable over on the settee. Then you may tell me about Holland's problem. I have the most lowering feeling that I may live to regret my willingness to lend an ear, however.''

His relaxed manner steadied Theresa and she was able to master her momentary weakness. Once seated, she proceeded to lay before the duke the particulars of Holland's case as she knew them. He listened without interrupting, a frown once crossing his face. When she was done, Theresa drew a breath and looked at him hopefully. ''Pray, do you think that there is anything that may be done?''

The duke glanced at her, coming back from dark memories. As Miss Thaleman was speaking, he had recalled another young man, one who had been perhaps more naive than Mr. Holland Bennett, and who had escaped an unwelcome marriage only by a freak of fate. ''I believe that there may be a solution, yes. And I assure you that I shall do whatever is in my power to do, Miss Thaleman,'' he said quietly.

Theresa flung herself into his arms, exclaiming, ''Oh, thank you, Hugo!'' His arms came up automatically to steady her, and Theresa found herself staring into the duke's face with only a hand's space between them. His breath was warm on her face. In his gray eyes there was a curious expression, and Theresa flushed suddenly. ''I . . . I am sorry. I never meant to . . . Pray forgive me,'' she stammered, drawing back.

The duke let her go with no discernible emotion in his expression. There was only a momentary tightening of his jaw to indicate strong feeling. ''You have no need to apologize, Miss Thaleman. The excitement of the moment was excuse enough, I believe.'' He stood up and offered his hand to her.

Theresa allowed herself to be drawn to her feet. He did not let go her hand, only clasping it more firmly in his. Theresa was unsure what to do. She felt very strange standing so close to him, and a moment before, when she had realized that she was in his arms . . . Her cheeks warmed again. ''I

suppose that I should be returning to my uncle's house,''
she said lamely.

"Yes.'' But the duke made no move to escort her to the
door, instead seeming to be reflecting upon something. He
lifted Theresa's hand, turning it over to glance at the ring
on her finger. "I had heard that you possessed a ring of a
certain design. It was mentioned to me because I once lost
a similar band, though that one was set with a greater number
of stones,'' he said in a curiously idle voice.

Theresa wondered at the duke's detached tone, even as
she registered surprise at his sudden revelation. "A
serpentine band such as this one, your grace? Why, this must
be the very one, then, for I found it buried alongside the road
to Rusland Park. It was just before I was to come to London,
and the twins had the ring done over for me into a set.''
Theresa suddenly realized what she was saying, and she
flushed with embarrassment. She snatched her hand from
the duke's clasp so that she could slip off the serpentine ring.
"Pray take it. It belongs to you, after all. And I shall have
the other stones returned to you as well,'' she said.

Hugo accepted the ring, but he did not slip it into his pocket
as Theresa had expected. Instead he looked at her in a way
that made her breath catch in her throat. "Miss Thaleman,
I find that I do not wish to have the ring back. I wish you
to keep it, with one condition if you should accept it.''

"What is that, your grace?'' Theresa asked.

He lifted her hand so that he could brush his lips lightly
over her slender fingers. "Miss Thaleman, I wish to call on
your mother and ask her permission to press my suit with
you. Would that be agreeable to you?''

Theresa was speechless. It was several long moments while
she was lost in the duke's soft gaze before she nodded.
"I . . . I would be most happy for you to do so,'' she said
shyly.

Hugo slipped the serpentine ring back onto her finger. "I
find that there are two other conditions,'' he said thoughtfully. "One is that you simply must abandon this distressing
habit of falling into formal address with me. The other is

that I am quite certain that I must kiss you before you leave."
He did not wait for her acquiescence but pulled her gently
into his arms and kissed her thoroughly. When he raised his
head to look down at her, he said laughingly, "My dear girl,
it is customary to close one's eyes."

"But I didn't wish to miss anything," Theresa said, smiling
at him. Her eyes were ablaze with happiness. She knew that
she would remember this golden moment all her days. She
now understood better what her girlhood friend Barbara
Trisham had already begun to learn months before her.
Falling in love could be a very wonderful thing. Theresa
reached up to put her hands around the duke's neck. "I
suppose that with practice I might become quite good at it,"
she said provocatively.

The duke made an inarticulate sound deep in his throat
and crushed her to him. His kiss was more demanding this
time and Theresa's lips parted beneath his. She was a pliant
slender reed in his arms, responding to him without
reservation. She was a heady wine to a gentleman who had
once believed himself jaded beyond recall. At last Hugo
forced himself to break away. His breath came hard and fast.
"My dear girl, I insist that you return home at once. Otherwise I cannot be held entirely responsible for my actions,"
he said hoarsely.

Theresa felt as though her veins ran with molten fire. Her
wondering eyes met the passion his gaze. She was suddenly
filled with a fierce gladness and yet also a soft confidence.
"Yes, Hugo. I shall go at once," she said. She reset her
veil and left the drawing room, lingering only a second at
the door to glance back at the duke before she was gone.

The Duke of Ashford made his formal request to Mrs.
Thaleman and was earnestly assured of her complete
approval. When he had taken his leave, Mrs. Thaleman
rushed out of her chair to fling her arms about her daughter.
"Dearest Theresa! How very proud I am of you. Why, you
are to be a duchess! I must write to your father at once. He
will be agog at the news. But I never doubted for a moment
that his grace was taken with you. Indeed not! And I think

just this once I shall interrupt dear Claudia's rest. She will be perfectly speechless. She has been such a cat about everything, as I am sure you are aware. I really cannot let another moment go by before relating the excellent news to my dear sister." Intent on her agreeable errand, Mrs. Thaleman bustled out of the drawing room.

Theresa stepped to the window and lifted the curtain, a happy smile playing about her mouth as she watched the traffic below. A quiet knock on the door was followed by the entrance of Miss Brown into the drawing room. Theresa smiled at her companion as she approached her. "Miss Brown, the most extraordinary thing has happened," she said, her voice lilting.

Miss Brown embraced her. "My dearest Theresa, there is no need to tell me. You are radiant with the news. I felicitate you, my dear," she said.

Theresa returned her hug. "Thank you, dear Miss Brown! But I have been thinking. What shall you do now that I am engaged?"

Miss Brown's mouth curved in a half-smile. "Your mother has very handsomely offered me the post of her companion."

Theresa regarded her with horror. "No, Miss Brown! Surely you would not!"

Miss Brown laughed and shook her head. "However well the squire and Mrs. Thaleman have treated me, I fear not. I hope to have other arrangements before that eventuality," she said.

"So do I hope also. You may count on a glowing reference should you need it, Miss Brown," Theresa said.

Miss Brown smiled again and civilly thanked her before turning the topic to the Duke of Ashford and possible wedding dates.

19

The official news of the Duke of Ashford's engagement to Miss Theresa Thaleman was the hottest *on-dit* of the Season. Suddenly Theresa found herself the center of all of society, a circumstance that she managed to handle with aplomb, thus earning her mother's high accolades for herself and several words of gratitude for Miss Brown. "And I do not mind telling you, Letitia, that you have done a splendid job in engendering the social graces in my daughter. I never had my doubts on that score, of course, but Theresa has completely exceeded all my hopes for her. A coronet and forty thousand a year! What more could a doting mother wish for her beloved daughter? The squire is very pleased. I wrote to him at once, naturally, and his reply was all one could hope for. The squire actually complimented the Duke of Ashford's good sense in making Theresa his choice," Mrs. Thaleman said on a laugh.

Miss Brown smiled at her employer. Mrs. Thaleman had been in high alt ever since the engagement had been announced. Her good humor had not been at all affected by Mrs. Bennett, whose acid comments and petulant glances ill-concealed her distemper that her sister had managed such a coup. Mr. Bennett had been surprisingly supportive of his niece's good fortune, even recommending to his wife at one point that she go soak her head if she could not bring herself to share in Theresa's happiness. Mrs. Bennett had been so shocked by her spouse's unlooked-for attack that she was struck dumb for several moments, much to Mr. Bennett's gratification.

When he happened to meet Theresa at a social function, George Bennett congratulated his cousin with utter sincerity. "I was meaning to call at the town house tomorrow to relay my congratulations. I know that you had few expectations of the Season, Teri, and to tell you the truth, so did I. You were such a hoyden that I was certain you would disgrace yourself before the end of the social rounds. But you carried it off just as you ought. And now you have knocked us all into the basket with this announcement. I wish you all the best."

"Thank you, dear George." Theresa smiled mistily at him.

"By the by, I saw Holland but an hour ago. He was extremely grateful to the Duke of Ashford, who apparently intervened on his behalf."

"I am so glad! And you need not look so quizzing, George. I admit it was very bold of me, but I simply had to ask Hugo to help poor Holland."

"I don't scold, cousin. Far from it. It but illustrates my own gathering conviction that one must seize upon the opportunity, as it were." George cleared his throat. He said hesitantly, "I have been giving some thought to making a change in my own life, you know."

Theresa looked up at him curiously. "Have you, indeed? What is it, George?"

After a false start or two, and feeling hot under his close-tied cravat, George finally managed to say what he wanted. "Theresa, I have decided to ask Miss Brown to become my wife," he said in a strangled voice. It was extremely difficult for him to make such an announcement, even to his cousin, whom he knew to be sympathetic, but he suspected that it would be more difficult when he was faced with Miss Brown's cool, inquiring gaze. But he felt easier for at last putting his intention into words.

Theresa resisted the impulse to fling her arms about him as she might once have done. She had learned that much self-control over the Season. Instead she gave her hands to him and squeezed his fingers. "I am so happy for you, George."

Holding her fingers tightly between his, George laughed. "She has not accepted me yet. I confess that I am a bit anxious about it all. Teri, what if she should turn me down?"

"Do not even think it, George. Oh, I know that you have irritated Miss Brown on occasion with your attentions, but I know that is only because she assumed that you were merely flirting. This puts quite a different light on matters, believe me. You must have faith that Miss Brown feels just as you do. And, George, do try to address her at least once as 'dear Letitia,' " Theresa said, twinkling up at him.

George sighed deeply. He drew her close so that he could rest his cheek against her hair. He knew now why he had chosen to tell his cousin first before all others of what he meant to do. "Thank you, Teri. I do not know that I could do it without your encouragement. I never knew myself to shy at a hurdle."

Theresa leaned back against his arms. "How foolish of you, George! You have only to recall all the mad coils that you and the twins have become embroiled in over the years, and not once did you ever waver. Surely you may derive some comfort from that!"

George laughed again and placed a swift kiss on her smooth brow. "I knew that you would say just the right thing to steady my nerves."

Unbeknownst to them both, several paces away the Duke of Ashford stood rigid with his fists clenched. His eyes were locked on the tender tableau before him. Though he could not hear what was being said, he thought he was well-versed enough in the games of love to guess the exchange. He had himself been in too many similar situations to mistake the tenor of this rendezvous. As the word formed in his mind, bolts of jealous rage shot through him. He could not bear to witness another second of the leave-taking between Theresa Thaleman and her fop of a cousin. Hugo turned on his heel and swiftly left.

When George left to call on his intended, Theresa returned to the company, positively itching to tell someone of George's momentous decision. She looked for the Duke of Ashford, thinking that he would be the very one with whom to share the news. She had come to rely on Hugo as one of her closest

friends, quite apart from their engaged status. When she did
not find the duke, she asked of him, only to learn that he
had left. Theresa was disappointed and somewhat puzzled.
She had reserved a waltz for him. It was strange that the
duke had left without first taking leave of her, but she
supposed that there must have been something of urgency
that had called him away. Theresa cheered at the thought
that he would almost certainly call on her on the morrow.
She would tell Hugo about her cousin then.

The following day the Duke of Ashford presented himself
just as Theresa had expected. She swiftly crossed the drawing
room toward him. Her expression was radiant with happiness
that he had come. "Hugo, I am so glad to see you. You have
no notion of the news I have," she said.

Hugo had spent the better part of the night torturing himself
with the burning memory of the *tête-à-tête* he had witnessed.
Over and over he had castigated himself for placing his trust
in Miss Theresa Thaleman. She was no better than all the
rest who had come to him, all those who had wanted to dip
their sticky fingers into his pockets or bathe in the aura of
his social standing. Now it seemed that she meant to break
the news of her understanding with her cousin to him, and
Hugo was pained by how much he minded. Full of disgust
for himself and his own weakness of character, Hugo flung
up a hand, stopping Theresa in her tracks. "Spare me your
effusions, Miss Thaleman," he said in a tone of unutterable
weariness. "I have come only to relate to you that your
brother has been set free and is at this moment on his way
home."

Theresa was completely at a loss. The news of Holland's
freedom was so overshadowed by the manner of its delivery
that she hardly comprehended the meaning of his words. She
studied the duke's set expression and the uncharacteristic
coldness of his eyes. "Hugo?"

"Let there be no more deceptions between us, Miss
Thaleman! I learned of your cousin, George Bennett,
yesterday evening," Hugo said harshly. He waited to see
her reaction to his abrupt announcement.

"But how . . . ?"

Theresa's expression of astonished confusion did not disappoint him, but rather served to confirm his conclusions. He spoke from between clenched teeth. "I was present during that most touching scene. I must applaud you, Miss Thaleman. You played it finely between the pair of you. But I must object to my role as the cuckold."

Theresa realized that something was terribly, horribly wrong. She did not know what he thought he had witnessed, but obviously it had nothing to do with George's visit to Miss Brown. "Hugo, what are you talking about? George and I are cousins only. He—"

The Duke of Ashford's laugh was short and hard. His eyes burned with bright anger. "Indeed, ma'am! I am to disbelieve the evidence of my eyes, then, and accept your innocence." His voice dropped as he advanced on her. "You are a jade. I should have known that from the first moment I saw you in those damnable breeches. Pray satisfy my curiosity, Theresa. When will you next go to meet your cousin, your lover?"

Theresa felt as though she had stepped into a nightmare. "It is not true, any of it!" As she stared into Hugo's cold, enraged eyes she realized that he was totally beyond reason. He had convinced himself of her guilt. The more she attempted to explain, the more she would damn herself in his eyes. Almost as a vague aside, she recalled that George had once described the Duke of Ashford as an unemotional man who had ice water in his veins. There was nothing unemotional about the duke at this moment. His expression was murderous.

Theresa sensed intuitively that only damage could come from this interview. It was imperative to call an end to it. Her thoughts tumbled erratically. Perhaps when the duke was calmer, when he learned of the engagement between George and Miss Brown, then he would be amenable to reason.

Her silence went on too long. The Duke of Ashford ground out a savage curse. His hands were rough as he yanked her to him, rocking her head on her neck. Theresa pushed against his chest, fearing what she saw in his expression. "Hugo, pray . . ."

The Duke of Ashford was unheeding. His jealousy was such that it consumed him. "Have you enjoyed his lovemaking, Theresa?" he breathed. He ran one hand down her slender back, pinning her to him. With the other hand he forced up her chin. Hugo stared down into her frightened face for one long second before he took possession of her mouth.

It was a brutal, punishing kiss, quite unlike anything Theresa had ever experienced or expected. She made an inarticulate noise of protest and fought him, but his strength was too great. When at last Hugo lifted his head and set her free, it was with an expression of contempt.

Theresa tasted blood where her lip had been smashed against her teeth. There was such a crippling pain about her heart that she could hardly breathe. The awful climax that she had sensed had not been avoided. Her thoughts were absolutely crystal clear. She had but one course left open to her.

"I do not care to see you again, your grace," Theresa said, her voice shaking. She pulled the serpentine ring from her finger and dropped it on the table.

The Duke of Ashford looked at her with the coldest expression she had ever seen on him. "As you wish, Miss Thaleman. The ring is yours, however. I do not reclaim tokens that I give to my ladies."

It was the worst of insults, and Theresa knew it. She turned white. She felt like bursting into tears, but her pride came to her aid. She held on to the chair back for support. "I think there is nothing more to say, your grace."

He bowed before he turned abruptly, snatched open the door, and left the sitting room. A footman stepped inside the open doorway. "Miss Thaleman? Is there anything that you require?" he asked.

Theresa took a shuddering breath. There was much that she required, but none of it could be provided by the footman.

"No, Hobbs. That will be all, thank you." He closed the door softly.

Theresa wandered aimlessly to the window, hardly able to put one coherent thought before another in her reeling mind. She lifted aside the lace curtain. The sun was setting and the street below was growing dark. It was the lonely, forlorn hour before the lanterns were lit and the *ton* began their nightly ritual of traveling to social gatherings. Theresa had never felt more isolated or more out of place. "How I wish that I had never left home," she said passionately, dropping the curtain.

The sitting-room door opened. "Teri? It is I, George."

Theresa turned swiftly. Her cousin entered, closing the door again behind him. His gaze was sympathetic, and it was what she needed. Theresa caught her breath on a sob. She ran across the carpet and flung herself into his arms. "Oh, George!" She buried her face in his shoulder, the tears spilling fast and furious.

For once George Bennett did not give thought to the preservation of his coat. He held his weeping cousin close, his cheek against her hair, and whispered nonsensical comfort. "Go on, Teri. That's the ticket. You'll feel more the thing in a trice. At all events, that is what they say." At last Theresa raised her head. She attempted a smile even though tears still coursed down her face. George placed a kiss on her brow. "There's my brave little cousin. I've never known a tumble to keep you down for long."

"Oh, George, this is not quite the same thing," Theresa said, letting go the hold that she had of his lapel. Sniffing, she rummaged in her pockets in fruitless search of a handkerchief. Seeing her plight, George offered his own, and Theresa took it with a mumbled word of thanks.

"Isn't it? Somehow I prefer to think of it that way." George went to the mantel and stared down into the fire, prodding the front log with the toe of his immaculate shining boot.

There was an uncharacteristic pathos in her cousin's voice

that caught Theresa's attention even through her own wretchedness. She stared at him, puzzled. "George? George, what is wrong?"

He glanced up at her. "Wrong? Why, whatever could be wrong? I have come from a delightful visit with my mother. Indeed, we seem to have established a common ground between us today, and—"

"George, you are deliberately throwing dust in my eyes," Theresa said. She went to him and stood close, searching his face. He could not bear her scrutiny for long, but averted his gaze to the flames. It was then that Theresa had a flash of intuition. "You knew what happened between me and Hugo without asking a single question. George! You offered for Miss Brown, didn't you? And she—George, I am so very sorry."

George Bennett shrugged one shoulder with but a vestige of his usual aplomb. "We are a pair, are we not? You have lost the duke and I . . . But I suppose that I never possessed Miss Brown's heart. It is so incredibly ironic, Teri. At first my flirtation with her was only a diversion to me, something with which to tease my mother's notions of suitability. But as I spent more time with Miss Brown, I began to realize her worth and her nobility. Little by little the question of her regard came to matter to me. But I never could bring myself to the point. This evening I finally screwed up the courage to ask her feelings, you know. Damned if she hasn't gotten herself engaged to another, some fellow called Winthrop."

Theresa recalled the look of absolute stunned recognition on both Miss Brown's face and Mr. Winthrop's when they had first met and how it had startled her. She wished very much that she had remembered something so important much earlier. "George, I don't know what to say."

George ran his hand through his hair and then smiled rather tiredly. "Nor I, Teri. If you shouldn't mind it, I believe that I shall head home. I feel peculiarly fatigued this evening."

"Of course I do not, George." Theresa walked with her

cousin to the front door, neither of them speaking. Before George stepped out on the steps, Theresa reached up to place her hand against his cheek. He smiled and nodded before he turned away.

20

Theresa could not recall ever having a more miserable evening. She had thought that defying her misery and attending the ball would lift her spirits, but she had spent the entire evening alternating between dread and hope that she would chance to meet Hugo among the company. The pull of her emotions served to give her a severe headache and left her feeling exhausted. Mrs. Thaleman, never one to see more than what was on the surface, commented that she was looking peaked and adjured her to pinch her cheeks to bring some color into her face.

Theresa did her best to appear normal, and she accepted several invitations to dance, until the pain hammering behind her eyes made it nearly impossible to see her partners. Then she begged off, citing breathlessness and a preference to sit and watch the company. She was eventually left alone, but with the pounding in her head she was hardly aware of her isolation as the company ebbed about her. Even Mrs. Thaleman abandoned her for the more lively company of another matron with whom she could exchange gossip.

When Lady Statten approached with the amiable proposition to join her at the gaming table, Theresa could not imagine anything less inviting. "Thank you, my lady, but I think not. I do not feel able to concentrate on the cards this evening," she said.

Lady Statten studied her with sharp eyes. "Theresa, you look positively hagged." With a tinkling laugh she said, "Forgive my blunt speech, my dear, but you do not look at all well."

Theresa made an effort to smile. "I appreciate your

concern, my lady. It is nothing, really. I but have the headache.''

"Then you must go home at once. I will make your excuses for you," said Lady Statten, not intending to do any such thing. Let the brat leave unnoticed and unlamented, she thought viciously.

"I doubt that will help," murmured Theresa to herself. She dashed a hand across her eyese. "How I detest London! I wish that I had never come."

Lady Statten was momentarily surprised. With the official announcement of the engagement, she had watched Theresa's meteoric rise to social prominence with gritted teeth, powerless to do much more than ingratiate herself with the little nitwit. Though she had been for the most part unsuccessful in wooing Theresa into dangerous company, the girl had never been backward in enjoying those entertainments that her respectable relatives deemed suitable. For Theresa to forswear London meant that she was operating under strong emotion of some sort. Lady Statten was swift of mind and she comprehended that there had been a lovers' quarrel between Theresa and the Duke of Ashford.

Her pulse quickened as she sensed the ripeness of the moment. She might yet be able to wean the Duke of Ashford from the puling brat, she thought. She glanced about as she seated herself beside Theresa, assuring herself that none of the glittering company was within hearing. With elaborate gentleness she laid hold of Theresa's arm. Her voice was sympathetic. "I see that it is more than the headache that troubles you, my dear. And indeed, I do not wonder that London has become closed-feeling after the swift pace you have set these past weeks. I know the very thing to pick one up, however, and that is a weekend trip into the country. I am myself posting down to Rusland Park this weekend. Why do you not join me?"

The old magic of her imaginings of Rusland Park struck a chord in Theresa. She gave the matter hardly any thought before she agreed to Lady Statten's suggestion. The invitation seemed a heaven-sent opportunity to escape for a time her intolerable situation in London. "I am grateful for your friendly concern, my lady. I shall be glad to accompany you," she said with a faltering smile.

"Good, good," breathed Lady Statten. She patted the girl's arm. "Now, you must go home to rest. I shall call on you tomorrow to set a time and place of departure. We shall make your excuses to our hostess this very minute."

"Thank you, my lady," Theresa said with a sigh. It was very pleasant to be able to put herself in another's capable hands. Lady Statten brought Theresa's malaise to Mrs. Thaleman's attention and she offered to see that Theresa was put into a carriage for home so that Mrs. Thaleman would not have to leave the company.

"How very kind of you, to be sure, my lady. But I would not dream of putting you to the trouble. No, indeed. Theresa, you will do well to take Lady Statten's advice and come home with me," said Mrs. Thaleman. She thought her rejection of Lady Statten's offer had been rather abrupt, and even though her ladyship had a shocking past, she was still a personage of consequence and therefore should not be made offended. Besides, Lady Statten had obviously meant well by Theresa. Mrs. Thaleman said with a conciliatory smile, "She is such a stubborn little thing, my lady. I am happy that you have been a friend to her, for she will never listen to me. I saw hours ago how it was, of course, but I held my tongue, knowing how useless it would be to argue with her."

Lady Statten smiled. She had never allowed even a hint of her impatience to seep through the mask of graciousness that she always wore for the clucking fool. "Indeed, Mrs. Thaleman. Theresa, I hope that you shall feel more the thing on the morrow."

"Thank you, my lady," said Theresa. She allowed herself to be docilely led to the carriageway and put into her carriage.

"Well, her ladyship has been most kind to you, Theresa. And after what I have learned of her reputation, I am somewhat surprised that she would bother with you," said Mrs. Thaleman.

"Yes, Mama," said Theresa, hardly paying attention.

Mrs. Thaleman was prone to rattle on about the ball but fortunately she did not expect her daughter to comment. Theresa put back her aching head against the squabs.

If Miss Brown was still awake, it would surprise her that Theresa and her mother had returned so early. Theresa only hoped that Miss Brown was already asleep so that she would be able to escape her companion's questionings, at least until breakfast, when Mrs. Thaleman was certain to make some reference to it. But by morning she thought she would be better able to fob off any suspicions that Miss Brown might have regarding the origin of her malady. She knew that Miss Brown was aware of her current unhappiness because that lady had dropped a leading statement or two that Theresa could not have failed to pick up. However fond she was of Miss Brown, Theresa still did not feel able to fully unburden her heart to her. Her impasse with the Duke of Ashford could not bear the scrutiny of a third party.

When Lady Statten had seen Mrs. Thaleman and Theresa off with expressions of solicitude and false cheer, she turned back into the crowded ballroom with a feeling of eminent triumph. At last, at last, she thought. She smiled at a gentleman acquaintance whom she had earlier snubbed, thus emboldening him to solicit her hand for a dance. Lady Statten graciously assented, her mood unusually mellow.

Lady Statten was in high spirits for the remainder of the ball. She did not leave until the small hours of the morning, and when she at last went home, she tumbled into her soft bed to sleep deeply and dreamlessly.

It was nearly noon when Lady Statten finally awakened. She stretched languorously, recalling with contentment the night before. She did not waste much time in reflection. Instead, she rose to begin her toilette and ordered her maid to pack for a two- or three-day stay at Rusland Park. Lady Statten unconsciously hummed a naughty ditty from a recent theater production. She planned to meet with Theresa

Thaleman, and then she would have the rest of the day in which to savor her coming victory.

Behind Lady Statten's back, the maid rolled her eyes. The mistress was in such good spirits only when there was a gentleman involved, she thought.

Lady Statten had a shrewd notion that Theresa Thaleman would attend an afternoon *al fresco* arranged by a prominent hostess. She was delighted to see that she had been right. She waited until Theresa was briefly left alone before she approached her. She did not want anyone to overhear what she said. "My dear Theresa, I am so happy to see you. I assume that you are feeling better?" she said, smiling.

Theresa looked at Lady Statten, recalling that she had accepted her ladyship's invitation to accompany her to Rusland Park. Upon awakening that morning, she knew that she could not possibly go. Her mother would never countenance either the trip or the company in which she was to make it. "I am much more the thing, my lady," she said. "Lady Statten, I must decline your kind invitation to accompany you to Rusland Park, after all. I do apologize, but I was not thinking quite clearly yesterday evening when you spoke to me of it."

Lady Statten's lips tightened a little. She managed to give a shrug of apparent indifference. "I understand, of course. It is a pity, however. Rusland Park is always such fun, and the usual good companions will be there, with the exception of the Duke of Ashford." She slanted a look at Theresa's face, calculating the effect of her words. "I understand that his grace is remaining in town this weekend because he has pledged himself to escort Lady Buffingsham to the ball tomorrow. Her ladyship is quite smitten with the duke, I hear. And of course he has known her family forever. The ball is to be a gala event and I almost wish that I was not committed to Rusland for the weekend, but so it is." She ended on a note of insouciance as she fiddled with her fan, seemingly unaware of her companion's stiffened frame.

Theresa's eyes were bright with anger and hurt. She could hardly believe that the Duke of Ashford had pledged himself to Lady Buffingsham for the ball. Somehow she had assumed that even though she would not be on his arm, he would not escort anyone else. How dare Hugo enjoy himself when she felt so miserable? she thought angrily. But two could play at that game. She would not give him the satisfaction of parading Lady Buffingsham in front of her. She would stay away from the ball altogether. But then it would appear as though she was sulking. Theresa felt a renewed surge of anger, mingled with defiance.

"I have seen an acquaintance that I must speak to, so I shall leave you now, Theresa. Perhaps I shall see you again when I return next week," Lady Statten said, and made to turn away.

"Wait!" Theresa put out her hand quickly, detaining Lady Statten, who looked at her with upraised brows. "My lady, I have decided that it would be the greatest of insults for me to decline your invitation. I should like to accompany you to Rusland Park after all. But I shall have to meet you after the dinner hour. Perhaps I might join you at your town house then?" She knew that her request was odd, and a slight flush rose in her face.

But Lady Statten appeared to notice nothing out of the ordinary. "Of course, Theresa. I had not meant to leave until this evening, in any event, because the earl keeps such late hours, and dinner at Rusland is never served before nine o'clock." Lady Statten smiled, her green eyes warmer than usual. "I am glad that you have changed your mind, Theresa. I promise that you will find it an unforgettable weekend."

"Oh, I shall not impose on your good nature for the entire two days, my lady," Theresa said, thinking quickly. Despite her defiance, she felt an echo of misgiving for her impetuous decision, but she could not back out now. She knew that her mother would never agree to letting her go to Rusland Park, and if she were to plunge into this illicit venture, she would have to arrange it so that no one ever suspected that she had gone there. "My father's estate is quite close to Rusland Park, so I thought that I would make mine but a brief visit to Rusland before I continued on to my home. I have not seen my father or brother since I came up to London, you see."

Once more Lady Statten exhibited complete understanding. "Of course, Theresa. It shall be just as you wish. Now, I really must not detain you any longer. Until this evening, my dear." She swept away.

That evening the Bennetts and the Thalemans dined quietly at home. Theresa chose her moment when the ladies had retired to the drawing room, leaving Mr. Bennett to enjoy his port in solitude, before she launched the first falsehood of her life. "Mama, if you do not mind, I think that I should like to go upstairs early this evening. I have still the headache," she said, stumbling a little over the lie. The color rose in her face when she met her mother's gaze.

"You do appear a bit flushed, Theresa. Oh, dear. I hope that you are not catching something. It would be simply too bad if you are to be ill just before the ball tomorrow. Have you a putrid throat?" asked Mrs. Thaleman.

Theresa shook her head quickly. She felt horrible. She had not realized before how difficult it would be to speak a bold-faced lie. "I know that I shall soon feel more the thing, Mama," she said quickly, hoping to lessen her feelings of guilt and shame. But it did not help.

"Very well, Theresa. I shall not keep you. Sleep well, my dear."

Theresa fled the drawing room. Mrs. Thaleman turned to Miss Brown. "I cannot but wonder at it, Letitia. Before we came to town, Theresa was never ill. This week alone she has had to lie down twice with the headache. I had dismissed as just so much nonsense those tales one hears on occasion of town life being so unhealthy, but now I am not so certain. Pray, do you think this malaise of Theresa's has anything to do with being in London?"

"Perhaps my niece has inherited my own tendency toward delicacy," said Mrs. Bennett, somewhat pleased by the thought. It quite put her in charity with Theresa, whom she had always thought of as being disgustingly robust for a delicately nurtured young woman.

Miss Brown had her own suspicions of the origin of Theresa's unusual complaint. She had noticed that the Duke of Ashford had not called at the town house for over a week. She rather thought that if she were to go upstairs to Theresa's bedroom at this moment, she might find the girl indulging in a hearty bout of tears. "Oh, I have no doubt of it whatsoever, Mrs. Thaleman. Theresa's headaches definitely stem from her arrival in London," she said quietly. She was disappointed that Theresa had not confided in her, but she thought she understood. Theresa was an independent young woman, and naturally she would attempt to sort out her feelings on her own.

Theresa quickly packed a portmanteau and then changed to a travel dress. It was a struggle to work the many small buttons on the dress, but she managed it at last, though she was flushed and perspiring from the effort. She spent a few moments penning a short note to her mother saying that she had become homesick and had decided to go home for a few days. As she reread the note, she sighed. It was all very complicated and reprehensible. But she was committed to her course and she had never been one to back away from a perilous jump.

She opened the door to her bedroom softly and slipped into the hall, her portmanteau in hand. She knew that coffee was being served in the drawing room to the ladies and Mr. Bennett, who would have left the dining room to join them. The servants would be occupied in clearing the dining room, so Theresa was fairly certain of being able to leave the house undetected through the back way. She gained the sidewalk without incident and was fortunate enough to immediately get a hackney cab.

Theresa was set down within a very few minutes at Lady Statten's address. She was let into the town house instantly and shown into the drawing room. When word was taken up that her guest had arrived, Lady Statten smiled in satisfaction. ''I shall be down in a few moments. Pray see that Miss Thaleman is comfortable until I join her.'' The servant bowed and left her alone once more in her private sitting room.

Lady Statten spent several minutes composing the letter that was to be carried to the Duke of Ashford. When she was done, she reread it with satisfaction. She carefully folded the note and dripped hot wax on the back flap to seal it. Just as she started to press her signet ring into the wax, she hesitated. It was likely that the duke would simply ignore a communication that was readily seen to be from herself. Making her decision, Lady Statten let the wax cool without marring its surface.

A few minutes later she tripped downstairs, wearing a bonnet and a travel dress. The sealed note was in her hand and she gave it into the care of her butler. ''Pray have it delivered directly to the Duke of Ashford, but not before morning,'' she said. The butler bowed his understanding and Lady Statten left her town house, laughing softly to herself as she envisioned the duke's expression as he read the note.

As the carriage containing Lady Statten and her young friend drove away, the butler glanced at the note in his hand. He grimaced, thinking that it was just like her ladyship to hand him a task to be done early in the morning, following his designated night of private drinking. With the head he would most likely have in the morning, he thought, he would forget the delivery of the note altogether, and then he would be in the suds. He decided to send the note on that same evening, assuring himself that if he sent it about ten of the clock and with the late hours that the gentry kept it was likely that the duke would not open the note until morning anyway. Thus the first thread of Lady Statten's revenge began to unravel before first light.

21

The mansion at Rusland Park was as grand as Theresa had ever thought it would be. Light blazed forth so that the night and the very stars above were eclipsed. The main house reflected the Tudor era in its steep slate roofs and deep windows. Each subsequent owner had added onto the main house, and now the wings of the structure were described as a "potluck of gables and turrets and tall windows." But Theresa thought it a veritable fantasy of grandeur and warmth.

Lady Statten did not remain with the carriage once she was aided down by a footman. Instead she walked up the steps, turning at the top to raise her brows at Theresa, who had hesitated after descending from the carriage. "Are you not coming, Theresa?"

Theresa flushed slightly, aware that she must appear a regular noddy to be standing about gawking up at the house. "Of course, Lady Statten," she said, and hurried to join her patroness. Satisfied, Lady Statten sailed through the open door, Theresa following along in her wake.

The butler met the ladies in the hall. "Ah, Lady Statten! I shall inform his lordship immediately of your arrival. Your usual rooms are ready for you, of course."

"Good, and for my young friend I wish very special accommodations," said Lady Statten, flicking a smile in Theresa's direction. She met the butler's knowing eyes. He gave a slight nod of understanding. Snapping his fingers at the footmen who had begun to carry in the baggage, he issued directions for its disposal.

"Pray do not go to any great lengths for me, my lady.

I desire only a little time to freshen up before meeting our host,'' Theresa said.

Lady Statten looked full at her. Her green eyes glittered and her lips curved in a slow smile. "I wish this weekend to be a particularly memorable one, my dear child. Pray allow me to indulge my little whims. I promise you that your expectations will be far exceeded."

Theresa laughed."Oh, very well. How can I say nay when you put it so artfully? Indeed, I am grateful that you have allowed me to accompany you. It has long been an ambition of mine to visit Rusland Park."

"Believe me, it is a visit that you will long remember." Then Lady Statten addressed the butler again. "My young friend is doubtless fatigued from our long drive, so I request that she not be disturbed until Lord Mumford wishes to receive us." She turned again to Theresa and put out her hand to catch Theresa's fingers in a quick squeeze. "We shall meet again at dinner, which is always served well after nine of the clock. Rest well, Theresa, for I promise you that the evening will wax long." Lady Statten laughed, and Theresa responded with a smile before she followed a footman up the stairs to her rooms.

When Theresa was alone, she pulled off her bonnet and laid it on the bed with a sigh. Until this moment she had not allowed herself to think of the Duke of Ashford, but the elegant surroundings and the quiet of the room created an atmosphere very conducive to the intrusion of his face and words into her memory. There was a leaden feeling in her breast. She had left London with little but the determination to prove that she could go on very well without Hugo. However, the way she and the duke had parted would not rest easily on her conscience, and Theresa discovered a distressing tendency toward tears.

She paced the bedroom a little while, occasionally giving a small watery sniff. It was not as though she did not love Hugo. She did, with all her heart. But she could not have done other than she had when he had proved what little faith he had in her.

For the hundredth time Theresa thought back over her relationship with the Duke of Ashford, trying to find some reason why he should suddenly show such full-blown mistrust of her. Even though his heightened sense of propriety and his natural reserve led him to deal with those about him with a certain distance of manner, he had always seemed to be amused by her flights of fancy. She had recognized from the first that there lurked a sense of humor beneath his polite exterior, and she had gone out of her way to tease it into the open. She had thought that he knew enough about her own character that he would have known that she could never betray him, and especially in such a despicable fashion.

Theresa finally came to the realization that the fault lay not with anything she had done, but with some part of Hugo's personality that heretofore had lain wounded and deeply buried for a very long time. Dimly she could perceive something in his actions that bespoke of hurt, and a plea for reassurance. She knew with intuitive certainty that she had put her finger on the problem. But it no longer mattered, she thought wearily. She was not likely to get the chance to put her theory to the test. Her life was her own once more. The Duke of Ashford need never concern himself again with whatever imbroglios she might fall into.

Theresa supposed that a notification of their dissolved engagement would soon appear in the newspapers. The resulting gossip in London would be impossible to ignore and equally impossible to bear, she thought. She shrank from the thought of being cross-examined about her suddenly-ended engagement to the Duke of Ashford.

Theresa looked around the lavishly appointed bedroom without pleasure or excitement. Somehow her long-held ambition to attend one of Rusland Park's grand entertainments seemed to have lost its luster. After this evening she would go home to stay and spurn all contact with fashionable circles, since the Duke of Ashford could be expected to be among society. She would most likely spend the remainder of her days dwindling into an old maid.

Theresa burst into tears and flung herself across the bed

for a hardy cry. When she was spent, she turned over to stare into the bed canopy. Finally she shook herself and left the bed to go to the washstand. She poured water from the pitcher into the basin and splashed her face. As she dried with a towel she thought that she felt a fraction better, which was all to the good, since she was shortly to meet the Earl of Rusland and his guests.

With the thought there came a knock on the door, followed by the entrance of a maid. "I am sent to help you dress for dinner, miss," said the woman.

"Oh, thank you. I was just wondering how I was to undo these hooks," Theresa said with a smile. The maid did not respond to her friendly overture, but went about her job with silent competency. Within a few short moments Theresa was freshly coiffed and gowned. She looked at herself in the cheval glass, a tiny frown between her brows. There was something odd about the way that the maid had done the ribbons on her gown. And then she realized that the ribbons had not been merely tied in a bow but had been positioned so high under her breasts that her bosom appeared fuller and more noticeable. She addressed the maid, who was shaking out her discarded traveling dress. "I should like the ribbons—"

The distant ringing of a bell intruded. The maid started for the bedroom door. "There be no time, miss," she said, opening the door for Theresa.

Hesitating in indecision for a brief second, Theresa finally gave the slightest of shrugs. Her dress scarcely mattered, after all. There would be any number of guests at the table, all more worldly and sophisticated than she, and they probably would not pay the least heed to a mere nobody's gown. Theresa's assurance to herself carried her into the drawing room, where, to her baffled astonishment, she immediately became the focus of all eyes. Theresa glanced around uncomfortably, giving a slight nod to those whose gaze she chanced to meet. She was acutely aware that the ladies as well as the gentlemen were looking her up and down, as though they measured her worth. Theresa was immensely relieved when Lady Statten appeared from out of a small group at the far end of the drawing room and approached her with a gentleman in tow.

"Lady Statten! I did not immediately perceive you," Theresa said. She gave the gentleman who accompanied Lady Statten but a cursory glance as she greeted her patroness. She was taken aback when the gentleman addressed her.

"Ah, fair one, the fates have decreed for us to meet again. You have become even more beauteous than ever," said the gentleman, catching up Theresa's hand to carry it to his rather full lips.

Theresa looked at him, completely awash. She had not an inkling who the gentleman was, but as she stared at his face it became vaguely familiar to her. Her eyes focused on his lips, pressed so warmly to her fingers, and suddenly she remembered. He was the same gentleman who a few weeks past had accosted her so familiarly in the park.

"Theresa, you did not tell me that you are acquainted with Sir Parke. Fie on you for a secretive little thing," Lady Statten said, amused.

"I am not acquainted with any such gentleman," said Theresa, pulling her hand from Sir Parke's insistent hold.

Sir Parke placed a hand slightly against his bosom. "My fair Persephone, have I truly no place in your memory? It was such an idyllic encounter, beneath the trees with naught between us but the breeze." He sighed gustily. There was a titter of laughter from those near enough to overhear him.

Theresa looked at Sir Parke with dislike. He had made it sound as though the two of them had kept an assignation, she thought indignantly. "You have forgotten my dear Miss Brown. As I recall, she thought your poetry rather bad. I have always admired Miss Brown's taste," she said pointedly.

There was outright laughter from one of the gentlemen, and Sir Parke grimaced. "Indeed, the dragon. Such a jealous guardian of virtue did she prove. The woman scarcely knew the meaning of the word 'civility.' "

"All rolled up, were you, Parke?" called another

gentleman before he guffawed. Sir Parke made an ironic bow in the gentleman's direction but otherwise ignored the raillery.

"The dragon has not accompanied the tempting morsel this evening, Parke," said a lady. She gave a low laugh, waving her fan slowly before her shockingly low décolletage. Her observation sent a ripple of amusement through the assembled company.

"Quite true, Athena. Perhaps my luck is in after all," said Sir Parke. He looked at Theresa, his tongue briefly wetting his lips.

A gentleman who leaned against the mantel with a half-empty wineglass at his shoulder rattled the dice box that he held in one hand. "Do you care for another set, Parke? A roll of best of three and I shall leave the field clear for you. But otherwise I shall demand my fair chance." The gentleman's glance met Theresa's, before his eyes boldly raked her form.

Theresa sucked in her breath, feeling as though he was stripping her of her gown. Her face colored under the gentleman's too-deliberate study of her anatomy and she made an instinctive protesting movement. She wished heartily that she had not only taken the time to have the maid redo the ribbons of her gown but also added a concealing shawl to her costume. Indeed, she had had quite enough of these obnoxious and rude individuals. They spoke of her as though she were some sort of calf on the auction block, she thought in confusion. "Lady Statten, I seem to have lost my appetite. Pray, will you not relay my excuses to his lordship and—"

"Nonsense, Theresa." Lady Statten took hold of Theresa's arm and slipped it inside her own, effectively holding her captive. "As for you gentlemen, pray curb your eagerness. My guest has yet to meet the earl," she said.

"So that is the way of it? A true pity," Sir Parke said, turning away with a negligent shrug.

Theresa glanced about and lowered her voice for Lady Statten's ear alone. "Truly, my lady, I would prefer to return to my room. This company is not at all what I am used to and I feel awkwardly out of place.''

Lady Statten smiled at her. ''It is only their funning way, Theresa. You will become used to it, I assure you. Surely you do not wish to rush off so quickly when you have yet to meet our host. You did tell me that you have long hoped to meet the Earl of Rusland, did you not? And here he is now. My lord, good evening. Allow me to present my little friend Theresa.''

Even as Theresa dropped a curtsy, she threw a puzzled glance up at Lady Statten. It was very odd that her ladyship had introduced her only by her given name. Theresa was not given time to correct the oversight, however, because the next moment she found her hand taken by the Earl of Rusland.

He lifted Theresa's hand to his lips to brush her fingers in greeting. ''I am happy to make your acquaintance, dear lady. In her note to me Lady Statten neglected to mention that she would be bringing a charming companion.''

Theresa felt more at ease with the earl's polished address. His lordship apparently did not share the same freakish manners of his guests. ''Thank you, my lord. I have been looking forward to this weekend at Rusland Park. It is such a beautiful place.''

The butler came to the drawing-room door to announce dinner. The Earl of Rusland politely offered his arm to Theresa. She was flattered beyond measure at the singular honor, and gave him a bright smile as she placed her fingers on his elbow. The earl looked at her consideringly. ''I anticipate a most enlivened weekend, Theresa.'' he said, then glanced at Lady Statten and gave her a fraction of a nod. Her ladyship smiled and dropped back a step to claim an escort of her own to the dining room.

The dinner provided was sumptuous and mouth-watering to those who were hungry. Theresa did not make one of that company, however, and merely picked at her food. She hardly spoke during the course of the meal, her glance flicking back and forth as she watched those who conversed. There was something strange about the company at the table. Ladies and gentlemen spoke with the ease of long familiarity, and there was much loud laughter at several sallies that Theresa did not in the least understand. Once when she did catch the meaning of what was said she felt her face grow warm. She cast down her eyes and wondered with a feeling of shock that any lady would allude to such private matters in public, and to a gentleman, no less. All in all, she was quite glad when the meal was done with and the ladies began to make motions of leaving the gentlemen to their after-dinner wine.

Theresa had no wish to make one of the group, and she was busily devising a plausible excuse to retire early when the Earl of Rusland leaned toward her and spoke in her ear. "I see that you do not care for the company, Theresa. If the truth be known, I am somewhat bored myself. If you have no objection, I would be honored to be allowed to show you my gardens. I have had lanterns strung in the trees and it is a vasty pretty effect," he said.

Theresa knew that going off alone with the earl was not the wisest course open to her, but she thought it might be simpler to extricate herself from his company than it had been to leave Lady Statten and the others. She laid aside her napkin. "I would like that, my lord," she said quietly.

Without further ado the Earl of Rusland rose from the table and offered his arm to Theresa. Together they walked out of the dining room. Theresa had been expecting someone to question their unorthodox departure, but no one seemed to notice their exit. She shook her head over the strange society she found herself in. It seemed that few if any of the polite rules that set the standards of propriety were in effect at Rusland Park. She would be glad to return to her own niche, where she knew what to expect and how to go on.

The earl stopped to open a French door and stood aside for Theresa to precede him. She stepped out onto a moonlit terrace. Before her was the garden, illuminated by lanterns that swayed gently in the night air, giving the effect of winking fairy lights. Theresa walked to the balustrade to rest her hands on the smooth stone. "It is beautiful, my lord. I have never seen the like before," she said, turning her head to smile at the earl as he joined her.

The earl nodded. "I am happy that my garden meets with your approval. Shall we take a stroll? I wish to show you the fountain. I have had lights put at the surface of the water and I think it quite the best feature," he said.

Theresa assented and allowed the earl to take her arm as they walked. The flagstone path they followed made a leisurely curve and the manor house became effectively hidden behind the shrubbery. The earl beguiled their progress by pointing out various types of greenery and flowers, which had taken on an extraordinary appearance under the moonlight and lanterns. "It is all quite beautiful," said Theresa, gazing about her. For the first time since those first disturbing moments in the drawing room, when she had felt nothing less than a sideshow for the amusement of the company, she began to enjoy herself.

The Earl of Rusland glanced down at her, calculation in his eyes. He gestured ahead as the path fanned open to encompass a large stone basin. "And here is the fountain that I spoke of. You must give me your honest opinion, Theresa."

Theresa stood still, thunderstruck. A white marble sculpture of a merman locked in deadly battle with a monstrous fish was set above the basin. Frothing water swirled around the sculpture and splashed up on the merman's muscular form and spewed from the fish's open maw. Myriad lights set under the inner edge of the basin made the water run like quicksilver and threw shifting shadows on the sculpture so that to the eye it appeared that the carved forms thrashed and strained. "They are so very lifelike," breathed Theresa.

"I had hoped for just that effect. Come, we shall sit on the bench under that arch and you may then enjoy the fountain for as long as you like," said the earl.

He drew her over to the bench and Theresa sank down

on the deep cushion, her eyes still fixed on the illusion of mortal combat. She more sensed than felt the earl's breath on her hair. She turned her head quickly, to discover that the Earl of Rusland's saturnine face was within inches of her own. "My lord!" Theresa drew away from him. She was shaken when the earl did not retreat but instead gave a low laugh.

"You are an enchanting young woman, Theresa," he said. He took hold of her hand, turning it over so that his thumb caressed her palm. "I am happy that my taste in sculpture pleases you. It speaks eloquently of your own sensual appreciation of art and nature."

Theresa was finding it difficult to breathe. She was horrified at the turn of events, having learned enough during her first Season to know what the earl was about. She jumped up from the bench, breaking away from him, and walked over to the fountain. Her hands twisted in front of her as she attempted to speak with unconcern. "It is indeed a wonderful piece. But I appreciate what I see in nature even more. I have always loved this countryside, for instance. A visitor would think that it never varies, but every season brings something new to delight the eye."

The Earl of Rusland had followed her with the intention of taking her into his arms, but he stopped, mildly curious at her words. "I was not aware that you were native to these parts, Theresa," he said.

Theresa turned toward him, at the same time taking a step backward to put more distance between them. She wished passionately that she had never agreed to keep Lady Statten company for the weekend. It had all gone awry. "Oh, yes, I have lived all my life here. I was born not three miles from Rusland Park. Until I went to London for the Season, I was used to spend my time riding over the entire countryside."

"I see." The earl was frowning as he studied her. "Would I happen to know your family, my dear?"

"I do not think so. At least, you have probably never had occasion to meet my family. My father is . . . is not one to socialize much with his neighbors,'' said Theresa, stammering a little. She knew that it would be the height of rudeness to inform the earl that her parents did not consider his lordship fit company for their daughter. However the earl behaved toward her, her own training was too ingrained to allow her to willingly inflict insult. She supposed it was different with gentlemen, and she only hoped that she could withdraw quickly and with dignity.

"Pray tell me, would your parent happen to be Squire Thaleman?" the earl asked.

"Why, yes," Theresa said, surprised. "Are you acquainted with Papa after all?"

"Damn her eyes!" breathed the earl, his hand clenching spasmodically.

"I beg your pardon, my lord?" Theresa asked, startled.

The earl glanced at her. "Nothing, dear child. About your father—we have met, yes. I have a great deal of respect for the squire," he said in a considering tone. He seemed lost in thought for several seconds.

Theresa was puzzled by his expression. He did not seem the least bit frightening now. Tentatively she said, "My lord, is there something troubling you?"

"What? It is nothing that need concern you, Miss Thaleman. I have only a bit of unfinished business with Lady Statten. Shall we go in?" The earl offered his arm, and after hesitating a fraction, Theresa accepted his escort. She did not know what had happened, but she was certain that she need not any longer fear the earl's advances.

They returned to the house and the earl escorted her past the drawing room, from which merriment could be heard, and led her directly to her bedroom door. He lifted her hand to his lips for a brief salute. "I shall wish you good night, Miss Thaleman. And may I suggest that you bolt the door tonight?" At her wide-eyed questioning glance, he smiled. "Some of my gentlemen friends are rakes, my dear. I should not like you to be surprised in your bedchamber by an unexpected guest."

"Oh. Oh, I see. Thank you, my lord. I shall do as you say." Theresa curtsied to his lordship and entered her bedroom. She glanced about to see that she was alone, for she knew that the earl waited without if he should be needed, and then she bolted the door. She heard the earl's footsteps fade down the hallway.

Theresa was not in the least sleepy. She decided to read some of the novel she had brought with her. However, her thoughts strayed from the story to dwell on her experiences that evening, and upon Hugo. A little over an hour later there came a scratching on the door. Theresa looked at the closed door in uncertainty. She did not want to open it without knowing whom to expect, and she had no reason to expect company at all. Her silence communicated her newfound caution to the person on the opposite side. "Theresa! It is I, Lady Statten. Pray open the door."

Theresa got up from her chair, book still in hand. She crossed to the door and put her ear against it. "My lady, are you alone?"

There was an impatient hiss of breath. "Of course I am! Whatever do you suspect me of?"

Theresa unbolted the door. Lady Statten surged in, her skirts swirling about her ankles as she turned to face Theresa. Her green eyes glittered and she seemed to be harboring strong feelings. "Lady Statten, is there aught wrong?" Theresa asked.

"Wrong? What could possibly be wrong?" Lady Statten made an effort to bring herself under control. It would not do to alarm the girl, she thought. She gave a credible laugh. "I have lost at cards and I am badly dipped. I am a very bad loser, I fear."

"I am sorry. I know how well you play, my lady. Facing an opponent that one suddenly discovers is superior in his play is never amusing," Theresa said sympathetically.

"Quite." Lady Statten took a restless turn about the bedroom. "Theresa, I find that this weekend is not at all what I hoped it to be. Will you be too disappointed when I tell you that I wish to return early to London? You may stay on alone, of course, but I do consider myself to be in the role of chaperone, and—''

''There is no need to utter another word, Lady Statten. I could not possibly stay when I have come as your guest, I shall hold myself ready to accompany you whenever you with to depart,'' Theresa said swiftly.

''Good, I had hoped that you would,'' Lady Statten said with a quick smile. ''I see that you have not yet gone to bed. I would like to leave within the quarter-hour. I shall meet you in the downstairs hall.''

Theresa was taken aback that Lady Statten wished to leave that very night rather than the following morning after breakfast, but before she could collect her wits and voice her surprise, Lady Statten had whisked herself out of the bedroom. Theresa rebolted the door, her brow knit in thought. It was very queer that Lady Statten should be in such a hurry to return to London. However, Theresa thought that such an unexpected opportunity to leave Rusland Park suited her down to the ground. Her reflections had led her to an unmistakable conclusion and she was anxious to put it to the test. She went to the wardrobe and began to pull out her gowns so that she could pack them into her portmanteau.

22

The Duke of Ashford returned from his last engagement of the evening after midnight. He discovered that his secretary had chosen to stay up late in the night with some paperwork in the study, and he joined Winthrop there, requesting of the butler that a cold collation and wine be brought in to them.

"A note was delivered earlier for your grace. It was a bit odd, I gather, for the butler informed me that the messenger was quite insistent that it should be opened only by you," said Winthrop, indicating the folded parchment on a corner of the desk.

Hugo picked up the communication, noting that it was still sealed. The note lacked identifying marks or direction, and the duke opened it. He read the few short sentences with a sense of growing rage, and though he did not readily recognize it, fear. He swept around and thrust the paper at his secretary. "I am off, Herbert."

Winthrop perused the note quickly as he followed the duke out of the study. "But what do you intend to do, your grace? Lady Statten has not said where she is taking Miss Thaleman!"

The duke had already called for his phaeton to be brought around and issued swift instructions to his butler regarding the household in his absence. "I intend to go at once to interview Miss Brown. Of anyone, Miss Thaleman may have confided in her."

"I shall go with you, your grace," Winthrop said.

The duke shook his head. "I will not need you, Herbert. You would do better to remain here to handle whatever inquiries might be forthcoming regarding my unexpected absence."

"I insist upon accompanying you, your grace."

The duke turned then, his brows raised in exaggerated astonishment. "I beg pardon?"

Winthrop's jaw was hard and his gaze was straight. "I shall not have Miss Brown bullied, your grace," he said quietly.

The duke was taken aback. He recovered quickly, and a half-smile flickered over his face. "Love is a harsh taskmaster, is it not? Come then, and protect your Miss Brown from my heavy-handedness," he said. The secretary bowed but did not vouchsafe a word to refute his employer's statement, instead following him out of the town house to climb up into the phaeton.

The duke took up the reins, threading them loosely between his gloved fingers. He nodded to the groom standing at their jibing heads. "Let them loose, Charles. I mean to spring 'em." The groom let go the leaders and leapt to one side as the duke flicked his whip. The horses sprang forward and the phaeton bowled down the cobbled avenue.

The Bennett residence was but a few minutes away. The town house did not boast many lights when the Duke of Ashford and Mr. Winthrop drove up to it. "Your grace, I believe everyone must be abed," Mr. Winthrop said unnecessarily.

The duke gave a ghost of a laugh. "Then they will soon be up again, Herbert." He leapt up the steps and banged the knocker. It took two more assaults on the knocker, accompanied by the duke's escalating impatience, before the door cracked open. The duke stepped back so that he could be better seen. "I am the Duke of Ashford, and with me is my secretary, Mr. Winthrop. I demand to see Miss Brown."

There was a short, astonished silence on the part of the servant. "But Miss Brown is in bed, as is the household, your grace!"

The duke uttered an exclamation and pushed open the door, sending the servant flying. "I repeat, my good man, I wish to see Miss Brown. If you will not wake her, I will.'' He started for the stairs, and the servant gave a bleat of prostestation. The duke stopped and looked over his shoulder, his brows raised.

The servant nodded. ''Very well, your grace. If you will allow me to show your grace and Mr. Winthrop into the drawing room, I shall go wake Miss Brown.'' He ushered the visitors into the drawing room and lighted two sets of candles to give some light before he retreated.

Mr. Winthrop watched the drawing-room door close and then turned his head so that he could see the duke's face. He had been appalled at the duke's rough handling of the servant, but it was not for him to object, and the duke's tactics had been effective. He saw from the duke's expression that his employer was not in the mood for small talk and he therefore seated himself and waited silently.

It was but fifteen minutes later that the drawing-room door opened and Miss Brown entered. She had taken the time to put on a wrapper over her bedgown and to braid her hair loosely. She looked from one to the other of her visitors, at once made anxious and amazed by this night visit. ''Your grace?''

The duke did not waste time. ''I am sorry for rousing you from your bed, Miss Brown. But I have come on a matter of some urgency. I received not an hour ago a communiqué that Miss Thaleman has left London and has done so in the company of one whom I do not hesitate to term irresponsible of her reputation and safety.

Before the duke finished speaking, Miss Brown's face had paled. She knew intuitively that what he said must be appallingly true. ''Theresa went upstairs very soon after dinner, complaining of the headache. I thought at the time it was unlike her to be ill, but it never occurred to me that . . . Oh, I cannot believe it!'' She made a movement toward the door.

The duke's sharp voice stopped her. ''You need not run to check whether Miss Thaleman is indeed gone, for my informant is the selfsame person who intended to accompany her. I have come to you in an effort to learn where Miss Thaleman and her companion could possibly have gone.''

"Theresa did not confide in me, but perhaps . . ." Her eyes turned from Winthrop's face to the Duke of Ashford and back again. "Herbert . . ."

Mr. Winthrop took gentle hold of her hand and covered her slender fingers with his. "Letitia, you must tell his grace whatever you might suspect of Miss Thaleman's whereabouts. The duke has a right to know," he said gravely.

She looked at Winthrop for several seconds before she sighed and nodded. Without a word she left the room, to return within minutes with her arms wrapped around a leather-bound journal. "There was a note addressed to Mrs. Thaleman on Theresa's pillow, which I did not open. But I have brought Theresa's journal. She is in the habit of writing in it each evening." The duke held out his hand peremptorily. Miss Brown took a step backward. "Pray, if we are to invade Theresa's privacy, at least let me be the one," she said in a tight voice.

The duke met Miss Brown's gaze. He realized that she had made an agonizing decision that went against everything she held sacred. His respect for her was reflected in his voice. "Of course, Miss Brown. You are Miss Thaleman's closest confidante."

Miss Brown sat down in a chair and reluctantly opened the journal. She turned to the back pages and read quickly. She gave a horrified exclamation. "Dear God! Theresa has gone to Rusland Park." She stared disbelievingly at the page.

"What!" Hugo's terse ejaculation startled Miss Brown so much that she jumped. He stared at her with a grim expression. "You cannot be correct."

"Yes, yes, it is all here! Theresa was in an unhappy frame of mind—I shall not elaborate further on that—and accepted an invitation from Lady Statten to accompany her ladyship to Rusland Park," said Miss Brown.

"Melanie!" exclaimed the Duke of Ashford in loathing.

His thoughts ran swift. "My God, she intends to bring ruin on Theresa. And that little fool goes unheeding to the slaughter."

Miss Brown was urgent in her effort to make the duke understand what she knew of her charge. "Your grace, Theresa knows nothing of the Earl of Rusland's style of entertaining. Even after these months on the town, Theresa will not know what to expect of that caliber of people. She will be completely adrift and unprotected." Miss Brown beat her hands together. "If only I had trusted my instincts so long ago and divulged to Theresa the sort of behavior that was reputed to be found at Rusland Park! But the squire and Mrs. Thaleman did not wish her innocence of the world to be tarnished. She was always kept so close, and even here in London, despite what anyone may say of her follies, Theresa has been protected and coddled as much as is possible. And now but see what it has all come to! Stupid, headstrong girl that she is, with her eyes and heart filled with fragile butterfly wings."

Alarmed by Miss Brown's strange flight of fancy, Winthrop knelt beside the chair and caught his love's agitated hands. "Letitia, calm yourself! You become hysterical and quite unintelligible."

"On the contrary, Miss Brown is making perfect sense." The duke smiled bleakly. "The fault for this particular coil lies more with me than anyone else, Miss Brown, as I think even you must agree. It is because of me that Theresa has felt compelled to leave London."

"I wish that she had confided in me. I would have taken her directly home to the squire, who dotes on her. Certainly there would not have been this hurried retreat to Rusland Park and in that particular lady's company. Lady Statten is . . ." Miss Brown broke off, realizing that she was on the verge of committing a *faux pas.* "Forgive me, your grace. I have no right to voice my opinion of one of your acquaintances in your presence."

The duke laughed at her. "I have no doubt that I would

agree with your observations on Lady Statten, Miss Brown. However, I think we have wasted enough time on recriminations. I intend to travel at once to Rusland Park.''

Winthrop got to his feet. His eyes were determined in expression. ''I shall go with you, your grace. I may be of assistance.''

The duke's first instinct was to refuse his secretary's offer, but he hesitated in the face of the man's obvious resolution. He made up his mind swiftly and clapped his hand on Winthrop's shoulder. ''Come, then. The assistance of a friend is always to be allowed. We shall endeavor to return to London with Miss Thaleman before she is missed by any of her acquaintances. Miss Brown, your servant.'' He strode to the drawing-room door and opened it, setting up a shout in the hall for his phaeton to be brought around to the front door.

Feeling a hand on his arm, Winthrop turned to find that Miss Brown stood beside him and looked up at him with a worried expression. He covered her fingers with his and pressed them reassuringly. ''Pray do not be anxious, Letitia. We shall bring her off without harm, or I know nothing of the duke.''

''Of course.'' Miss Brown's frown lightened as she gave a lopsided smile. ''I do wish that I were going as well. Believe me, I do not anticipate the task of reassuring Mrs. Thaleman when she rises in the morning to find Theresa gone.''

Winthrop laughed and dropped a light kiss on her brow, causing her to blush. ''That's my girl. I have every confidence in you, my dear. When this business is settled, I intend to address a matter close to my heart, and that is your immediate retirement from Mrs. Thaleman's service.''

''But I cannot leave until Theresa's future is settled,'' protested Miss Brown.

The duke put his head inside the drawing-room door. ''Winthrop! What are you standing about for? Let us depart on the instant.'' He disappeared.

"Somehow I think that it has already been settled," Winthrop said with a gleam of humor. He disengaged himself from Miss Brown's clasp and hurried after his employer.

As Winthrop left the drawing room on the run, Mr. Bennett entered. His face wore a sleepy, bewildered expression, and a resplendent silk dressing gown was wrapped around his rotund frame. "Miss Brown! What is toward? It is not as though I mind that you receive gentleman callers, but must it be in the small hours of the morning? Really, it is quite shocking in you."

Miss Brown, still warmed by the attractive color in her face, began to laugh. She covered her mouth a moment until she had sobered, then said, "Indeed, Mr. Bennett, I am very sorry. Pray, may I confide in you? It is a matter of some importance and I very much wish your counsel on how the matter should be handled."

Mr. Bennett was startled and yet flattered. He had never before thought of himself as a wise man, but someone of Miss Brown's superior intellect would hardly mistake the matter. "Certainly, Miss Brown. Most happy to oblige," he said expansively. His confidence was shaken when Miss Brown firmly closed the drawing-room door. He eyed her askance, and his uneasy forebodings ruptured into full bloom with her first words.

"It is Theresa, sir. She has left London in the company of Lady Statten to spend the weekend at Rusland Park."

Mr. Bennett's eyes started from their sockets. "My word, Rusland Park! Why, what is the girl thinking of?" His shocked thoughts graduated naturally to what he assumed to be Miss Brown's request. He took a step backward, clutching the sash of his dressing gown. "No, no, Miss Brown, I could not possibly. My niece and all that, of course, but I could not possily set chase. Why, I have not ridden in years. Not a horse up to my weight, you see, and—"

Miss Brown attempted to stop the swift spate of words. "Certainly you cannot give chase, sir. I would not ask it of you."

Mr. Bennett's expression cleared. "You are thinking of George! Quite so, we shall send a man around immediately to rouse him out of his bed." He started toward the bell-pull beside the mantel.

"Mr. Bennett, pray do listen to me. I do not wish for Mr. Bennett to fly off half-breached in pursuit of his silly cousin. Really, sir, there is no need to look at me like that. I am quite in possession of my faculties," said Miss Brown, her temper beginning to fray. "Mr. Bennett, the Duke of Ashford and Mr. Winthrop are already on their way to Rusland Park. That was who left the house but moments ago."

Mr. Bennett stared at her with a frown. "Then what is it you require, dear lady? If it is reassurance, I tell you that I am now confident that my niece will come to no harm. At least, she will not at the earl's hands. What the duke sees fit to do with Theresa, I give him in advance my hearty approval. My niece is leading him a pretty dance, 'pon my word!"

Miss Brown abandoned her usual respectful civility and interrupted Mr. Bennett to come straight to the point. "Sir, what are we to tell Mrs. Thaleman and Mrs. Bennett if the duke has not returned Theresa to us by morning?"

"Tell Mrs. Thaleman and . . ." Mr. Bennett was immediately filled with acute dismay. " 'Pon my word, I never gave a thought . . . Miss Brown, we are in the suds."

"I agree, sir. What shall we do? Of all people, you must know best how to soothe those ladies when they become agitated."

Mr. Bennett gave something between a laugh and a snort. "Oh, indeed! You are far off there, Miss Brown. No, that is George's forte, and . . . George! By Jove, there's a capital notion. We shall have George in to breakfast."

"Indeed, sir, a capital notion," said Miss Brown, smiling on him as though he was a particularly backward pupil who had just accomplished the task set before him. It was the very decision that she had come to several moments before, but propriety as well as the personal circumstances between herself and George Bennett barred her from sending a communication to him herself.

"I shall send a man around to his lodgings directly. There's not a moment to be lost if he is to have time to attend to his toilette. George won't step out-of-doors without his appearance to his satisfaction, whatever the urgency of our summons," said Mr. Bennett. He pulled on the bell rope, hoping that his son would indeed be available to join the household at breakfast. If not, he thought that he just might breakfast at the club. A pity about Miss Brown, though. She would have a time of it alone.

23

The Duke of Ashford and Mr. Winthrop made good time to Rusland Park. In fact, Mr. Winthrop was fairly certain that if bets had been laid, the duke would have beaten all odds. The phaeton swept up to the front of the mansion. A blaze of light came from nearly all its windows, and even outside there could be heard the buzz of loud voices and laughter and music.

The duke snubbed his reins and leapt down, giving a terse word to the stableboy, who had appeared from nowhere, that he would be needing his cattle again and just to walk them a few minutes. He ran up the front steps and pulled the bell impatiently. Mr. Winthrop followed the duke's example more slowly, his bones aching from the jarring he had taken on the road, for even as well-sprung as the phaeton was, it still bounced as it bowled along.

The front door was opened. "Your grace! This is a most pleasant surprise," the butler said. The Duke of Ashland brushed past him and Mr. Winthrop followed behind in his wake.

"Your master. Where is he?" the duke asked sharply.

The butler was taken aback by the duke's terse tone and stern expression. He gestured toward the ballroom. "Allow me to show you in, your grace."

"That will not be necessary," Hugo said, and thrust open the ballroom door. He swept the crowded assembly with cold eyes, looking at once for Theresa and the Earl of Rusland. When he found the earl, he bore down on him with determination, not acknowledging the greetings of those who recognized him. Winthrop waited at the door to await his employer's orders.

The earl looked up as his ear caught a gathering wave of whispers and dying laughter. He met the angered gaze of the Duke of Ashford. "Pray excuse me," he said to his lovely partner, and went to meet the duke. "Hugo, you need not bother to tell me why you have come. Come outside into the hall, where we shall have a bit more privacy." He guided the Duke of Ashford back into the hall and waved at the butler to shut the ballroom door. When that was done, he drew the duke to one side. "Rumor has it that you have become affianced to a chit of a girl, Hugo, specifically one Miss Theresa Thaleman," he drawled.

"Where is she?" asked the duke shortly.

"When I discovered Miss Thaleman's identity, I escorted her at once to her bedroom and advised her to lock herself in for the night. You know what it is around here, Hugo. I could not have trusted any one of them to leave her be."

"And you, my lord?" Hugo asked softly, dangerously.

"Good God, man! Have you lost your senses? Miss Thaleman is the daughter of my neighbor, Squire Thaleman, who is a high stickler if ever there was one. I prefer to keep relations with my neighbors as amicable as possible, for obvious reasons. I hardly want to be run out of county for ravishment of the locals' daughters! Besides, I had every reason to believe in the truth of the rumor of your engagement, and however much we have drifted apart, Hugo, I still consider you my dear friend." The earl sighed as he flicked a speck of dust from his coat sleeve. "It has been a distressing business, to say the least. I would have preferred to have gotten Miss Thaleman out of the house at once, but there is not a decent woman under this roof who could escort her. In the morning I meant to have my own nurse, who is living in a cottage on the estate, make the journey with her to London."

"I shall spare you the trouble and take Miss Thaleman off your hands. Where is she?" asked the duke.

"Come, I will myself take you to her. I warned her not to open the door to anyone, even the maid, but I suppose that she might be expected to make an exception in your case," the earl said with a sly grin.

The duke did not bother to reply, but followed the earl upstairs. The earl paused outside a closed door and raised his hand to knock. The door swung open, startling both him and the maid who was standing inside. "What are you doing in there?" the earl asked sharply. He pushed open the door to reveal an empty room. The Duke of Ashford strode past him into the bedroom and turned about, looking for some clue. His sharpened gaze found a soft white square on the carpet. He picked it up and in its corner was embroidered the initial T. His fist closed about the linen, crushing it.

"Why, I be cleaning the grate, m'lord," said the maid, her eyes wide at her employer's tone of displeasure. "Ye did say that the bedrooms must be kept readied at all times, m'lord."

The earl turned on her. "Where is the young miss who was staying in this bedroom?" he demanded.

The maid began to feel unsure of herself. "Why, the other lady and the miss left together, m'lord. I 'ave just come from m'lady's room, you see, so I know."

"Lady Statten!" exclaimed the Duke of Ashford. He strode quickly from the bedroom and down the hallway, not sparing a moment to observe the courtesies and take leave of the earl.

The Earl of Rusland dismissed the maid, who scurried off looking back over her shoulder at the peculiar-acting gentlemen. He narrowed his eyes, remembering his interview with Lady Statten. She had been enraged and had sailed from the library without a word, he recalled. Even at the time he had thought it odd that Lady Melanie Statten should forbear to make a rash announcement of her feelings and intentions. He had shrugged it off, rather grateful to be spared a scene, but now he regretted that he had not detained the troublesome woman a moment longer. There had been a look about her eyes that he had not liked.

"Damn her," he breathed. It was not to his taste that he should be obligated to make certain of Miss Thaleman's fate. Especially now, when he had guests in the house, and in particular one very lovely and willing young woman who had flashed him an unmistakable glance before he had left her in the ballroom. If he was not careful, that young woman would be snapped up by one of the hungry wolves that restlessly scouted his parties.

Miss Thaleman had been under his protection, however ironic that was, and he was bound by honor to pursue Lady Statten. For a second only, the earl entertained the thought of simply washing his hands of the matter. After all, Hugo was already on the scent. But he could not shrug off his seldom-aroused sense of responsibility. The earl sighed and made his way downstairs, having come to the decision to call for his carriage. "Breeding will always win out," he murmured with irony.

24

The murky shadows were thrown back by the crackling fire in the grate. A few candles had been lit, but the flickering light did little to illuminate the far corners of the room. Theresa looked about her surroundings with a feeling of dread. She had thought that Lady Statten was taking her back to London, but now she was not so sure that was what the lady intended.

She had been inordinately thankful when Lady Statten had abruptly announced that they would be leaving Rusland Park. She had been both confused and frightened by the earl's guests and what had been said. The earl himself was not at all what she had expected. He had made her very uncomfortable at first, but that had all changed as they had talked. She had been surprised and pleased that he knew of her father. After all, the squire had never given any sign that he had even met the Earl of Rusland, and he had certainly not been what one might term a friendly neighbor.

The earl in some subtle way had changed toward her during the course of their conversation, so that Theresa had begun to feel quite easy in his company. But she knew now why her parents had thought it best for her not to associate with those at Rusland Park. She simply did not fit into that circle. The realization had not brought with it inquietude, but instead content. Theresa knew at last where she belonged, and in particular with whom.

Lady Statten's decision not to remain at Rusland Park for the weekend had therefore been very welcome. It had seemed a little odd that they would depart well into the small hours of the night and without taking formal leave of their host, but Lady Statten had said that she had made their good-byes already, and Theresa had not questioned her too closely. Theresa was in a fever of impatience to communicate what she had learned about herself to a particular gentleman. As soon as she returned to London, she thought, she would at once apologize to Hugo and everything would be right again.

But she was not in London. She had barely settled herself for the long drive when the carriage came to a stop. She had looked inquiringly at Lady Statten, but that lady had said not a word. Instead Lady Statten had opened the door and stepped out. Theresa waited several moments before she followed suit and got out of the carriage. Gravel crunched underfoot and she looked up at the windows of a darkened house. The coachman had approached her then. Pulling on his forelock, he told her that Lady Statten was inside. When she asked why they had stopped, the coachman mumbled something about a pulled fetlock in one of the horses. His vague tone of voice left her with a sense of dissatisfaction, and Theresa allowed herself to be led into the house so that she could speak to Lady Statten. After showing her into the room, the coachman had retreated.

The parlor that Theresa stood in had obviously not been aired in some time, and smelled of dank must. Dust covers shrouded the furniture, except for the settee and a table set before the hearth. Altogether the place had an eery, damp feel to it. Theresa shivered. The fire that had been lit was too small to warm the room. As she bent to hold her hands to the flames, she abstractedly noticed that the poker had been left lying in the coals, and she was about to move it when she heard voices.

Lady Statten entered and closed the door behind her. Theresa straightened at once. "My lady! I have been anxious to speak with you. Why ever have we stopped? Your coachman mentioned an injury to one of the team, but he was so hesitant in his answer that I thought he was improvising excuses."

Lady Statten stood a moment longer in front of the door. Her face was partially shadowed until she moved into the pool of light before the hearth. "Indeed, Theresa! Sometimes you surprise me with your perceptiveness. It is nothing to worry your head over, however. Pray, won't you be seated? I have had a bottle of the finest burgundy brought in for our enjoyment while we talk." She sat down on the settee and lifted a wine bottle from the table.

Theresa eyed her companion a moment, uncertain what she should do. Lady Statten appeared perfectly calm, but there was about her something that was unnatural, unsettling. In the midst of pouring the wine, Lady Statten looked up inquiringly, her thin brows raised. Theresa sighed and took her own seat on the opposite end of the settee. Lady Statten held out one of the two filled wineglasses. Theresa took the glass and sipped at the wine experimentally.

Lady Statten watched her a moment, faintly smiling. "It is not poisoned, Theresa," she said gently.

Theresa flushed, embarrassed that the flash of her thoughts could be read so easily. But then, why should Lady Statten wish her harm? she thought. The lady had been more than gracious to her. The unfounded uneasiness she felt was just that and nothing more. Theresa set aside the wineglass. "Thank you, my lady, but as you know, I am not a true connoisseur."

Lady Statten laughed. "Are you not, Theresa?" She threw back her head and emptied her wineglass in one swallow. When she lowered the glass it was to hold it against her full underlip. Her eyes glittered over the rim. "Are you not a connoisseur, Theresa? One must take leave to differ with you, for you have singled out the most eligible gentleman in society. You must consider yourself very clever."

Theresa was bothered by her companion's strange behavior, but she endeavored to act as though they were engaged in a normal conversation. "I think myself fortunate that the Duke of Ashford chose to offer for me, of course. His lordship is a wonderful gentleman."

"Oh, indeed! He is quite wonderful. His person and rank and wealth make him a prime catch. And naturally you are in love with him," said Lady Statten.

Theresa did not like her companion's implication. "My lady, I accepted his lordship for himself, not his position."

"I beg pardon, Theresa. I had forgotten that you are the complete innocent," Lady Statten said. She poured herself another glass of wine.

Theresa stood up. "My lady, I think that we have tarried long enough, do not you?"

Lady Statten leaned back, laying a casual arm along the back of the settee. She ignored the younger woman's words. "You playact the high-bred lady quite well, Theresa. But I think that I would make a far more convincing duchess."

Theresa realized of a sudden what their odd *tête-à-tête* was about. She said slowly, "I am sorry, Lady Statten. I did not know that you were attracted to his lordship."

Lady Statten sat up abruptly. Her fingers were curled tight about the wineglass stem. "You little half-wit! Is it not plain to you yet? Hugo was mine until you interfered. Something interfering—that was what Madam told me. And it was you. All those months ago, it was you!" Between her clenched fingers the wineglass stem popped in two. With a violent movement Lady Statten threw the broken wineglass, shattering it against the floor. She stood up, breathing hard.

Theresa stared at the dark smear of blood on Lady Statten's hand. She took a careful step backward. There was no doubt in her mind that she would never share a coach with this woman on this night or any other. She would walk back to Rusland Park and beg transporation. Better yet, she would make her way to her own home, which was a few miles further, but infinitely more reassuring to strive for. How very much she wished that her dear papa or the twins would walk through the door.

Lady Statten bent to the fire. When she straightened up, she held the poker. Its glowing tip shimmered dull red. Studying it, Lady Statten spoke quite calmly, even reflectively. "Madam said that I must destroy whatever interfered between me and Hugo. And I tried so very hard to do so. I introduced you into the least reputable crowds.

I taught you to gamble for high stakes. I encouraged every bit of folly that entered your foolish little head. And you were so amazingly grateful to me for taking you under my wing. Foolish Theresa! But all my efforts went for naught. Time and again Hugo saved you from the consequences of your folly. By his very presence he threw an impenetrable cloak of respectability about you. As my last bid I brought you to Rusland Park. Once it becomes known that Miss Thaleman spent the weekend in the sort of company that surrounds the Earl of Rusland, Hugo's pride will give him no choice except to renounce the engagement. I meant for you to be debauched, you see. But the fates once more worked against me. It seems that the earl has an aversion to seducing the daughters of his neighbors. So I am left with but one last option. It is a pity, actually. I rather liked playing cat's-paw with you.'' She turned her head and her gaze was hard and flat.

Theresa stared in disbelief, her throat suddenly constricted with fear as she read the horrible determination in Lady Statten's eyes. She backed up. Lady Statten followed her in a leisurely fashion that was macabre. Theresa found her voice at last. ''My lady! Think what you intend!''

''Oh, I have. Why do you think I had the coachman stop here at the dower house? Very few visit it, you know. Rusland's owner has no use for it except as a place of assignation.''

Theresa put the settee between her and the madwoman, for that was how she thought of her ladyship. Her thoughts spun quickly. ''An assignation,'' she gasped. ''Yes, I overheard the earl mention the dower house to someone. He . . . he said that it would be open for them.''

Lady Statten stopped and her exquisite brows puckered. ''The door was unlocked. I did not need to use the key that I bribed that slattern of a maid for,'' she said vaguely.

Without daring a glance, Theresa sensed that she was very near the closed parlor door. If she could only distract Lady Statten's attention a moment longer, then she might escape unscathed. "Someone is certain to come. You will be known. Think of it, Lady Statten." As she spoke, she let go the back of the settee and edged toward the door. Without taking her eyes from the woman who menaced her, she groped behind her for the doorknob.

Lady Statten stood still, the poker dropping slightly. There was a diverted expression in her wide green eyes. "I will be known. The scandal—"

"Yes, yes! The scandal will be ignominious for you. Hugo is very correct. He could not marry—"

"Hugo! How dare you!" Lady Statten's voice hissed. Her eyes narrowed to mere slits. She seemed to swell with rage, and to Theresa's horrified eyes she appeared to change color as dark splotches appeared on her face and neck. "You dare! You dare call him by his given name. You stole him from me! And you dare . . ." Screaming incoherently, Lady Statten rounded the settee and sprang at Theresa.

Theresa whirled and threw herself at the door. She twisted the brass knob frantically, her head turned so that she could watch her enemy's rapid progress. With absolute horror she saw the poker swing up and begin its swift arcing descent. The knob gave in her hand. Sobbing a prayer, Theresa flung herself aside, her fingers still clutching the knob, and the door came open.

The poker struck heavily against the edge of the door, at the exact level of Theesa's head. Lady Statten cursed and swung around. There was a mad glitter in her eyes. She raised the poker again. "You shall not escape me, Theresa. I promise you that," she said clearly.

Theresa stumbled backward, her breath sobbing in her throat, and fell against a heavy armchair shrouded in a dustcloth. Lady Statten rushed toward her before she could rise. Theresa screamed and threw up her arm to ward off the deadly blow.

A hand shot over Lady Statten's shoulder to catch the poker before it found its target. Lady Statten whirled. She fought savagely for possession of the poker, but it was wrested from her grasp. A hail of curses fell from her twisted lips. She flew at the gentleman who had frustrated her desires, her fingers spread like claws.

The Duke of Ashford ducked the long striking nails and caught Lady Statten's wrists in a steely grip. "Lady Statten! Enough, do you hear me? The game is done." He locked stares with the woman that he held prisoner, and for several moments the atmosphere was palpably tense.

Then the fight seemed to seep out of Lady Statten. She sighed and relaxed against him. "Oh, Hugo, everything could have been so different," she whispered.

The duke looked over her bowed head to meet the gaze of his beloved. Theresa had gotten to her feet, and when she gave him a faint smile of reassurance he returned his attention to Lady Statten. He hardly recognized her. Her red hair had tumbled out of its pins and there was blood on her cheek where she had unthinkingly brushed it with her wounded hand. He wondered at the brand of desperation that had led her to stoop to such straits. Even now he had difficulty believing that this woman was the selfsame lady that he had once contemplated for his choice of bride. It seemed a very long time ago. "Perhaps once, Melanie," Hugo said. There was almost a note of pity in his voice.

Lady Statten heard it, and she immediately pulled free of his loosened hold. She slapped the Duke of Ashford across his hard cheek. "Damn you! Go to the nitwit, then. She'll bore you within a fortnight. And as for you, Hugo, you're all kinds of fool. You deserve one another!"

The Duke of Ashford made an ironic bow to her and then walked over to Theresa. Lady Statten watched with clenched fists as his grace enfolded the young woman in his arms. Theresa turned into his embrace with a soft sigh.

There was loud applause, and Lady Statten turned quickly. The Earl of Rusland came away from his place in the open doorway, where he had leaned to observe the unfolding scene. "Marvelous, Melanie. I have always harbored suspicions that if you so desired, you could make a sumptuous living from the stage,'' he said sauvely.

"I? Tread the boards? You must be mad!" exclaimed Lady Statten.

"After this night's work I think madness must be your forte, my dear lady,'' the earl said, his mocking expression suddenly shifting to a sterner cast. "I have admired you for a very long time, Lady Statten, and up to now I have found amusement in your foibles. But one must draw the line somewhere. One cannot have a countess who threatens to murder a respectable neighbor's daughter. That would put one quite beyond the pale, even for one of my reputation.'' He shifted his gaze to the couple standing in the parlor. "Ah, Hugo. True love has struck at last, I see. I felicitate you, of course, and may I proffer my sincere good wishes to you as well, Miss Thaleman. I know that you will both accept my excuses. I must return to my guests. We left in such a scurry that the gossip will be running rampant. It will be amusing to hear. Pray make free with the dower house for as long as you like. This dwelling has been used many times before as sanctuary against a cruel and intruding world.'' He gave a mocking salute and exited the parlor.

Lady Statten's green eyes flew wide. "Sanctuary! That was the word Madam used! Charles! Charles, do wait for me.'' She rushed out of the parlor, and her voice floated back. "Pray do not leave me, my lord! I must speak with you.''

The Duke of Ashford laughed softly. "Somehow I do not believe that the earl will be much inclined to give the lady an audience.''

"How did you find me?" Theresa asked. It was not quite the most important question, but it would do for the moment.

"Lady Statten very thoughtfully sent a note to me that she had taken you off with her, and promised me that I would soon learn of your true colors. She did not disclose her destination and so I immediately went to Miss Brown, thinking that you might have confided in her. It was she who had the brilliant notion to read the last entry in your journal. The poor lady agonized over breaking into your privacy, but fortunately her good sense overrode her sense of propriety,'' the duke said. He reached up to smooth her soft hair.

"Miss Brown once told me that my journal would stand me in good stead,'' Theresa murmured.

"I do not care to contemplate what might have happened if Miss Brown had not learned of your journey here to Rusland Park with Lady Statten,'' the duke said a shade grimly. "As it was, it was sheer chance that I caught sight of Lady Statten's carriage stopped in front of the dowèr house. Her driver attempted to dissuade me from entering, but Winthrop surprisingly enough has very good form with his fists.''

"What will happen to Lady Statten?'' Theresa asked hesitantly.

"Nothing at all. At least at first. Then, as bits and pieces of this night's work become known or speculated about, she will find fewer and fewer acquaintances willing to take up with her. She will gradually slip into obscurity, which for someone like Lady Statten will constitute an unimaginable hell,'' Hugo said somberly.

Theresa found she did not want to talk of Lady Statten. Her terrifying experience at the lady's hands had left her more shaken than she wanted to acknowledge. Theresa laid her head against Hugo's shirtfront and her fingers slid up to cling tightly to his coat lapel. She was not thinking any longer of Lady Statten, but of the gentleman who held her so comfortably close. "I am so very glad that you are here, your grace,'' she said in a low voice.

His arms tightened about her. His warm breath ruffled her hair as he spoke. "Are you, Miss Thaleman? I seem to recall that you stated quite strongly that you never wished to see me again. Actually, I cannot blame you, for I made an utter fool of myself. I had time during that nightmare drive here to realize it and come to my senses. I beg your forgiveness, Miss Thaleman.''

"I hope that you do not take to heart every foolish or cross word that I might have uttered," Theresa said, raising her head. She cleared her throat, uncomfortable of a sudden. How did one go about letting a gentleman know that tone wished very much to marry him after all? she wondered. "Hugo, I am so very sorry that I—" She got no further, for the Duke of Ashford took swift possession of her mouth. His deep kiss reduced Theresa to incoherent thought. When he finally released her, Theresa blinked in disorientation.

"What was it you wished to tell me, Miss Thaleman?"

In answer, Theresa rose on tiptoe to place her lips firmly against his. The duke's response was most gratifying. His arms tightened about her so hard that her ribs seemed in immediate danger of cracking, but Theresa did not care. She and her beloved Hugo had at last come to a perfect understanding.